RUMOURS THAT RUINED A LADY

Marguerite Kaye

MILLS BOON®

First published in Great Britain 2013
by Mills & Boon, an imprint of Harlequin (UK) Limited.
Harlequin (UK) Limited, Eton House, 18-24 Paradise Road,
Richmond, Surrey TW9 1SR

© Marguerite Kaye 2013

ISBN: 978 0 263 89859 0

Printed and bound in Spain
by Blackprint CPI, Barcelona

AUTHOR NOTE

Almost all of my books have their genesis in the characters of the hero and heroine. This one was different, and began life as a whole lot of disjointed concepts and ideas, something I've learned the painful way was a *big* mistake!

While writing THE BEAUTY WITHIN, my previous book about the Armstrong sisters, I decided that Caro's story was going to be very dark, and as such did some minor setting-up, hinting that there were goings-on in her life without knowing myself what they were. I wanted Caro—on the surface the most compliant and dutiful of sisters—to have a deep, dark secret, and I wanted that secret to be revealed in layers, so I decided that I would begin her story at some tragic pivotal point and then reveal how she got to there. I wanted to write a love story that extended over a long period of time and, just to complicate matters, I decided I wanted there to be a strong gothic element in it too—without actually having defined what I meant by gothic.

I made Caro a murderer. I invented a twin brother for Sebastian. I made his father physically vicious as well as emotionally cruel. I decided that being a murderer wasn't dark enough for Caro, and turned her into a long-term opium user. And I invented a mother for Sebastian based on the character of Jane Digby, whose biography I was reading. She was a beautiful and outrageous society beauty, with a string of husbands and lovers, who ended up living as a Bedouin and married to a sheikh. (If you want to know more about Lady Jane, then I can highly recommend Mary S. Lovell's book, *A Scandalous Life*.)

As you'll see when you read Caro and Sebastian's story, very little of this made it into the final version. There's no twin brother, no murder, only a little opium and the only link to Lady Jane's life in Damascus is the mention of an Arabian horse! The problem was, I think, that concepts don't make a romance. People and characters do. I *did* get my lovers with a history, though, and I have structured the story in a non-linear way. Writing this book has been a long and sometimes very painful process, though ultimately it's produced a story I'm extremely pleased with. I hope you'll agree.

I'd like to thank my editor Flo for her enthusiasm and support, without which I think I might just have given up on Sebastian and Caro. I'd also like to thank Alison L for suggesting Lady Jane's biography to me, and for coming up with Hamilton Palace as the model for Crag Hall. And finally I'd like to thank all my Facebook friends, for all your suggestions and encouragement during the writing of this book. You helped get me there in the end!

Chapter One

⁂

London—August 1830

Sebastian Conway, Marquis of Ardhallow, glanced wearily at his watch before returning it to his fob pocket. Just gone midnight. Ye Gods was that all! He'd expected the evening to be substantially more entertaining, especially since this house had a reputation for hosting the raciest parties on the *ton*'s social circuit.

The recent death of King George the Fourth having caused many social gatherings to be cancelled, there was a very healthy turnout at this one. The relative earliness of the hour meant that the veneer of respectability cloaking the main salon was still more or less intact.

The ladies sat clustered in small groups, idly swapping gossip, artfully posed to display their ample charms. Their gowns cut fashionably but daringly, they comprised the so-called fast set, women long-enough married to have done their duty by their husbands, who therefore considered themselves to have earned the right to conduct the kind of discreet *affaire* which frequently both began and ended at a party such as this. On the other side of the room the gentlemen gathered, sipping claret and appraising their quarry with a practised eye. The air crackled with sexual tension. Everything was the same, just exactly as he remembered, and none of it interested him one whit.

Sebastian exited the drawing room. In the adjoining salon, for those eager to lose their wealth rather than their reputation, card tables had been set up. The play was deep and the drinking which accompanied it deeper still, but he had never been interested in games of chance. Out of curiosity he made his way to a room at the back of the house which had been the subject of salacious rumour.

The chamber was dimly lit, the windows heavily shrouded. He paused on the threshold. The atmosphere inside was thick with a sweet pungent smell which hung like incense in the air. Opium. As his eyes became accustomed to the gloom, he could make out several prone figures lying on divans, some lost in the dream-like state induced by smoking the drug, others clutching their pipes to their mouths, eyes glazed, attention focused inwards.

The room had been decorated in the Eastern manner, strewn with low divans, the rich carpets covered in jewelled and fringed cushions of silk and velvet. He had seen numerous such places on his travels and his own, single, experience of the drug in Constantinople had been, on the whole, pleasant. His dreams had been highly sensual, heightening the pleasure of the release he sought afterwards in the adjoining seraglio. He knew that others endured waking nightmares and grotesque hallucinations while under its influence, or suffered shivering sweats in the aftermath, and so counted himself fortunate. Perhaps if he indulged tonight, it would make one of the beauties so patently on offer in the salon more tempting.

A low, grumbling objection from one of the smokers reminded him that he was still holding the door ajar. Closing it softly behind him, he leaned against the oak panelling and scanned the room. In the centre, a low inlaid table held the complex paraphernalia required to vaporise the opium. A selection of bamboo pipes with their bowls and saddles were set out on a lacquered tray beside several opium lamps. Scrapers, scoops and tapers were scattered across the table, and the drawers of the little cabinet which contained the opium itself were askew. His host, that most flamboyant and failed of poets, Augustus St John Marne, had married an heiress, he now recalled. It must be she who was funding her husband's hobby, which was like to be very expensive, especially since he was supplying his guests' requirements so generously.

The poet wafted into the room at that very moment, waving distractedly at Sebastian. St John Marne was a wraith-like figure who had in his youth, if one were to believe the gossip, had the ladies swooning over his beauty and the breathless romance of his verse. A few of the other faces in the room were frighteningly familiar, men he had known all his life. Rich, titled, dissolute and purposeless, they looked much older and more jaded than their years, though many were the same age as he.

Slightly sickened by this realisation, Sebastian deciding against partaking of the drug and was turning to leave when a long tress of hair caught his attention, stopping him in his tracks.

It was far too long to belong to any man. The colour, that of burnished copper, made his heart freeze for one long, terrible moment. He had never known another with hair that precise colour, but *she* would surely not frequent a place such as this.

The woman was lying with her back to the door, her figure obscured under a swathe of shawls and embroidered throws. It wasn't her, and even if it was, he had sworn he would have nothing to do with her ever again. If she chose to make herself insensible with opium, it was none of his business.

Thus spoke his head. Sebastian's feet were already moving of their own accord towards the divan, his heart thudding hard and fast in his chest, his skin suddenly clammy with sweat. If it was indeed her, and he simply couldn't bring himself to believe it was, then the wisest thing he could do would be to turn around and leave forthwith.

Now!

He leant over the divan and roughly pulled back the covering from the comatose woman's body. She did not stir. Sebastian swore heavily, reeling with shock. He barely recognised her. Thin, painfully so, under the emerald gown which hung loosely around her, the only sign of life was the pulse fluttering under the fragile skin at her temple. He cursed again. Her eyes were closed. Wisps of copper hair clung to her high forehead, which had a glistening sheen of perspiration. Her hand, when he touched it, was clammy. The skin which had once been so milky-white was ashen. Her cheekbones were too prominent, flushed not with health but fever. Her mouth, whose sensual, teasing smile he had once found irresistible, was drawn into a tight grimace. Beneath her lids, her eyes fluttered. Her hand gripped him like a claw and she moaned, a tiny, hoarse sound of protest against the opium-induced hallucination she was experiencing. Hers had always been the kind of beauty which reflected her mood, sometimes in full bloom, at others so withdrawn into itself as to make her look quite plain. Now, she looked more like a cadaver than a living, breathing woman.

Scarcely-breathing woman, Sebastian corrected himself as he bent his head towards her face. Her breath was the merest whisper upon his cheek. What had happened to her? The woman he knew was so strong, so full of life, so vibrant. She had been patently unhappy when last they met, but this stupor went way beyond the seeking of painless escape. What had befallen her to make her so careless of her life?

Telling himself again that it was none of his business, he knelt down next to the prone figure, a terrible suspicion lodged in his head. Her lips were cracked and dry. He bent closer and touched them with his own, the merest contact, yet enough to confirm his fears. She had not smoked the drug but consumed it. *Dear Lord*.

'Caroline.' He tried to rouse her by shaking her shoulder. Still, she did not stir. 'Caro!' he exclaimed, more sharply this time.

There was no response. Getting to his feet, Sebastian turned towards his host, who was fastidiously preparing a jade pipe on the table in the centre of the room. 'How long has she been like this, St John Marne?'

The poet blinked at him owlishly. 'Who?'

'Caroline! Lady Rider. How many other women have you here, for heaven's sake! How long?'

'I don't know. I do not recall…' Augustus St John Marne ran a hand distractedly through his over-long blond hair. 'Two hours? Three at most.'

'Three! And she has not stirred in all that time?'

'I'm the host, not a governess, for goodness'

sake. I can't be expected to keep an eye on all my guests. Let her be, she'll come round. Obviously she has misjudged the quantity.'

'She has not taken it in a pipe, St John Marne, she has ingested it.'

'Egad!' Suddenly the former poet was all flapping concern. 'Are you sure? You must get her out of here. This is very pure—the best, I only ever serve the best. What can have possessed her. Take her away, get her to a doctor, give her a purge, just get her out of here right now, I beseech you.'

Sebastian told himself yet again to walk away. Caro was a grown woman. Given the four year age gap between them, she must be seven-and-twenty and therefore more than capable of taking care of herself. Except that there was something about her that told him she no longer cared for anything. The way her hair fell about her in lank tresses, the pallor of her skin, the outmoded gown. Her breathing seemed to be growing ever more faint.

In all conscience Sebastian could not leave her here, but he had no idea where she lived. A terse question prompted St John Marne to look at him in surprise. 'Did you not you hear? Rider threw her out. Caught her *in flagrante* with the boot boy, according to the *Morning*

Post. Turns out that the boot boy was merely the latest in a long line, and Rider being the up-and-coming man in Tory circles, he really had no option but to be shot of her.' The poet tittered. 'Quite the social outcast, is Lady Caroline. She has lodgings somewhere. My footman will know, he knows everything.'

Sebastian struggled with a strong and perfectly unjustified desire to smash his fist into his host's supercilious face. 'What of her family?' he demanded tersely. 'Surely Lord Armstrong…?'

St John Marne sneered. 'Oh, the great diplomat is off saving the world, I believe—the Balkans or some such place, last I heard. The house on Cavendish Square is shut up. That frumpy wife of his must be in the country with her brood of boys. As for the sisters—not one of 'em left in England now, save for this one and the youngest, who has apparently eloped.' He looked contemptuously over at the comatose figure. 'You could say, you really could say, that poor Lady Caroline is quite alone in this world.'

Pity overwhelmed Sebastian, and anger too. Whatever she had done—and he simply could not bring himself to believe those scurrilous allegations—she did not deserve to be abandoned. Whatever had happened to her, she had obviously given up hope. He would regret what he was about to do. He would curse himself for it, but he could not leave her alone in this state when there was no one else to care for her. Wrapping a black velvet cover around her body, Sebastian lifted her into his arms and strode, grim-faced, from the room.

Killellan Manor—Summer 1819

The sun beat down remorselessly from a cloudless sky as Lady Caroline Armstrong made her way towards the rustic bridge which spanned the stream at the lower border of Killellan Manor's formal gardens. She paused on the pebbled banks, tempted to pull off her shoes and stockings and dip her feet in the burbling waters, but knowing she would then be in full view of the house she resisted, her desire to be alone much more powerful than her need to cool down.

Not that anyone was at all likely to be interested in her whereabouts, Caro thought dispiritedly. At sixteen, she already felt as if she had endured enough upheaval to last her a lifetime. She barely remembered Mama, who had died when Caro was five. Celia had taken her place, but two years ago Celia too had abandoned them to accompany her new husband on a diplomatic mission to Egypt. Her eldest sister's departure had left the four remaining sisters quite bereft. The murder by renegade tribesmen of George, Celia's husband, had shocked Caro to the core, though not nearly as much as the subsequent developments which saw Celia happily ensconced in Arabia and married to a Sheikh. Of course Caro was glad Celia had found happiness but she couldn't help wishing, just a little selfishly, she had found it a little closer to home. She missed Celia terribly, especially now that things had changed so drastically at Killellan Manor.

Pausing in the middle of the bridge to carry out the ritual of casting a twig into the waters, waiting only long enough for it to emerge, bobbing and bumping along in the shallows on the other side, Caro took the path which led through the woods to the borders of her father, Lord Armstrong's estate. It was quiet here and cooler, the sun's rays dappling down through the rich green canopy of the leaves.

She made her way along the path almost without looking, her thoughts focused inwards. They had always been close, the five sisters, but Celia had been the glue which bound them. Since she left they had all, it seemed to Caro, retreated from each other in their own way. Cassie, who always wore her heart on her sleeve, had hurled herself, in typically melo-dramatic fashion, into her coming-out Season. She had already fallen wildly in love with the dashing young poet Augustus St John Marne and had taken to declaiming long tracts of his terrible poetry, at the end of which she inevi-tably collapsed dramatically in tears. Caro, for what it was worth, thought Augustus sounded like a bit of a ninny. Cressie had simply locked herself away with her precious books. And as for Cordelia—well, Cordelia always was as mysterious as a cat.

The only thing which united the sisters these days was their enmity towards Bella. Caro kicked viciously at a stone which lay in her path, sending it flying into a cluster of ferns. Bella Frobisher, now Lady Armstrong, their fa-ther's new wife. Their new stepmother. Cassie had summed it up best. 'Bella,' she had said dismissively, 'has no interest in anything but usurping all of us by providing Papa with a son and heir. As far as Bella is concerned, the sooner she can empty Papa's nest of its cur-rent occupants and replace us with her own little cuckoos the better.' And that prediction had proven to be wholly accurate. Bella made her indifference towards her stepdaughters quite plain. And as for Papa, once he had ensconced his new wife at Killellan, he was as absent a father as ever, wholly consumed by his political manoeuvrings. Not even Bella, it seemed, was as important as the diplomatic affairs which sent him to London, Lisbon and goodness knows where he was just now.

It could be Timbuktu for all Caro cared. Except she did care, no point denying it. Papa was all she had left. She wished that he would, every once in a while, put his family before his country. She knew he loved her, he was her father, after all, but there were times, like now, when she was completely miserable and it would be nice to have some evidence of the fact. She kicked even harder at another, bigger stone. The pain which stabbed her toe was comforting, a physical reflection of her inner mood.

The woods came to an abrupt end at a boundary wall. On the other side, the lands belonged to the Marquis of Ardhallow. Rich and holder of one of the oldest titles in England, the marquis was a virtual recluse. His wife had obviously died long ago, for no mention was ever made of her. Papa was one of the few visitors permitted access and always made a point of visiting the marquis on the rare occasions when he was at Killellan long enough to pay calls. 'The Marquis of Ardhallow has one of the most prestigious titles in the country. If he chooses to live in seclusion, it is not for us to question, or to annoy him with unwanted invitations,' he had once informed Celia, who had inadvertently roused Papa's anger by inviting the marquis to dinner. 'It is a shame the man decided not to take up his seat in the Lords for he's a Tory to the core, and one must never underestimate the power he could wield if he chose to.'

Lord Armstrong's enigmatic words had unwittingly given rise to a myth. Propping her chin on her hands, gazing across the meadow at the house in the distance, Caro recalled the many tales she and her sisters had spun about their elusive neighbour. Tall and very thin, he could have been a handsome man were it not for the meanness of his mouth, the coldness in his eyes. Upon the rare occasions she had come across him out on his estate—for Caro and her sisters were wont to trespass there often when out playing, when they were much younger—the marquis's haughty stare had frozen her to the bone. He wore the powdered wig and wide-skirted coats of his youth too, giving the appearance of having stepped out of a portrait. When he spoke, it was with a strange lisp at odds with the iciness of his tone, which terrified them. For the Armstrong sisters, the marquis had come to epitomise the evil, brooding monster in their darker make-believe games. Crag Hall was their haunted castle. It was Cassie who gave him the nickname Marquis of Ardhellow. Papa, who was somewhat in awe of the man, would be appalled by the liberties his daughters had taken with his neighbour's prestigious title and spotless reputation.

Without her sisters, trespassing upon the Crag Hall estate had lost much of its appeal. Today however, the spirit of rebellion which she had to work so hard to suppress, combined with a need to put as much distance between herself and her own home, prompted Caro to climb over the boundary wall and into the grounds for the first time in years. She would welcome an encounter with the intimidating owner, she told herself. Though she was not exactly sure what she would say to him, she was certain she would not simply turn tail as she had done when younger.

The house was vast, three storeys of blond sandstone with six sets of windows placed either side of the huge Palladian Corinthian frontispiece giving it the look of a Roman temple. Two sets of stairs led up the pillared entrance-way, the pediment of which was carved with the family motto and the Ardhallow coat of arms. Only Papa had ever been inside, and Papa was not inclined to describe in any sort of detail a house of which he was clearly envious. Caro imagined a whole series of opulent rooms opening out the one on to the other, hung with tapestries and huge historical paintings, the kind usually seen only in churches.

Skirting the path which led around the west wing to the rear, avoiding the large walled kitchen gardens, she headed for the rose garden. It was then that she spied the riderless horse. A beautiful creature with a coat the colour of golden sand, it was galloping full-tilt across the paddock towards her, bucking and snorting in its efforts to rid itself of the empty saddle. Surprised and entranced, she felt a fleeting sympathy for the animal, followed by a much stronger desire to ride the untamed creature, to feel the exhilaration of trying to control such an elemental force of nature. The horse came to an abrupt halt right in front of her, flanks heaving, eyes staring wildly. Unthinking, Caro stretched out her hand to touch the soft velvet of his nose.

'No!'

She froze.

'For God's sake, are you out of your mind? Can't you see he's spooked? He'll take your fingers off.'

She dropped her hand and stared in astonishment. Striding towards her, dressed in breeches, top boots and a shirt, all of which were covered in a film of fine dust, was a young man wearing a furious expression. He was also carrying a riding crop which, by the look of him, Caro reckoned, he would happily use on her.

Later, she would notice that he was also a very attractive young man. Later, she would also notice that he was well built, with the natural grace of an athlete. But for now, it was that riding crop and the furious look in his eyes which made her glare at him defiantly, and just as defiantly reach out once more for the horse, clucking softly in the way that never failed, and did not let her down now. The young stallion tossed his head once, then nudged her palm, snickering contentedly.

'What the devil!'

Caro cast him a triumphant look. 'It is simply a question of empathy. Animals respond to gentleness,' she said, with a pointed look at his whip. 'If your riding is as aggressive as your language, Mr Whatever-your-name-is, then I am not surprised this magnificent beast threw you.'

For a moment, she really did think she had gone too far. He glared at her, delivering a look even darker than her own. Then he threw his head back and laughed, a deep, rumbling and intensely masculine laugh.

He was younger than she had first thought, probably not that much older than she was herself. His hair was close-cropped, very dark brown tinted with bronze, which seemed to reflect the colour of his eyes. She had thought him austere in his anger, but in humour his face was quite changed. His expression softened when cleared of its frown, though his mouth was still intriguingly turned down at the corners. The day's growth which darkened his jaw, the smattering of hair she could see through the open neck of his shirt, the deep tan on his forearms and neck, all added to a general impression of wildness which appealed to Caro on a fundamental level, in the mood she was in.

His frown returned as he watched her stroking the horse's pale blaze. 'Let me assure you, young lady, that if this animal let you close enough to inspect his flanks, you would find not a trace of violence. Who the hell are you?'

'I'm Caro. I live over there.' She waved vaguely in the direction of her home.

'You mean Killellan Manor, Lord Armstrong's place? I met one of his daughters once. Haughty female, tall. Lady Celia, I think her name was.' He frowned, peering into her face, and raised his eyebrows in surprise. 'Yes, I can see the resemblance now, though you are not so tall, and your hair...'

'Is more carrot than Titian. Thank you for pointing that out,' Caro said.

'Actually, it is more like copper. Burnished copper. I don't think I've ever seen anything like it.'

'Oh. That was a compliment.'

'A very badly worded one, I'm not surprised you took it amiss. I'm Sebastian, incidentally.' He made a face. 'Actually, Sebastian Conway, Earl of Mosteyn.'

Caro's eyes widened. 'Good grief, you are the marquis's son!'

'For my sins.'

'I can't believe our paths have never crossed until now,' she said blithely.

'I don't live here, when I can avoid it. I find

that my father and I deal best when we are not confined under the same roof.'

'Well, you must deal very badly indeed if you cannot stand being under such a very large roof,' Caro replied. Realising too late that she had been both rude and probably hurtful, she covered her mouth with her hand. 'I'm sorry. I didn't mean...'

Sebastian shrugged. 'No need to apologise, it's the truth. My father finds my presence offensive. Nothing about my person pleases him and nothing I can do will change his mind. He packed me off to Harrow at the first opportunity. I went straight from there to Oxford of my own accord. In the weeks since I came down, my mere presence here has offended every bone in his stiff-necked body. Fortunately, I am not obliged to please him, having come into some money of my own. I'm off to London next week, and shall be more than thankful to shake the dust from this place for ever.'

Though the picture he painted was painfully bleak, his tone was flippant. 'My father is lately remarried,' Caro said. 'There is only so much influence he can accrue by marrying off his daughters, you see. He has decided the time has come for him to produce some sons.

Or at least, for Bella to produce some sons. Bella is my new stepmother. She hates me.'

'And so you are trespassing on my father's grounds in order to escape.'

'It will have to suffice since *I* have not the means to run off to London, unlike some,' Caro said, ignoring the lump which had risen in her throat at the unexpected understanding in his voice.

'You'll be there soon enough for the Season, no doubt.'

'Yes.' Though she had never considered any other future save the marriage her father would arrange for her, the idea was depressing. 'Well, naturally,' Caro said, forcing a smile, 'making a good match is what Papa expects of us, though he has Cassie and Cressie to manage before it is my turn.'

'Manage! You make it sound like some sort of game.'

'Oh no, indeed not! I mean, that is what Cressie says, she calls it marital chess, but she is quite—I mean I am sure that Papa wants only the best for us. It has been difficult for him, losing Mama when Cordelia was just a baby. We owe it to him to—it is natural to want to please one's father, is it not?'

'So I am told.'

It had seemed important to explain herself to him for some reason, but in her earnestness, she had quite forgotten how the conversation had taken this turn. Sebastian looked morose. 'Things cannot possibly be so bad as you think, can they? I know that fathers and sons do not always see eye to eye. Indeed, sometimes fathers and daughters disagree fundamentally,' Caro said, thinking of Celia's second marriage, to which it had taken Lord Armstrong a considerable time to reconcile himself. She put a tentative hand on Sebastian's arm. 'I sometimes think my father doesn't care for me at all, but I know that is just—he is simply not affectionate by nature. At heart I am sure...'

He brushed her arm away angrily. 'My father has no heart. Look, I am sure you mean well, but you know nothing of the circumstances and furthermore it's none of your business. I can't think why I—but we will drop the subject, if you please.'

He wasn't looking at her, but frowning off into the distance, intimidatingly remote. She was abruptly conscious of her youth and her presumption. How pathetic she must have sounded. No wonder he was angry. The best thing she could do was to leave him in peace, even if it was the last thing she wanted.

'I beg your pardon for intruding, and for trespassing, I will not do it again,' Caro said in a small voice. 'I can see that you would prefer to be left alone, so I'll just…'

'No, I'm sorry. It's this place, I find it always blackens my mood.' Sebastian was not smiling, but his frown wasn't quite as deep, and he was looking directly at her. 'Stay a moment and make my horse's acquaintance properly.'

Did he mean it, or was he just being polite? She found him difficult to read, but she wanted to stay, and so decided to take him at his word. 'He's very beautiful. What is his name?'

'Burkan.'

'Is he a true Arabian? I have never seen one, they are very rare are they not? How on earth did you come by him?'

'He is only half-Arabian. He was a gift for my nineteenth birthday.'

'You see!' Caro exclaimed. 'Your father is clearly not as black as you have painted him if he is capable of such a generous present.'

Sebastian may as well have donned a suit of armour, so clear was it that he had no desire to say any more on the subject. Curious as she was, Caro bit her tongue. 'May I ride him?' she asked instead.

'Don't be ridiculous. He's barely broken.'

It was her one talent. She had not Celia's diplomacy nor Cassie's looks, nor Cressie's brain nor Cordelia's wit, but she could ride. 'I'm not being ridiculous. You saw how quickly I gained his trust. He won't throw me. I am certain of it.'

'Lady Caroline…'

'Caro.'

'Caro. You are barely broken yourself. You are simply not up to handling a horse of his size and power.'

'I can do it.'

Sebastian smiled down at her. A frowning smile. A dismissive smile which was both hurtful and annoying. 'You are the strangest girl I have ever met.' He touched her cheek. 'But I cannot take the chance. If you fell and were hurt…'

The rebellious mood in which she had set off from Killellan returned. Confused by the way Sebastian's touch made her feel, knowing that he would laugh at her innocence if he knew the effect he had on her, Caro broke away. She was tired of being dismissed. In one leap she was over the fence, the bridle in her hands. The stirrup was high, her petticoats a major obstacle, but she had scrambled into the saddle before he could stop her, and was away, urging Burkan into a canter and then a full gallop around the paddock. A fleeting glimpse over her shoulder gave her the satisfying view of Sebastian standing confounded, hands on hips, unable to do anything but look on helplessly.

The horse was nervous, but Caro was not. She sat straight astride in the saddle, heedless of her skirts. It was a talent she had discovered while very young, her affinity with horseflesh. She had never, however, ridden any animal so highly strung nor so powerful. Burkan took all her strength and determination to control for two circuits of the paddock. Confident that she had proven her point, Caro tried to rein in. The stallion however, was enjoying his freedom and refused to co-operate. Leaning over his neck, Caro tightened the reins and tried to soothe him, but the slender thread of communication between them seemed to have been severed. The horse bucked. She clung tight, but he bucked again and Caro found herself soaring over his head, landing with a horrible thud on her bottom.

Sick with mortification, dizzy with pain, she was struggling to her feet when Sebastian reached her. 'Devil take it, are you hurt?'

She hurt all over, if truth be told, and her pride had been severely dented, but there was no way on this earth that she'd let him know that. 'I'm perfectly fine.'

Sebastian swore. He swore a lot, it seemed to Caro. She envied him the freedom. 'You're quite pale, are you sure you're unharmed.'

'It's my hair. Red hair and pale skin always go together.'

'Your hair isn't red, it's copper, and you are not a healthy shade of pale. Are you going to faint?'

She gritted her teeth and breathed deeply. 'No. Absolutely not.' Trembling now, at her own temerity as much as anything, she realised, too late, how childish her behaviour must have looked. 'Burkan, is he hurt?'

'He's fine. I was rather more concerned about you. You could have been killed.'

'Oh, I'm a lot less fragile than I look, I assure you.'

Sebastian caught her as she staggered. 'You're a bold little thing, I'll grant you that. Weren't you scared?'

'No.' His hands were warm on the thin sleeves of her muslin gown. She hadn't realised until now how tall he was. And how solid, compared to her. He smelled of sweat and horse and summer, a heady, intoxicating combination. Her heart was racing. She felt strange. 'I'm sorry,' Caro said belatedly.

Sebastian smiled his frowning smile. 'No, you're not.'

She couldn't help but smile back at him. 'I would be, if Burkan had been harmed by my poor horsemanship.'

Her hair had escaped its ribbon. She could feel it, hanging in long straggles over her face and down her back. Her hands were dusty. Her gown must be filthy. Caro was not usually aware of any of these things, but now she wished—she wished...

What she wished, she realised with a horrible sense of shame and excitement, was for Sebastian to kiss her. She'd never been kissed. She had never found the idea of kissing someone anything other than repugnant until now. The way he was looking at her though—was he thinking the same? It was absurd. 'I should go,' Caro muttered, blushing, hiding her blush beneath the fall of her hair.

Sebastian blinked and released her. It seemed to her he did it reluctantly, but she knew she must be wrong. She was not much more than a child to him—he had said as much—though she didn't feel anything like a child just at the moment. 'I'll walk you back,' he said.

'No, thank you, I shall be…'

'I wasn't asking for permission.'

She had nothing to say to that and so, terrified of appearing gauche or worse still, betraying her shocking thoughts, instead simply shrugged in a very good impression of indifference, and began to clamber over the paddock fence, quite forgetting that she could easily have opened the gate.

They walked through the woods in silence. There was between them an awkwardness, an awareness which she could not describe. She did not want their walk to end, but it did, and too soon. 'This is where I leave you,' she said, pausing to the wall at the edge of the woods, waiting—for what?

Nothing, it seemed. Sebastian held out his hand. 'Goodbye, Caro.'

She took it briefly. 'Goodbye, Sebastian.' Without another word, she climbed over the wall and took off through the woods, refusing to allow herself to look back.

Chapter Two

Crag Hall—August 1830

Caro slowly came round to consciousness. She felt as if she had swum to the surface of a deep, dark pool, exhausting herself in the process. Her head was thumping. Her eyelids were gritty and sore, as if she had been rubbing sand in them. What was wrong with her? Pushing herself upright, she opened her eyes, wincing as the room spun sickeningly. The ceiling was ornate, with rococo gilding on the cornicing. The bed hangings were green damask, as were the curtains. Tulip wood, she thought distractedly, running her trembling hands over the bedstead with its gilt carving. A dressing table set by the window was draped in white lace. The walls were painted a pale green and hung with a number of portraits. A white marble mantel upon which a large French clock sat, was carved with cupids.

It was, or had been, an elegant room. As her senses slowly unscrambled Caro began to notice the shabbiness, the fine layer of dust which covered the furniture, the faded fabric, the musty air of neglect. Where was she?

Breathing deeply to quell her rising panic, she threw back the sheets and stumbled over to the window, pushing open the casement. Fresh country air flooded in. She was clearly not in London, then. Outside, it was dusk. There was a paddock. Gardens. Woods. And in the distance, the chimney pots of another house. A very familiar house. Oh, dear heavens, an extremely familiar house. Killellan Manor. Which meant that this house was…

She looked around her in consternation. She pinched her hand, something she'd always thought people did only in novels. It hurt, but she didn't wake up because she wasn't asleep. She really was here, in Crag Hall. Appalled, she tottered back to sit on the edge of the bed. How did she get here? Frowning hard, her head aching with the effort to concentrate, she tried to recall. Her memory came back in flashes.

Her father shouting, then coldly formal. Her storm of tears followed by an urgent need to forget, to obliterate it all, just for a moment.

Who had told her of the room in Augustus St John Marne's house? It didn't matter. She remembered it now, the sweet smell, the bitter taste, and then the dreams. A great bear with yellow teeth and malevolent eyes. A fish with bleeding scales. An endless corridor with door upon door which led to a sheer drop. She had fallen and fallen and fallen and not once landed. Dreams. Nightmares. Visions. But how had she come to be here?

A tap on the door made her clutch foolishly at the bedcover, pulling it up over her nightgown. *Her* nightgown. Had someone then packed her clothes? And who had dressed her? She watched the door open with a heart which beat far too fast and a growing sense of dread.

'You're awake.'

Her heart plummeted. Sebastian hovered on the threshold. Caro froze, terrified to move lest her emotions boil over. She mustn't cry, she must *not* cry. His frown was deeper than she remembered, and the shadows under his eyes were darker. He looked older. Sadder? No, but not happy either. Which was no concern of hers. She must remember the last time they had spoken, how disillusioned she had been, how hurtful he had been.

'You said you never wanted to see me again,' she said, opting for attack to cover her mortification and confusion, 'so what am I doing here?'

He flinched, and she could not blame him for her voice sounded much more aggressive than she had intended, but she had to keep hold, she had to keep sufficient control of herself to get out of here. 'The last thing I remember is Augustus St John Marne's party.'

Sebastian closed the door and leaned against it. He was wearing riding breeches and top boots, a shirt, open at the neck. He was tanned. She didn't like the way he was looking at her. She had forgotten that way he had, of making her feel as if he could read her mind.

'If I hadn't stumbled across you there and rescued you, it would most likely have been the last thing you ever remembered. Or perhaps that was your intention,' he said.

'Of course not!'

'You came pretty close, Caro.'

'Nonsense.' She swallowed uncertainly. Her throat was sore. An image of herself, retching into a bowl, popped into her head, making her face flame. 'I am sure you exaggerate.'

Sebastian shook his head decisively. 'If the doctor hadn't given you a purge, I doubt you'd still be with us.'

Which answered that question, Caro thought, now thoroughly mortified. 'How long have I been here? And more to the point, *why* am I here? I'd have thought I'd be the last person you'd want to keep company with, after our last meeting. In fact, even more to the point, where are my clothes? I suppose I should thank you for rescuing me, not that I believe I needed rescuing, but I am perfectly fine now, and will relieve you of my presence just as soon as I am dressed.'

She jumped to her feet, staggering as a wave of dizziness swept over her. Sebastian strode across the room, catching her before she fell. '*Dammit*, Caro, you have been at death's door.'

How could she have forgotten how solid he was? And how quickly he could move. He smelled of fresh linen and soap and outdoors, hay and horse and freshly turned soil. She had an overwhelming urge to cry, and fought it by struggling to free herself. Not that she had to fight very hard. He let her go immediately. As if he could not bear to touch her. Caro sniffed. 'Was I really so close to...'

Sebastian nodded.

She sniffed harder. 'I truly did not mean to—you must not think it was deliberate. It was just—I was just...' Her voice trembled. She took a shaky breath. 'I merely wished to blot everything out. Just for a while. I don't suppose you understand that, but...'

'Oblivion. I understand that need very well. As I think you remember,' Sebastian said curtly.

Oblivion. It was Caro's turn to flinch. 'I should go.'

'Don't be ridiculous.'

'Sebastian, I know you don't want me here.' She tried to push past him, though where she thought she was going dressed only in her nightgown, she had no idea. He caught her, pulling her firmly up against him. Heat of a very different sort flooded her, taking her aback, as her breasts were crushed against his chest.

For the briefest of seconds, she saw the same heat reflected in his eyes, then he blinked, his face set and he released her, taking up a post at the window, as far away from her as the room would allow, she noted without surprise. 'May I ask where you plan to go?' he asked.

Caro shrugged. 'Back to my lodgings, where else?'

'I took you there from St John Marne's. I couldn't believe it when I discovered you don't even have a maid. I paid that vulture of a land-lady to watch over you once the doctor had given you a purge, and when I came back the next morning she was nowhere to be seen. Your trunk was packed. She left me a note requesting me to leave the key in the lock.'

It hurt, more than it should, for she should be accustomed to being an outcast by now. 'One more place where I am *persona non grata*,' Caro said with a fair attempt at nonchalance. 'There are plenty other landladies. I must assume, from your decision not to return me to the bosom of my loving family, that you are aware that I have been cast out?'

'I heard that you and Rider had separated.'

She felt her cheeks flame. 'It is not like you to be so polite, Sebastian. I can tell from the way you hesitated that you have heard significantly more than that. You have not asked me how much of it is true.'

'What difference would it make? Besides, whatever you may think of me, I am no hypocrite. My reputation is hardly snowy white.'

She smiled faintly. 'No, but it is different for a man.' This was such an incontrovertible fact that he made no attempt to answer, for which she was strangely relieved. Whatever he had heard, he had not judged her. It was the smallest of consolations, but it was a balm nonetheless. 'My father came to see me earlier on the day you found me at St John's. He was just back from the Balkans. He was so angry that I, the one dutiful daughter he thought he had, should be the cause of such a dreadful scandal. It is ironic,' Caro said with a twisted smile, 'that of the five of us, I am the only one to have gone through with a match of his making, if one does not count Celia's first marriage, and it is that very match which is now the subject of every scandal sheet in London. He told me—he said to me—he said he was ashamed of me.'

She dug her nails into her palms. To cease feeling sorry for herself was one of her new resolutions. 'He told me that I had brought disgrace to the family name. That I was not fit company for my brothers, and that—that I am no longer his daughter. I know it was weak of me, but at the time—for that to happen on top of everything else, it was the final straw. You must believe me when I tell you that I had no intention of doing myself any fatal harm, but I confess that for a few hours, I really didn't care whether I lived or died. I am grateful to you for coming to my aid,' she finished, blinking furiously, 'truly I am, but I am perfectly capable of looking after myself.' She ran her fingers through her tangle of lank hair. 'I must look a fright.'

'Yes, you do,' Sebastian said, forcing her to laugh, for he never had been one for empty compliments. 'What will you do, Caro?'

She got to her feet and joined him at the window, looking out at the paddock. 'I don't know, but I obviously can't stay here.'

'London is hellish uncomfortable in the summer months. Sitting alone in a dingy set of rooms with nothing but your thoughts for company isn't going to solve anything. You're not nearly as strong as you think, in body or mind. You need respite, a place to recuperate, a change of scenery.'

'Then I shall go to Brighton, or Leamington Spa, or Bath. I don't care where I go, and it's none of your business.'

'Why do so, when you can stay here?' Sebastian dug his hands deep into the pockets of his riding breeches. 'Tell me honestly, Caro, was it that night which caused the rift between you and Rider?'

That night. She had grown up in more ways than one that night. '*That night* was two years ago, Sebastian,' she said coldly. 'What came between myself and my husband was entirely my own fault. If you are offering me sanctuary to assuage your conscience, let me tell you there is no need.'

'I'm offering you sanctuary because you need it! Why must you be so pig-headed!'

'I am not being pig-headed, I am being considerate,' Caro snapped, roused by his anger. 'Very well it would look, for the Marquis of Ardhallow to give house to a fallen woman whose own family are his neighbours. I can see the chimney pots of Killellan Manor from this window, for goodness' sake. The county would be in an uproar.'

To her surprise, he grinned. 'You know my reputation. One more fallen woman is neither here nor there.'

She smiled reluctantly, trying not to remember how that upside-down smile of his had always heated her. 'I could not even consider it. Papa would be mortified.'

'Isn't that all the more reason for you to stay? He has treated you appallingly, I can't believe you're going to lie down and take it.'

She opened her mouth to protest, then closed it again, much struck by this.

'You don't owe him anything, Caro,' Sebastian urged, as if he could read her thoughts. Which he used to do, remarkably well.

'Papa told me I had fallen as low as it was possible to fall,' she said bitterly.

'Then show him that he's wrong.'

She was absurdly tempted, but still she shook her head. 'It is very kind of you, but...'

'Kind! I am never kind,' Sebastian broke in harshly. 'I thought you knew me better.'

She looked at him wonderingly, playing for time as she tried to make sense of his motives. Though they had known each other for more than ten years, the time they had spent together had been fleeting. Though they had shared the most intimate of experiences, *that night* if nothing else should have proven to her that she had been wholly mistaken in him. 'I barely know you, Sebastian, any more than you know me. We may as well be strangers.'

He looked hurt, but covered it quickly. 'Not complete strangers. We are two renegades in the wilderness with nothing to lose, we have that much in common.'

'I am not—you know, I think you may be right. I have lived my entire life bending to other people's will, perhaps now it's time to live my own life. Whatever that may be.'

'Then you'll stay?'

Her smile faded. 'Why, Sebastian? Truthfully?'

'Truthfully?' He stared out of the window. 'I don't know. I swore I'd have nothing to do with you again, but when I saw you at St John Marne's—no, don't bridle, you were pathetic then, but you are not pitiful. I suppose, despite all, I don't think you deserve the bad press you have received...'

'And that feeling resonates with you?'

She knew she should not have said it, that it was deliberately provocative, but he had always had that effect on her, and to her surprise he smiled ruefully. 'Perhaps.'

It was this rare admission that decided her. 'Then if you mean it, I will stay. For a little while. Until I have recovered my strength and am in a better position to decide what to do.'

'Good.' Sebastian nodded. 'I—good.'

The bedchamber door closed softly behind him. What on earth had she done? Caro looked out the window at the rooftop of her family home, and discovered that her strongest emotion was relief. A lifetime's obedience to the call of duty had backfired spectacularly. She was done with it! The shock of coming so close to death made her realise how much she valued her life. Whatever she would become now, it would be of her own making.

London, Spring 1824

The room in which the séance was to be held was dimly lit. Sebastian's knowledge of séances and mediums was confined to one slim volume. *Communication with the Other Side* it had been titled, written by Baron Lyttleton. He had come across it in the vast library of Crag Hall on his latest—brief as ever—visit. The tome described the author's conversations with the departed. Arrant nonsense, Sebastian had thought derisively. He had not changed his view.

Kitty, however, seemed genuinely to believe in the whole charade. His current mistress had, to his astonishment, become sobbingly sentimental upon the subject of her dead mother from whom she had parted on poor terms when she had first embarked upon her fledgling career as a courtesan. Kitty had resorted to tears in her efforts to persuade Sebastian to escort her here tonight. 'If I could just talk to Mama once, Seb, I know I could explain, make her proud of me,' she had said.

The fact that she was naked at the time save for her trademark diamond collar, having just performed expert, if somewhat clinical fellatio upon him, made Sebastian somewhat sceptical of the point Kitty was making. He had gritted his teeth at her use of the diminutive of his name, something he had always loathed, but there was little merit in constantly correcting her. He was already bored with Kitty, and under no illusion about her feelings for him either. His rakehell reputation made him a desirable catch for her, but there were so many other fish swimming in her pond that it was only a matter of time before her avarice overcame her promise of exclusivity, and exclusivity was one of the very few principles to which Sebastian held true.

He had already purchased the diamond bracelet which would be her farewell gift after tonight's entertainment. Though he had no doubt it would prove to be a clever hoax, the séance had at least the merit of being a novel experience. God knows, after more than four years in the *ton,* there were few enough of those left to him.

They were a strange collection, the other guests in the room, some surprisingly well-heeled. He recognised at least two grand-dames, bedecked in black silk and lace, who turned quickly away from him, though whether it was because they were ashamed to be caught dabbling in the black arts, or ashamed to be seen in the company of the notorious Earl of Mosteyn, Sebastian could not say. More likely the latter, though.

'Do stop staring, Seb, it is not at all the thing.' Kitty, resplendent in red silk, her justly famous bosom demurely covered by a spangled scarf, tugged reprovingly at his arm. 'And take that cynical look off your face. These people are seeking solace from their loved ones, just as I am. Do not mock them, or me, for that matter.'

Sebastian eyed his about-to-be-ex-mistress with some surprise. 'You really do believe in this balderdash, don't you?'

'Yes, I do. And so too do the rest of the audience, so you will please me this one last time, and refrain from disrupting the proceedings.' Kitty adjusted her bracelet over her evening glove, then drew him a very candid look. 'Oh yes, I know your mind better than you think. I am perfectly well aware that you are about to give me my *congé*, so I will accept your promise to behave as the gentleman you were raised to be in lieu of any more prosaic payment.'

'Alas, I had already purchased diamonds for you. But if you are sure…'

'Then of course, it would be very rude of

me to decline them,' Kitty said with one of her sweetest smiles.

'You may have my promise and the jewellery both,' Sebastian said, making the smallest of bows, 'and please accept my compliments too. Our time together has been most pleasurable.'

'Naturally it has. My reputation is not undeserved.' Once more Kitty adjusted her bracelet, a smile playing on her lips. 'Nor indeed is yours, my lord. The pleasure has been quite mutual.'

He would have been flattered had he cared, but he did not. They were both adept at giving pleasure. They had both had many years' practice. They were skilled enough to have turned love-making into an art and indifferent enough to ensure that it remained exactly that—a pleasant pastime which was neither necessary nor encroaching, an indulgence of the senses which was no drain on the emotions.

Which, thought Sebastian, as he watched the other attendees begin to seat themselves around the large table placed in the centre of the room, explained why he was so bored. He needed change. And he needed distance. That last interview with his father preyed on his mind. Having the marquis threaten to disown him unless he mended his profligate ways should have felt like a victory, but the truth was, Sebastian's taste for scandal and his reputation for refusing no wager, no matter how dangerous, had become as tedious to him as they were repugnant to his father. Perhaps he should consider the Continent.

There were still two empty spaces at the table. As the maidservant circled the room dimming the lamps, one of the chairs was taken by a lady. Tall and slim, he could not at first see her face, which was obscured by her neighbour, but there was something, a prickling awareness, which drew his attention. Unlike the other women, she did not wear an evening gown, but a plain muslin dress with long sleeves, cut high at the neck. Her hair was piled in a careless knot on top of her head. Even in the dim light, he could see it gleaming. His memory stirred.

The arrival of the medium, an impressively large woman bedecked in lilac, intruded on his view. Mrs Foster, *spirit guide and conduit to the hereafter*, to give her her full billing, took the remaining empty chair. The lights were extinguished and the séance began.

Grateful for the anonymity afforded by the dark, Caro concentrated on trying to get her breath back. Bella, with Cressie in tow and no doubt the cause of their tardy departure, had only just left Cavendish Square for the Frobishers' ball, resulting in Caro having to run all the way here, unwilling to risk waiting for a passing hackney cab, lest she miss the beginning of the séance. She had come on impulse, pretending a headache after a piece on Mrs Foster in the *Morning Post* had piqued her interest. Her sensible self told her that it was silly to expect to make contact with her mother, who had been dead nearly fifteen years, during which time her ghost had stubbornly refused to appear. Her sensible self told her that even if Mama did want to communicate in some way, it was highly unlikely that she would do so through Mrs Foster, with whom Lady Catherine Armstrong had never, to the best of Caro's knowledge, been acquainted. So spoke Caro's sensible self, but her secret self was slightly desperate and could not help but hope.

'Let us all join hands.'

Mrs Foster had surprisingly large, meaty hands, more suited to a butcher than a medium. Her fingers, which rested on Caro's, were warm in contrast to those of the man seated on her other side, which had the quality of parchment and made her shiver. *Like someone walking over your grave,* melodramatic Cassie would say. Could this woman really conjure voices from *beyond* the grave? As the room grew suddenly cold, Caro began to think it possible.

'Concentrate,' Mrs Foster intoned in a deep, sonorous voice, 'concentrate on summoning the spirits of the dear departed.'

The silence intensified, becoming thick as treacle. A smell, a terrible noxious stench, horribly like something emerging from a crypt, drifted into the room, carried on wisps of strange white smoke. One of the women seated round the table began to whimper. Caro's hand was clutched painfully tight by the man at her side. On her other side, Mrs Foster's hand had become icy and cold, like marble.

Caro tried not to panic. Part of her was sure it was a charade, but another part of her was afraid that it was not. She had assumed that speaking to Mama would be reassuring, that knowing Mama was there for her would make it easier to bear the absences of those who were not—Papa, Cassie, Celia—and accept the presence of the one person she wished really would go away, Bella. But whatever presence was in this room, it was not benevolent.

The smoke drifted towards the ceiling, and the smell changed, from acrid and dank to something sweeter. Lilies perhaps? The clutching man next to her gasped, making Caro jump. Of its own accord, the table rattled, and the muslin curtains at the long windows blew gently as a light breeze wafted through the salon. One of the female guests squealed. Caro, her leg pressed too close to Mrs Foster's voluminous skirts, had felt the woman's knee jerk upwards, but was it before or after the table moved? She could not be sure.

The medium began to speak, her voice tremulous. 'I have someone standing behind me. Catherine.'

Catherine was Mama's name. A cold sweat prickled Caro's spine.

'Catherine.' The medium's voice grew higher in pitch, like the whine of a recalcitrant child. 'Is Catherine there? She wishes to speak to Catherine.'

To Catherine. The disappointment was so acute that it made Caro feel sick and slightly silly. It hadn't occurred to her that Mama may have to wait her turn, if she appeared at all. She almost jumped out of her skin when the woman on the other side of the table spoke up, claiming this ghost as hers.

'Mama?' the woman said uncertainly. 'Mama, is that you? It is I, Catherine. Kitty.'

'Kitty.'

The voice, the same strangled, whining voice which had emanated from Mrs Foster, now seemed to be projected from the other side of the room. A trick? Surely it must be a trick. Had the medium's lips moved? Caro couldn't see.

'Catherine. Kitty. It is your mama.'

A muffled shriek greeted this statement. 'I am so sorry for our quarrel, Mama. Can you forgive me? I know you disapprove of my— my career, but it has brought me prosperity and security. Please try to be proud of me.'

'Of course I am, my darling daughter. I am at peace now, Kitty. At peace.'

The voice trailed away. Still, Caro could not tell if it came from Mrs Foster or some other presence. The table rattled again. The smell of lilies grew sickly sweet, and the medium spoke once more, this time in a deep growl. 'George?'

There was no answer. The attendees waited, it seemed to Caro, with bated breath, until the name was uttered again. More silence.

'Edward?' Mrs Foster ventured, in that now familiar high-pitched voice.

The clutching man at Caro's side let go of her hand. 'Nancy? Could it be my Nancy?'

'Edward, it is your Nancy. It is I, my dear.'

She wanted to believe it, but it struck Caro that Mrs Foster's messages from beyond the grave seemed to rely on information provided by the audience rather than the spirit world. It had to be a trick. Of course, she'd known it would most likely be so, but all the same...

Her fear turned to anger. It was not fair, to give out the promise of false hope. What an utter fool she had been to think it could be otherwise. Even if Mrs Foster hadn't been a charlatan—yes, there went the table again, and this time Caro was sure that the medium's knee jerked *before* and not after—even if she had been *bona fide*, even if Mama had made contact, what comfort could she have given her daughter? Bella still hated her. Papa still acted as if he cared nothing for her—or any of his daughters. And Caro was still faced with the prospect of either making a good match to please him or spending the rest of her life looking after Bella's many progeny. Her stepmother had already given birth to two boys, and she was increasing again. Killellan stripped of all of her sisters would be unbearable. Cressie, in her second Season, was bound to make a match in the near future, and Cordelia made no secret of her desire to wed as soon as possible in order to escape home, where Bella and her infant sons ruled the roost. Caro sighed. Why was it that doing one's duty seemed sometimes so unrewarding?

Having assured George that his Nancy, like Kitty's mama, was very happy and at peace, Mrs Foster slumped back in her chair with a deep, animalistic groan which distracted Caro from her melancholy thoughts. Her hand was released. As if by magic, though obviously with the impeccable timing of practice, the maid appeared to turn up the lamps. Caro rubbed her eyes. Across the table from her, a woman was sobbing delicately into her kerchief. The aforementioned Kitty, she presumed, and obviously wholly convinced that she had just communed with her mother. Lucky Kitty, to be so easily placated.

Caro stared at her, fascinated. The woman was voluptuously beautiful. Tears sparkled on her absurdly long dark lashes, but signally failed to either redden the woman's nose or make tracks down her creamy skin. When Caro cried, which she hated to do, her nose positively bloomed and her skin turned a blotchy red.

A prickling feeling, a sense of somebody watching her, made her drag her eyes away from the beauty to the man at her side. Her heart did sickening somersaults as she looked quickly away. It could not be he, it simply could not be. She sneaked another glance. *It was him!* What on earth was Sebastian doing here? Surely not, like her, in the hopes of communing with his dead mother!

It was almost four years since they had met, four years since she had tumbled headlong into that girlish crush which she ought to have recovered from long since. Which of course she had recovered from! It was a shock, that was all, seeing him here, looking even more raffishly handsome than she remembered. He had garnered a frankly wicked reputation in that time, while she had turned him, in her imagination, into her dashing knight in shining armour, riding to her rescue in her dreams, taking her away from the tedium and loneliness of her life at Killellan.

Kitty appeared to be his companion. There was something proprietary about the way the woman put her hand on Sebastian's arm. And something not quite proper in the way she was dressed. Too much bosom on display, even if it was quite magnificent. Caro's eyes widened. She must be his mistress. Yes, definitely his mistress, and a—what was the saying?—yes, a pearl of the first water, more than worthy of

Sebastian's reputation. Of a certainty, someone of his poise and experience would not look twice at a gauche stork-like female with carrot hair and no bosom to speak of. Except that he was staring, frowning at her, oblivious to his mistress's tears.

He looked shocked. It hadn't occurred to her until now, so taken up with her foolish hopes had she been, but she supposed her presence here was a bit shocking. And now she was blushing. Caro pushed her chair back, intent on leaving before he could approach her, because though the thing she wanted most in the world was to talk to him, the thing she wanted least in the world was to be chastised by him, especially in the presence of his beautiful companion. Stumbling from the table, she was halfway across the room when Sebastian caught up with her.

'What the devil are you doing here?'

Caro turned. He was not quite so tall as she remembered, though that was probably because she had acquired so many extra inches as to make her a positive maypole, according to Bella. And he did seem bigger—broader, more solid, more intimidating, if she was of a mind to be intimidated, which she was not! 'Good evening, my lord. I seem to recall you asking me a similar question when we last met in your grounds. I see your manners have not improved much in the interim.' Her voice sounded quite cool, she was pleased to note. 'As to what I am doing here, I could easily ask you the same question. I had not thought you the kind to be interested in the afterlife.'

'One life is quite enough,' Sebastian replied feelingly.

Damned right, was her instinctive reply. She swallowed the words with a small, prim smile. 'If there is such a thing as an afterlife, I doubt very much that Mrs Foster has access to it.'

'I am relieved to hear that you were not taken in by the charade. What the devil brought you here, and alone too?'

His eyes were shadowed, with lines flanking the corners of them which had not been there before. Two more lines drew his brow into a permanent furrow. His mouth still turned down in that fascinating way. He had not the look of a happy soul. 'If you must know, I came here for the same reasons as everyone else—yourself excepted. I had the stupidest notion that I might contact my mother. I thought—oh, it doesn't matter what I thought, Sebastian, it is none of your business.'

'Does your father know about this escapade?'

'Certainly not. *He* has no interest in speaking to Mama. Oh, you mean he would disapprove of my being here. You may rest assured that he is quite oblivious, as is he seems to be of everything I do, provided it does not damage the prospects he has lined up for me.'

'His game of matrimonial chess has begun then,' Sebastian said.

'You remember that!'

Sebastian grinned. 'You almost gave me an apoplexy when you leapt on to Burkan.'

Goodness, but she had forgotten the effect his smile had on her. Caro tried and failed to suppress her own. 'I don't know why I did it, except that you were so very certain I should not.'

'And is that why you are here tonight, because you know you ought not to be?'

'What a very false impression you have of me. I will have you know, that of the five sisters, I am known as the dutiful one.'

At this, he gave a bark of laughter. The deep, masculine sound of it brought the attention of everyone in the room, including the beauty he had escorted who, having recovered her black-velvet evening cloak, was sashaying towards them, all creamy skin, black-as-night hair and voluptuous figure. Caro felt her own shortcomings acutely.

'My lord,' the beauty said, 'I am much fatigued by this experience, and would return home.'

Sebastian was looking suddenly extremely uncomfortable. Obviously, introducing his mistress to his neighbour's newly-out daughter was not a task he relished. His discomfort stirred the devil in her. 'My lord,' Caro said, 'will you not introduce me to your companion?'

Now he looked appalled. Emboldened, she held out her hand. 'How do you do? I am Lady Caroline Armstrong.'

Kitty, herself looking slightly taken aback, dropped a curtsy. 'Miss Garrison. I am honoured, my lady. Mrs Foster has a remarkable gift, has she not?'

'I'm afraid Lady Caroline is rather more of a sceptic than you, Kitty,' Sebastian drawled.

'Lady Caroline prefers to keep an open mind,' Caro said pointedly. Did he not realise that his mistress was most likely content to be duped? 'Really, Sebastian, you are every bit as rude as I recall.'

And a good deal more attractive to boot.

Heavens, but she must not let him see the effect he had on her, it would be mortifying. 'It was a pleasure to meet you again,' Caro said, 'but I must go.'

Sebastian took her hand and surprised her by bowing over it, brushing his lips over the tips of her fingers. His mouth was warm on her skin. His kiss was no more intimate than many she had received since coming out, but it felt very different. She wondered what it would like to kiss him properly, and suddenly remembered wondering the exact same thing that first time they had met. It was a struggle to retain her composure, but she managed. Just.

'Sebastian, I think we had best be on our way,' Kitty said with a pointed look at her lover. 'All this excitement has quite overset me.'

Caro snatched back her hand. Sebastian clasped his behind his back and rocked on to the heels of his polished Hessians. No evening wear for him, despite his mistress's attire. Had he come here straight from her bed? The thought made her stomach churn. She conjured up a faint smile. 'You are quite correct, Miss Garrison. I must bid you both goodnight, it was a pleasure.'

'You have a carriage waiting, I assume?' Sebastian asked.

'No, I shall have Mrs Foster's servant hail a hackney.'

He looked at her, aghast. 'You surely would not travel alone at night in a public carriage.'

'Really, it is no distance, and…'

'Sebastian is quite right,' Kitty Garrison interjected. 'Better that he escort you and I will make my own way. No, pray do not protest, I am far more capable of looking after myself on the streets of London than you are. Nor need you have any qualms that you are interfering with our plans for the evening. We have agreed we no longer suit, is that not so, my lord?'

Sebastian bowed. 'With regret.'

Kitty Garrison laughed softly. 'No regrets, my lord, only diamonds. You may have them sent round in the morning.'

She was gone in a flutter of silk and velvet, leaving behind the faintest scent of rosewater. 'I must apologise,' Sebastian said curtly. 'If it was known that you had been exchanging pleasantries with Kitty Garrison…'

'Why should that worry you?'

'It doesn't, but it should worry you.'

'Oh, *my* reputation is spotless. No one would believe it.'

They were in the small reception hall. Caro pulled on her cloak. It was made of serviceable wool and quite unadorned, worn for its all-enveloping properties, as was the wide, plain hat she had chosen. Sebastian tucked her hand into his arm as they went down the steps of Mrs Foster's house and began to walk along Great Russell Street. It was not quite dark, but the lamps were already lit on the few carriages which passed. The air had a tang to it which Caro could not get used to, of coal and dust, so different from the sharp, clean smell of the air at Killellan. As always at this time of the evening, with the night stretching ahead, there was a sense of excitement, a tension, of a city waiting for the cover of dark to fall before bursting into life.

'You know perfectly well that you should not have been at that woman's house tonight without even your maid to accompany you,' Sebastian said.

'What Papa and Bella don't know cannot harm them,' Caro responded flippantly. 'It seems to me that if they knew that *you* were accompanying me across London in the dark, they'd be a lot more concerned than if they discovered I'd attended a séance and conversed with a courtesan.'

'Their fears would be quite groundless. I never seduce innocents. Dammit, someone ought to be keeping a closer eye on you.'

'Oh, but they think they are. However, as I discovered tonight, it is remarkably easy to dupe people into believing one is doing as one ought when they don't actually care. Papa leaves us girls to Bella, and Bella is so very taken up with her darling boys that she has very little time to supervise us.'

Sebastian threw her a strange look. 'I would have thought that Lord Armstrong would show a great deal of care about who you do—or do not—spend your time with, since the whole point of the Season…'

'Is to make a match. Papa *has* taken a great deal of care. He has drawn up a list, and handed the list to Bella, whose job it is to orchestrate the introductions, while it is my job to make myself charming, as you would have noted for yourself had you frequented any of the numerous parties or balls I have dutifully attended.'

'I have no wish to become the prey of some matron determined to snare a husband for her daughter. There is no more terrifying creature in all the world than a mama with the scent of marriage in her nostrils.'

Caro laughed. 'It is true, there are times

when I feel as if I am being paraded around like a prime piece of horseflesh. I am twenty years of age, and my entire life is already mapped out for me. A Season to catch a husband who will embellish my father's position, a few years of docile matrimony to produce the requisite heirs, then I shall no doubt be retired to the country to rear them while my husband enjoys himself in the town as every other husband does.'

'That is a very jaded point of view.'

'Oh, I don't really mean it. I am merely a little—it is nothing. What else is someone like me to do, if not marry?'

'Attend séances.'

'Oh, tonight was a—a temporary aberration.' Caro gave herself a little shake. 'I am perfectly content to marry one of the men Papa has picked out for me. Though Cassie and Celia have made excellent marriages, they were neither of his choosing. It is only right that one of his daughters does as he bids, for it seems to me that Cressie—never mind, it doesn't matter.'

'It obviously does. Tell me.'

She hesitated, but he did seem to be genuinely interested, and the urge to confide in someone was strong now that even the prospect of hearing from Mama had disappeared. 'I know Cressie is not happy, though when I ask her if anything is wrong, she tells me that there is nothing. But I know there is. She tries so hard to pretend, but I know she hates going to dances and she would much rather be alone with her mathematical books than talking about fashion over the teacups.'

'Mathematics!'

'Cressie is the clever one. She is practically a genius,' Caro said proudly. 'She has been working on a mathematical theory of cards, something to do with probability and chance. It's all a bit over my head, but she claims that the system she has developed for faro is foolproof. I would love to be able to surprise her by proving that it is.'

'And how would you propose to do that?' Sebastian said warily.

'You are a great rake, are you not? Well, you must be, because they call you the Heartless Heartbreaker.'

'A stupid name. I doubt any of the women I have had dealings with have a heart to break.'

'Rakes are notorious gamesters.'

'Cards are not one of my vices.'

'Drink then. Though I confess, I've never understood the attraction. What is the point of drinking to excess, if you cannot remember, the next morning, whether you enjoyed yourself or not?'

'Or whether you had done anything scandalous or not,' Sebastian added drily.

'Had you had too much wine then, when you drove hell for leather in the curricle you raced to Brighton, or when you swam the length of the Serpentine in the depth of winter for a wager, or when you climbed to the top of the clock tower of St Paul's?'

'Had I been in my cups when I climbed St Paul's I would most likely be dead. It might surprise you to know, Lady Caroline, that I am not accustomed to drink to excess.'

'It is Caro. What possessed you to do such dangerous things?'

'What possessed you to ride a horse you could not control?'

She was forced to smile. '*Touché.* Would it cause a great scandal if you were to take me to a gambling hell?'

He stared at her for a moment, then burst into laughter. 'Not at all, that would be perfectly acceptable since you and I are acquainted. I recommend we try Crockford's, known as Fishmonger's Hall amongst the savvy. The stakes are prodigious there, and their reputation for fleecing every flat who enters the hallowed portals is second to none. Your sister's mathematical system will get a thorough examination, and if it works you will earn a small fortune in the process. I am jesting, I hasten to add, before you get any silly ideas.'

She had not been entirely serious, but Sebastian's teasing dismissal raised her hackles just as it had four years ago, when he told her she could not ride his horse. Were it not for the turn the conversation had taken, she would never have dreamed of doing any such a thing as visiting a hell. But she was sure she'd heard Cressie crying in her room last night. How pleased she would be when Caro presented her with the validation of her theory—if she could just persuade Sebastian to accompany her.

They were walking along Margaret Street, a few minutes from Cavendish Square. The nearer they came to her father's house, the less Caro wanted to arrive because then Sebastian would leave her. She was acutely conscious of her gloved hand on his arm, of her cloak brushing against his leg. It was sheer chance which had brought them together tonight, for they moved in very different circles. Four years since their last meeting, and most likely there would be the same before their next. 'You may be jesting, but I am in earnest. I would very much like to visit this Crockford's,' she said impulsively. 'It would make Cressie so happy.'

'You are being ridiculous.'

'It is surely not entirely without precedent for ladies to frequent such establishments, wearing either masks or veils. I may indeed be fleeced, if Cressie's theory is wrong, but I am unlikely to be ravished.'

'Caro, you can't mean it.'

She didn't, yet part of her did. There was a strange pleasure to be had in challenging him, just to watch his reaction, but there was too the fact that she would be flaunting the rules just a little. Besides, she would also be helping her sister. 'I could go disguised as a man, if you thought it would be safer that way,' she said hopefully.

'Good grief, no, you would fool no one.'

'Truly? I am so thin, I would have thought…'

'Caro.' They were at the corner of Cavendish Square, yards away from her father's house. Sebastian pulled her into the shadow of the corner building, away from the lamplight, and pushed her veil up from her face. 'It is true, you are slim enough to slip through rain, but believe me, there is nothing in the least bit boyish about you.'

He held her lightly, his hands on her arms. Not quite an intimate embrace, not quite wholly respectable either. 'Why don't you escort me there, since you are so concerned for my well-being?'

'Are you out of your mind!'

'With you as my protector I would surely be safe, and...'

'Caroline! Enough of this nonsense, you have gone too far.'

She studied him carefully. His mouth was set in a firm line, his expression stern. 'My apologies. I see now that I would be placing you in a most uncomfortable position, which is unfair of me.'

'Dammit, it's not about me. I have no reputation worthy of losing.'

'That's not true.'

'What do you mean?'

'It strikes me that you have put an enormous amount of effort into building just such a reputation.'

'It strikes me that you are doing a very poor job of winning me over.'

'I can see you are resolved not to assist me, and so I will make my own arrangements.'

His hands tightened on her arms. He pulled her the tiniest bit closer. She could feel his breath on her face. Her heart hammered in her breast. She was hot. Her stomach was churning. She felt as if she were hovering on the edge of a cliff, that giddy temptation to leap into the void almost overwhelming.

'You would not dare,' he said.

No, she would not, but nor would she back down now. 'Did I falter when faced with the challenge of riding your unbroken horse?' Caro asked.

Sebastian swore under his breath. 'You would, wouldn't you? No, don't answer that.'

'So take me then, Lord Chivalrous, it is surely your duty to do so. Your father would certainly expect it of you, to protect his neighbour's daughter.'

Sebastian's smile turned immediately to a frown. 'I could easily inform your father of tonight's events and this discussion, but you will note that I do not threaten any such thing, even though it is what any responsible man would do.'

The sudden change in his demeanour shocked her. She had quite forgotten what he had said of his relationship with his father, having dismissed it as a mere passing quarrel, but things had obviously not improved. 'I beg your pardon, I meant only to tease.'

'It doesn't matter,' he replied, though she could see that it patently did. 'Caroline, you cannot—must not—go to Crockford's alone.'

She refrained from making any further comment, aware that she had come very close to overstepping the mark. Her heart thudded as she watched him wrestling with his conscience. Her own was beginning to bother her. It was unfair of her. And wrong. But she had come too far to back down now.

She was eventually rewarded with a weary nod. 'Very well,' Sebastian said, 'you leave me with no option, Crockford's it is. But I earnestly hope we do not live to regret this rash decision.'

Chapter Three

Crag Hall—summer 1830

'So this is where you've been hiding.'

Sebastian looked up wearily from the account book to find Caro standing in the doorway. She wore a simple gown, cream striped with pale green and lemon. The scooped neck showed the soft swell of her breasts, the fragile hollows at the base of her throat. Her hair hung in soft, fiery tendrils over her shoulders. There were still shadows under her eyes, but her skin, no longer ashen, had regained the rich creaminess which had always fascinated him. There remained a fragility about her, she was still far too slim, but she had come a long way since he had brought her here. His mouth went dry as he met her eyes, the blue of a summer sky. Even after all that had passed, even with all that he knew of her, just looking at her was like a kick in the stomach. 'You look better.'

'Thanks to several good nights' rest and a bath. Your housekeeper told me I would find you here. It is very—cosy.'

Convenient was the word he would have used, for the room served as his dining room, study and parlour. Seeing it through Caro's eyes however, Sebastian realised that it was also cramped and rather shambolic. The large walnut desk stacked with account books, papers and tomes on all aspects of agriculture took up much of the available space. Two wingback chairs faced each other across the hearth. A bookcase occupied another wall, and the small table with two matching chairs took up the only remaining space, leaving little room for manoeuvre. 'I find it adequate for my simple needs,' he said defensively. 'I am close to the stables, I don't have to employ a small army of servants, and it suits me well enough.'

'Mrs Keith told me that you kept the staff to a minimum, so I suggested I eat here with you from now on to avoid being an additional burden to the household.' Caro picked her way across the room to the table and sat down. 'She looked most disapproving. I suspect she thinks we do more than eat together.'

'She may disapprove, but she won't gossip, if that's what you're worried about.'

Caro rested her chin on her hand, eyeing him speculatively. 'Are you having second thoughts, Sebastian? Mrs Keith may not gossip, but you know what it's like in the shires, my being here will probably already have been discussed over the breakfast cups at every house in the county.'

Sebastian pulled out a seat and joined her at the table. He had been so engrossed in his accounts that he'd failed to notice that it was set for two. Having persuaded her to stay, persuaded himself that his motives were purely chivalrous, her remaining closeted in her room these last two days had allowed him to fool himself into thinking that he had quite forgotten her presence. This unexpected domesticity rather took him unawares. 'I told you,' he said, 'I don't give a damn what the county say of me.'

'It's certainly clear that you have made no effort to endear yourself.'

'What the devil do you mean by that?' Sebastian demanded, irked as much by the cool confidence of her tone as by her words.

'Look at this room, it is as if you are camping out and will pack up and leave at any moment. As to the rest of the house—Sebastian, it cannot have escaped your notice that it is sadly neglected. Mrs Keith tells me all the rooms save yours are shut up. She said that I am the first person to stay here since your father died. She said…'

'She said a great deal too much. It was my father who let the house go, if you must know. It was like this when I returned from my travels.'

'Perhaps it was like this because you did not return from your travels earlier.' Caro dropped her coffee cup with a clatter. 'I'm sorry. That was unpardonable, I have no right to pass comment on your behaviour.'

'It was. And you don't,' he said tightly.

She buttered a slice of bread, cut it carefully into four triangles and began to nibble on one, saying nothing, but he was aware that she was studying him from under her lashes. Sebastian poured himself another cup of coffee and sipped it broodingly. 'I don't see what my neglecting my house has to do with what the damned county think of me,' he said.

'No?'

She shrugged, and started on a second triangle of bread. She had very white teeth. She had a very sharp mind. He had no need to justify himself to her. 'Besides, I have no time for the upkeep of this great barn of a place. Keeping the land in good heart takes all of my time and energy. Not that I get any thanks for that either.'

'I expect it's difficult for you to understand the way of things here. You told me the first day we met,' she added, in response to his questioning look, 'that you spent as little time as possible at Crag Hall. It is hardly to be expected that you would know how to manage such a large estate.'

Much as he would have liked to, Sebastian could not argue with this fact. 'An inevitable state of affairs, since my father had no more desire for my company than I had for his,' he said brusquely.

'Well, that is one thing we now have in common then,' Caro said after a short, uncomfortable silence. 'I used to think that my father was simply not the affectionate type. I was sure he loved me, even though he never gave any sign that he did. Then Bella had James, and Papa haunted the nursery, and it was the same with Henry and George and Freddie. He was never like that with us girls.'

'Caro, I'm sure…'

'No. No, there is no point in pretending. If he loved me he would not cast me off. He did not even ask if any of it was true. He took my husband at his word. They went to the same school, you know, though Papa is a good twenty years older.'

He was tempted to ask her for her side of the story, but refrained, telling himself that he did not care, that it was nothing to do with him, that her being here was merely transitory. Her attempt to smile was admirable. Though every word she said was true, he could not doubt the pain which lay behind her acceptance of such unpleasant facts, for he knew how much it had meant to her, to try to please the man. 'You seem very philosophical about it all,' he said.

'That is what happens when you come close to death. It rather gives you a perspective on your life,' Caro replied drily. 'Sebastian, why do you keep the house shut up like this?'

He threw his unused napkin onto the table. 'Dammit, can't you leave it?'

'If you were to open it up, to invite your neighbours to tea…'

'Tea! Do you honestly think they'd allow their wives and daughters to take tea with the Heartless Heartbreaker?'

She chuckled. 'I expect most of their wives and daughters would readily take anything you were prepared to offer them.'

Her eyes were alight with humour. She had a mouth made for smiling, though he was willing to bet she hadn't done much of that recently. And for kissing. It caught him unawares, the memory of her lips on his, the sweet floral scent of her, the silken softness of her glorious hair. He realised he was staring at her, and poured himself another cup of cold and unwanted coffee. She had changed, he thought. She was right, he didn't really know her at all.

'My sisters and I used to call your papa the Marquis of Ardhellow,' Caro said, interrupting his thoughts. 'We used to speculate about what the house was like. We were desperate to see inside. It is ironic that it took an overdose of opium for me to be granted my wish. From the little I have seen of the place, Crag Hall would live up to every one of the terrible tales we used to spin. It is quite Gothic in its state of neglect.'

She always did have a way of turning things on their head. That much had not changed. Sebastian pushed his full coffee cup out of reach. 'The Marquis of Ardhellow. I suppose you think the title fits me even better than it did my father.'

She pursed her lips. 'What I suppose is that you would like it to be so. You seem almost to relish your poor reputation.'

'Why not? It was hard-earned.'

Caro looked at him appraisingly. 'What a strange thing to say. And I suppose my being here can only help your cause. So, you really do intend to walk in your father's shoes after all?'

'What is that supposed to mean?'

'Shut up here, never seeing anyone. Just as he did.'

'I see people every day.'

'Tenants. Villagers. Stable hands. Your bailiff. Servants. But you don't have any friends to dinner. You don't call on your neighbours.'

'There is the small matter of your presence here. And the fact that my nearest neighbours happen to be your family.'

'Sebastian, do not be obtuse. How could you have guests call on you here, in this room which is smaller than some of your tenants' parlours? You don't even employ a cook. Such a beautiful place this is, and so obviously unloved, it is a shame.'

'I am not the one who neglected this damned pile.

'Perhaps your father stopped caring because he knew you did not.'

Sebastian pushed his chair back angrily. 'If I had known you would be so damned inquisitive about matters which do not concern you I would have...'

'Left me to die.'

'No! Caro, I did not mean that.'

'I wouldn't blame you if you did. I did not mean to poke my nose into your affairs. It is simply that—oh, you will think I am being melodramatic, but you saved my life. I wanted to help save yours.'

'Thank you, but I do not require saving.' She looked as if he had slapped her. He felt as if he had. Dammit, he would not let her get under his skin. 'You will excuse me now, but I have important matters to attend to,' Sebastian said. 'My father may have neglected both me and the house but he never shirked his duty when it came to the estate, and nor shall I. Last year's harvest was poor, and this year's looks likely to be no better. Despite my lack of experience, I am very much aware of the impact this will have on the labourers.' In fact, it was a problem which kept him awake at night, for the resulting unrest threatened to turn very nasty indeed. Sebastian was determined to do all he could to alleviate any suffering, but his lack of experience made it a difficult business, giving him ample cause to regret the ignorance he had so deliberately cultivated. 'Like it or not, I am the Marquis of Ardhallow now.' Nodding curtly, he left the room.

Alone at the table, Caro dropped her head into her hands. All the brightness of the new day seemed to have disappeared. The dark clouds which had enveloped her of late loomed large. She sat up, squaring her shoulders. She had problems enough of her own without trying to solve Sebastian's. In fact, it was probably a desire to avoid thinking about her own problems which had made her turn on him as she had done.

She got to her feet and began to tidy the breakfast things. It was the least she could do, since Mrs Keith was so short-handed. Two years ago, he had finally destroyed her silly notion that she was in love with him. Two years ago, he had destroyed the last of her illusions about him. She had always laughed at the notion of his being the Heartless Heartbreaker, but perhaps after all that was exactly how it was. Like the Hall, Sebastian's feelings on the subject were locked away and shuttered. His heart was as cold and empty as the house he inhabited.

Picking up a stack of plates, she made her way carefully across the untidy room. The problem was, if he really had wanted to live up to his name, he would surely have left her to die. What was it he'd called them? Two renegades. She smiled to herself, finding that she liked the idea very much. They had always been thus, back then. Cocking a snook at the world. That night at Crockford's for example…

London—1824

A week had passed since Sebastian had left Caro outside her father's house at Cavendish Square following the séance. A week, during which time he'd almost convinced himself that she would see sense and change her mind, until her note had arrived that morning. It had been terse and to the point. Her father was still abroad, her stepmother was temporarily confined to bed, her aunt was unavailable to act as duenna, Cressie had of a sudden come down with a head cold and was also confined to bed, and so Caro was free tonight to accompany Sebastian to Crockford's. *If this in any way inconveniences my lord, then be assured that I am perfectly capable of accompanying myself,* it finished.

'No, you most definitely are not,' Sebastian had exclaimed aloud. 'Why the devil I allowed you to persuade me in the first place...'

Why? Because she was different and he was bored. Because it would be nice to be of service to someone, even if she had virtually co-erced him into it. Because if he ever spent any time at Crag Hall, they would be neighbours.

'In fact, I have a duty to protect the chit from herself,' he muttered under his breath later that day as he donned his evening clothes of black trousers, a silver waistcoat and a black coat.

Having thus reassured himself that his motives were entirely chivalrous, Sebastian arrived in his town coach at the corner of Cavendish Square at the appointed hour. It was late, after ten in the evening, when Caro slipped into the carriage beside him, wrapped once more in her voluminous evening cloak. He was aware of something large placed upon her head, but in the dim light could make out little. He was seriously beginning to doubt the sanity of the whole undertaking. He tried, for the bulk of the journey, to persuade her that the prudent thing to be done was to turn the coach around. He was entirely unsuccessful.

'Hush Sebastian,' Caro said, 'pray do not lecture, for there is no point. Remember, I am doing this for Cressie. You would not wish me to let her down.'

'She knows you're here?' he asked incredulously.

'No, of course not, it is to be a surprise, but you would not wish me to deprive her of it, I am sure. Stop trying to persuade me to turn tail and tell me instead what to expect.'

Resigning himself to the inevitable, he decided that the only thing he could do was mitigate the damage. 'I think you had best explain your sister's precious theory to me.'

The system, as far as he could make out, played to the percentages. He could see how it might prove reasonably effective, were it not for the fact that the faro table would undoubtedly be fixed. He considered telling Caro this, but decided it would be best for her to discover it for herself. If she lost, she would be far less likely to attempt to repeat the exercise.

The folds of her cloak brushing his trousers, the alluring scent of her, something light and flowery, and the suppressed excitement in her voice, distracted him. He had the distinct feeling that he was caught in a net from which he should escape, but he had no idea how to fight free. 'You do understand the rules of faro, I take it?' he asked.

'Cressie taught me. She has studied several games of chance in the name of mathematics. Cressie loves mathematics, though strangely enough, she's not the least bit interested in gambling. She will be relieved not to have had to put her theory into practice herself.'

He couldn't help but laugh at her enthusiasm. He was touched too, at her motives. Though it seemed the years had separated the various sisters, at some fundamental level it was obvious that they cared very much for each other. He wondered what it would be like to have a sibling, then dismissed the thought contemptuously. He would not wish his own experience on anyone. 'That reminds me,' he said, 'you must endeavour not to speak while we are there. There are bound to be acquaintances of your father present tonight.'

'And of your own?'

'My father is a stickler for propriety. Were he to discover any of his acquaintance were in the habit of gambling, he would damn well drop them immediately.'

'Do you always swear so much?'

'I was not aware that I did. Do you always ask such personal questions?'

'I expect swearing is another aspect of being a rake which you deliberately cultivate. I confess I find it shockingly attractive,' Caro said.

Her remark made him uneasy. He was four-and-twenty and had been loose on the *ton* for four years, while she was but twenty and only just out. To his relief, the carriage began to slow as it eased its way along St James's. 'We are nearly there. Are you absolutely sure about this?' he asked.

'Absolutely certain,' Caro replied firmly.

He, on the other hand, was now having serious qualms. Crockford's may be one of the more respectable hells, but it was a hell none the less. If Caro was spotted here, her reputation would be in tatters. He should have made that clear. He was about to embark upon trying to do this when the carriage came to a halt and she handed him something. 'Can you tie this for me, please?'

It was a mask, one of those silk affairs that covered the eyes only. He was both impressed and appalled at her level of foresight, for while the lightskirts who haunted such places made a point of showing every charm they had, the very few women who came to gamble made a point of keeping their faces covered in exactly this way. Some men too, wore hats, shades and masks, though they feared more that their expressions would expose the strength of their hand rather than that their true identity would expose them to scandal.

Sebastian tied the strings of Caro's disguise as best he could, given the lack of light and the large creation she seemed to be sporting on her head. His fingers touched the bare skin at her nape, and a tiny quiver of awareness shot through him. It would not do, he reminded himself guiltily. The sooner they were out of the intimacy of the carriage the better. 'Come,' he said, leaning past her to open the carriage door, 'let us go and see how your sister's theory holds up.'

The impressive red-sandstone building with its portico front which constituted the latest in the erstwhile fishmonger's long line of clubs, was one of a number of copper and silver hells on St James's. William Crockford hired thugs to prevent any but his own sharps from entering its portals, and to ensure also that the clientele had at least the appearance of respectability—the ladies of the *demi-monde* excepted, of course. For this reason, Crockford's was frequented by those females of the *ton* who wished to play deep, and Crockford had the business acumen to reward his employees well for their discretion in order to encourage such well-heeled patrons.

Sebastian had never understood the thrill of staking a fortune on the turn of a card. Helping Caro down from the carriage, he was struck afresh by the lunacy of this escapade as she emerged into the blaze of light which emanated from the beacons in the club's entranceway. She looked preposterous, like a child playing dress-up. Headstrong, naïve, absurdly well meaning and utterly oblivious of the risk she was taking, she was actually smiling at him mischievously, inviting him to admire her outfit. The enormity of what they were doing, of the responsibility he was assuming for her, hit him with full force. 'Devil take it, this is not a game,' he exclaimed.

Caro's face fell. 'You think I shall be discovered?'

'I doubt your own sisters would recognise you, which is not the point at all. Where on earth did you get that hat?'

She patted the monstrosity which adorned her head. 'It is a turban, not a hat. I—er— liberated it from my stepmother's wardrobe.

I needed something big enough to cover my hair, you see. Red is most distinctive.'

'Your hair is not red, it is copper.' He shook his head, torn between amusement and trepidation. 'Take my arm, keep that damned thing on your head, and stay close.'

Caro did so willingly, he was relieved— and a little surprised—to note. She wore black lace gloves, leaving her fingertips bare for the cards. Her attention to detail was second to none. 'I confess I am suddenly rather nervous,' she whispered. 'I am very glad I have your lead to follow, and extremely grateful that you agreed to escort me. I doubt I would have managed on my own.'

'Admit it, you would not have come on your own.'

'Yes I—well, no, I would not, you are quite right. Only please, we are here now, do not say we have to leave.'

He knew he should do exactly that, but meeting her eyes, pleading with him from behind her mask, he realised what he wanted to do, despite her turban and her gloves, despite the fact that she had coerced him into this foolhardiness, was to kiss her. Dammit! She was not the kind of female he kissed. He was here simply to keep her safe and for no other reason.

But as he led her up the steps and into the garish reception hall and waited while she dispensed with her cloak, Sebastian found himself having to work very hard to stop himself grinning. She made him angry and she made him laugh and she made him want to shake her and yes, even to kiss her. The one emotion she did not provoke in him was boredom.

Having checked the looking glass in the room set aside for ladies and satisfied herself that none of her tell-tale hair was showing under the turban, Caro stood on the edge of the crowd in the reception hall. She had never in her life been so nervous. The enormity of what she was doing was only now beginning to sink in. She was surprised Sebastian hadn't noticed her trembling when he tied the strings of her mask. Not that she could in all honesty attribute the trembling wholly to nerves. She was no longer sixteen, but she was still very much attracted to him.

I doubt any of the women I have had dealings with have a heart to break. She had neither the age nor the experience of the women Sebastian consorted with. She would be a fool to think he would look twice at her. What's more, if he thought there was the least danger of her falling in love with him—not that she would be so very stupid—then he would make sure their paths never crossed again, something she would do very well indeed to bear in mind.

Holding her head straight in order not to upset the balance of the surprisingly weighty turban, Caro picked her way carefully across the bustling reception hall. The perfume from many and varied scents which had been applied liberally by the fastidious added a top-note to the sour smell of the sweating bodies in the throng of people making their way to the gaming rooms. The reception hall was a blaze of light, the proportions elegant, though the décor was rather too overwhelmingly gilded for Caro's taste. She had expected it to be more subdued somehow, for gambling was a serious business, but there was a buzz of anticipation in the air. Voices were shrill, the laughter raucous.

When she finally reached Sebastian, she stifled the urge to give a little twirl, for she was really rather proud of her disguise, and the expression of utter astonishment on his face, though it was quickly hidden, was most gratifying. She was not altogether surprised, for the dress she had 'borrowed' from Bella was vulgar in the extreme. Turkey-red silk, embroidered with gold fleur-de-lis, it clashed horribly with the walls of the room in which they stood. Since the robe was far too large for her slim form, she had stuffed her corset with an assortment of stockings and gloves in order to fill out the revealing *décolleté*, achieving a matronly cleavage which she was forced to drape with a spangled fichu for fear that her padding might be detected. Working on the assumption that the more dazzling was her *toilette*, the less likely it was that anyone would pay attention to the person wearing it, Caro had tied another spangled scarf around her waist, and draped the brightly embroidered mantilla which her father had brought Bella back from Spain around her shoulders. A paste necklace which her Aunt Sophia, whose taste in jewellery was execrable, had given her as a birthday present, a pair of garnet earrings, another of Aunt Sophia's presents, this time to Cressie, and a reticule of silver net, completed her rather extraordinary ensemble. 'Do I pass muster, my lord?' she asked, making her curtsy.

Sebastian's eyes narrowed, but his mouth twitched. 'As a gaudy peacock likely to draw both attention and comment then yes indeed, you pass muster. Since the circumstances require you to be both anonymous and incognito however, I am struggling to muster anything other than a headache. I fear you are not taking this seriously. You could at least have worn less ostentatious jewellery.'

'This necklace was a gift from my father's sister.'

'Your aunt appears not to value you as she ought.'

Caro tucked her hand back into Sebastian's arm. 'On the contrary. Aunt Sophia thinks that I am a most dutiful niece. She herself is a stickler for propriety.'

'Are you quite sure you're related?'

She giggled. 'There are times when I wish we were not. No, that is unkind of me. Aunt Sophia may look like an ill-tempered camel, but she has always been most—most conscientious in her care for my sisters and I.'

'And you are most conscientious in acknowledging it, even if you cannot hold her in affection,' Sebastian said. 'Come, let's extricate ourselves from this mêlée.'

The room into which he led her was on the first floor, the dim lighting and concentrated hush a stark contrast to the noise and glitter they had just escaped from. At the centre stood a faro table, presided over by an extremely tall, thin man of about fifty. None of the other players paid Caro and Sebastian any attention, for all eyes were focused on the game. The atmosphere was tense, an air of almost palpable excitement hung over the room. She was not the only woman present, Caro was relieved to note. Catching sight of the large piles of gold on the table however, she began to feel quite sick.

She had gone round and round the problem of raising funds for the last week, but her conscience would not allow her to sell any of her jewellery even if had she known how to go about such a thing, and she could not think of a single reason which Bella would accept for her asking for an advance on her allowance. Still she had managed to amass what she considered a small fortune, certainly more than the annual salary of a laundry maid. She had been quite sure this vast sum would more than suffice for one night of deep playing, but now she was having her doubts. 'Sebastian, what is the minimum stake?'

'Twenty guineas.'

'Twenty!' she squeaked. 'But I have only fifteen in total.'

Rather than curse her naivety, Sebastian seemed to be biting back a laugh. 'Keep your guineas, we will use mine. And before you

tell me that would be wrong, let me point out
that firstly, I am more than wealthy enough
to bear the loss, secondly, I am happy to do-
nate the funds in the name of scientific exper-
imentation, and thirdly, you lost the right to
champion propriety the moment you bribed me
into bringing you here.' He produced a weighty
purse and tried to put it into her hands.

Caro shook her head. 'I cannot risk gambling such huge sums. What if Cressie is mistaken? What if I lose?'

'Ye of little faith. What would Lady Cressida say, to hear you doubting her?' Sebastian wrapped her fingers round the purse, and
steered her towards the table.

Though the minimum wager seemed astro-
nomical to her, Caro was astounded to discover
that almost no one bet so low. Despite—or perhaps because—the money at stake was Sebastian's, she could not bring herself to do other
than bet much more modest amounts. She lost
steadily regardless.

'Perhaps I have misunderstood Cressie's
theory,' she said, struggling to hide her rising
panic after half an hour's play and not a single
win. 'I think we should leave.'

'No, no. You must stick to your guns and

trust your system,' Sebastian said, 'any hardened gamester would tell you that.'

But she was not a hardened gamester, as Sebastian knew perfectly well. Was he punishing her? She could detect nothing in the bland look he gave her. The dealer turned another card, and she lost another twenty guineas. She was not enjoying herself one whit, and was very sure that despite her mask and her turban, her feelings were apparent to everyone else around the table. The other players, in contrast, seemed most adept at masking their emotions. Only the widening of the man in the olive-green coat's eyes, the slight tic at the side of that man in the yellow waistcoat's mouth, the way the man with the fair curly hair compulsively tucked an errant lock behind his ear betrayed them when they lost.

Half an hour later, the purse which Sebastian gave her was decidedly lighter and Caro had had enough. 'It's not working,' she said miserably. 'Cressie was mistaken. I would like to leave now.'

'Nonsense. Why not carry on? I'm sure your luck will change.'

'Sebastian, it's got nothing to do with luck.

Cressie says…' She stopped, remembering Cressie had miscalculated. 'Shall we go?'

'Aren't you enjoying yourself?'

'You know perfectly well I'm not. I was wrong and you were right and I'm sorry, but please, Sebastian, I'd like to go home now.'

He pressed her hand. 'That is your first sensible decision of the evening. Let's get out of here.'

It was a relief to leave the claustrophobic atmosphere of the club. Alone with Sebastian in the carriage, Caro pulled off her mask and turban, casting both on to the floor in disgust. Turning towards him, she braced herself for a setting down. 'You were right. I should not have gone there. It was awful and I put you in a terrible position and you have no doubt been bored senseless and—well, I am sorry.'

Sebastian, to her astonishment, laughed. 'I haven't been bored. I admit I was angry at first, but with myself, not you. I should not have allowed a mere chit of a girl to blackmail me, but you know, I am quite glad that you did.'

'Glad! I have lost you a small fortune.'

'But of course you have.'

'You knew that Cressie's system would not work?'

'Yes, but it was nothing to do with her mathematics. I am sure the theory was sound. The problem is, it didn't take account of the reality of the situation.'

'You mean I was too inexperienced a player?'

He laughed again. 'Certainly, your inexperience contributed. They had you marked out as a little lamb to be fleeced the minute you placed your first bet. Caro, no system can work when the cards are stacked. No matter how long you play, your luck will never turn in a hell like that. Only the banker will ever win.'

Her eyes widened. 'You mean the cards were fixed? You mean the banker was cheating?'

'What else did you expect? There is a reason these places are called gaming hells. That is the reason—one of the many reasons—why they are no place for an innocent like you.'

She took a moment to digest this information. 'If you knew that, why then did you not tell me?'

'Would you have paid any heed?'

No, for the embarrassing fact was that she had been so intent on trying to impress him with her nerve that she had not, until she arrived at the club, thought about the risks. 'I have spoilt it all,' she said.

Sebastian shifted closer to her on the squabs. 'Quite right, you have. I am utterly disgusted with your brazen behaviour.'

She eyed him sceptically, but his face was difficult to read in the gloom of the carriage. 'I would not have thought it would be so easy to shock such a hardened rake.'

He took her hands between his, rubbing warmth into her fingertips. 'I was not playing the rake tonight, but your knight errant. My motives for escorting you were purely chivalrous.'

His touch was sending shivers up her arms that had nothing to do with the cold. His thigh brushed her skirts. The toe of his evening shoe lay against her slipper. 'Now that, I know to be a lie,' Caro said. 'Were you truly a gentleman you would have taken the simple step of informing Bella of my intentions.'

'And were you truly a lady, you would not have cast that point up at me. I find it extraordinary that you are known as the dutiful one amongst your sisters.'

'But I am. Only you make me—ah! Now I see that you are truly a rake, for that is your skill, to make perfectly respectable and extremely dutiful young ladies behave outrageously.'

Sebastian's fingers tightened on hers. 'I have

never in my life been interested in respectable young ladies. I know only one with outrageous tendencies, and she is sitting right next to me.'

This was whispered into her ear. The carriage had come to a halt just out of the reach of the glow of a street lamp. Caro's mouth went dry. Not fear, she wasn't frightened at all. 'You are saying we are equally to blame, then, for we have each encouraged the other.'

'What I am saying is that I would like very much to kiss you.' His mouth hovered over hers. Her stomach clenched in anticipation. His breath caressed her cheek. Then he sighed, a strange, guttural sound. He lifted her gloved hand to his mouth and brushed his lips over her fingertips. 'There, you see, it appears I am not such a confirmed rake after all. It is late. Let me check that the way is clear, and I will escort you safely to your door.'

'No!' Without thinking, she pulled him towards her. Her heart was hammering. She felt giddy with a kind of fluttering excitement. It seemed she was every bit as outrageous as he said, and more. 'No,' she said, 'don't go. I want you to kiss me.'

Sebastian hesitated. He ought not to, he knew he ought not to, but he could not resist her. He knew the moment his lips touched hers that it was her first kiss. That should have made him stop, but instead it set him on fire. The soft uncertainty of her touch, the way she puckered her mouth, as if she would kiss a child, and the tiny little gasp when he ran his tongue over her lips to open her to him, sent the blood rushing to his groin.

Caro twined her arms around his neck, her mouth pliant, soft, her body melting against his. She tasted like honey. No, ridiculous thing to think. Nectar. Peaches. She tasted so sweet.

Gently, he disentangled himself. 'Too sweet,' he said, as if it would explain. 'Caro, you know this is wrong.'

She said nothing.

'Caroline, *I* know it is wrong. I beg…'

'Please don't say you're sorry, Sebastian. Not unless you mean it.'

He swore. Then he laughed. 'Outrageous. I am not sorry, but nor am I sorry I stopped.'

'I don't suppose I'll see you again now for another four years,' she said in a small voice.

She was right, their paths were not likely to cross save by the purest of chance, for they inhabited very different worlds. Save that he was very bored with his world. Hadn't he been thinking only this morning that he needed a change? And tonight, he had not been bored at all in Caro's company. Perhaps more of such company would give him some perspective on his life. 'Perhaps,' Sebastian said, 'my father had a point for once in his life.'

'Your father?'

'He told me to seek out more respectable company.'

'You mean me? But you've just told me I'm outrageous.'

'Ah, but you are respectably so.'

Caro laughed uncertainly. 'Do you mean to develop a taste for polite society?'

'I rather think I do,' Sebastian replied, to his own amazement.

Chapter Four

London—1824

Caro placed the glass of fruit punch on the table next to her stepmother, who was fanning herself frantically. 'The heat in this place is unbearable, I feel as if I am about to melt,' Bella gasped, taking a grateful sip.

Standing by her side in a ball gown of pale yellow that did nothing for her complexion, Cressie looked hopeful. 'Perhaps we should leave.'

'Certainly not,' Bella snapped. 'Not only is our hostess our country neighbour, but Lady Innellan's ball is recognised as the high point of the Season. You surprise me, Cressida. I am sure that Mr Peyton is here, and will be most disappointed not to be given your hand for at least one dance.'

Cressie's smile was more like a grimace. 'I was thinking only of your condition,' she said. 'I am sure Papa would not wish to put your unborn child at risk.'

Bella patted the swollen mound of her stomach, which seemed to Caro to be growing at a frightening rate. 'I am perfectly well, thank you. I know my duty. Your father is most eager to have you off his hands, Cressida. Besides, you would not wish to spoil your sister's chances. Not when she is doing a fine enough job of that on her own, by allowing *that man* to pay her such attentions. If he is here tonight, Caroline, you will oblige me by granting him a solitary dance. You are looking very well, I have to say. It would be a shame to waste it on someone who has absolutely no intentions whatsoever of offering for you.'

Startled by her stepmother's acuity even more than the back-handed compliment, Caro could only stare blankly.

'You wonder how I know such things,' Bella said with one of her tight little smiles. 'I would remind you, Caroline, that I am responsible for you in your father's absence, and I have no intention of incurring his wrath by allowing you to make a fool of yourself. It was your Aunt Sophia who tipped me off about the Earl of Mosteyn's shocking reputation.' Bella pursed her lips and shook her head. 'I confess I am at a loss as to why he seems to have changed his habits so radically these last two months or so.'

It was a question Caro would be hard-pressed to answer herself. When Sebastian had turned up at a *ton* party the week after they had visited Crockford's, she had been gratified and a little uncertain as to how to behave. Recalling how very boldly she had flirted—yes, *flirted*!—with him, positively demanding that he kiss her, made her blood run hot and cold.

But that kiss, her first kiss, she could not regret, no matter how improperly she had behaved. The first time he had appeared at a ball, bowing in front of her, asking her hostess to introduce them, she had been unable to stop blushing. But when he smiled at her, that curious upside-down smile, she had been carried away with the thrill of knowing that this man, this sophisticated, fascinating, wildly attractive man, was here solely because of her.

She had been captivated ever since, though she had been very careful not to let Sebastian see how very enthralled she had become. If she was honest, she was in serious danger of falling in love with him. She had forgotten all about the reasons for her being here, her dutiful desire to make a marriage to please her father, her resolution to be a good daughter and not to cause a scandal as her elder sisters had done. Not until Bella had cautioned her tonight had it occurred to her that she was coming close to crossing the line.

Sebastian made her laugh with the shocking things he whispered in her ear when they were dancing. He made her skin tingle when he touched her. He made her wish she did not have to dance with anyone else. She knew he flirted with her only because he was sure—and she had been at great pains to make sure he was sure—that she understood it meant nothing. She knew it would end, and she would eventually come back down to earth, but she didn't want to land with a bump just yet.

He had scrupulously avoided placing her in any sort of compromising situation. He had not been alone with her. He had not once made any attempt to kiss her again. Yet despite repeatedly reading herself a lecture on the subject of Sebastian's lack of intentions, she couldn't help but hope, for he *had* singled her out, and he *did* sometimes look at her in a way that made her hope for the impossible.

'Perhaps,' Caro said to her stepmother, tentatively testing the water, 'Sebastian—I mean Lord Mosteyn—is reforming his ways and should therefore be encouraged in his endeavour?'

Bella snorted. 'A rake is a rake and always will be. 'Tis only in the pages of a novel published by the Minerva Press that they are reformed.' She snapped her fan shut, eying her stepdaughter beadily. 'I have not spoken until now, Caroline, for I had hoped your own good sense would guide you. You are an obedient little thing on the whole, but there is a wilful streak in you which must be curbed. This flirtation must come to an end before you ruin your chances. I know you will not wish to heed me on this, so I must warn you that I have already taken the precaution of speaking to your father on the subject.'

'Bella! There was no need to do so. I assure you, I am perfectly well aware that Lord Mosteyn's intentions are—that he has none.'

'Which makes your encouragement of him quite incomprehensible,' her stepmother replied implacably. 'Do you wish to be known as an inveterate flirt? I will not sully your ears with the vernacular, but I assure you, it is not a phrase you would wish to have associated with your person. You may have one dance tonight, during which you will inform the earl that his attentions are no longer agreeable to you, and you will hitherto avoid his company.'

'And that, dear sister,' Cressie whispered in Caro's ear, 'is a warning you would do well to appear to heed. I know you don't want to hear this, but Bella is right you know. Lord Sebastian is most certainly *not* on Papa's list of eligibles. I couldn't bear for you to be hurt, dearest.'

'I won't be, I promise,' Caro said, squeezing her sister's hand. 'It's just that Sebastian is—he is—oh, I can't explain. I know he has a dreadful reputation, but...'

'Caro,' Cressie said urgently, 'Caro, Bella is right about that too. Rakes do not reform; it is not in their nature. Please tell me you are not in love with him.'

'*No!* No, of course I am not. That would be perfectly—foolish.' Was she blushing? No, it was just very hot in here. She wished she had Bella's fan. She met her sister's concerned gaze unwaveringly. 'I am perfectly safe, I promise you. I know my duty, and I will do it, just—just not quite yet. In any event, it is your turn first.'

She said it lightly, meaning merely to turn the conversation away from herself, but Cressie looked troubled. 'If only it was that easy,' she muttered.

'What do you mean?'

But Cressie, seemingly reassured, was now distracted by the sight of Giles Peyton making his way towards them across the dance floor. Cressie did not seem to Caro particularly happy about this. In fact Cressie seemed to Caro positively unhappy these days. She'd tried to talk to her, only to be assured entirely unconvincingly that she was perfectly fine.

Continuing to watch her sister out of the corner of her eye, Caro smoothed down the folds of her evening gown. Cream silk brocade, embroidered with tiny sprigs of greenery, it was in the latest fashion, fitted to the waist with a scooped *décolleté* trimmed with cream lace, the puffed sleeves and the skirt both wide. The shape, which made more generously proportioned females look rather galleon-like, suited Caro's slim frame perfectly. Tonight her hair was behaving itself, piled elegantly on top of her head, leaving an expanse of neck and shoulder exposed, which looked creamy rather than white for once. She would never be beautiful like Cassie or Cordelia, but tonight her mirror had told her that she'd pass muster. Which pleased her for her own sake, and absolutely not because she hoped Sebastian would notice.

Though she knew he would notice. He always did. She caught him looking at her sometimes, his eyes darkened with an intent that excited her, but it was always quickly masked. Even if he did find her attractive, it would come to nothing. She must be careful, very careful, not to let herself forget that.

Where was he? Frowning, she scanned the ballroom. It was very late. Perhaps he would not show up on this occasion. Perhaps he had tired of society after all. He never made any promises when she told him artlessly which events she would be attending, but in the last seven—no, it was eight—weeks, he had been there at most balls, and several parties. Was she spoiling her chances, as Bella had suggested? She hadn't thought about it until now, and she didn't want to. She was but twenty years old, and Sebastian was not actually much older, no matter how experienced. Who cared about the future, who cared about stuffy things like blood lines and pedigrees—she was not a horse! And if other people wanted to label her a flirt—well then, other people were simply jealous that Sebastian sought *her* company and not theirs.

For goodness' sake, where was he? Consulting the dance card which dangled from her wrist, she saw that the waltz was next. She had saved it for him. Beside her, Cressie was accepting Mr Peyton's hand. The band played the opening chords, and the dance floor began to fill, obscuring the flutter of very late new arrivals in the doorway. One of them was tall, with close-cropped hair. The dance had started. Cressie would be a good dancer if she kept her mind on the steps, but she never could, for her mind was filled with numbers. Mr Peyton was making a terrible hash of steering the pair of them round the floor. The tall man in the doorway had familiar dark brown hair. Caro's heart did a silly flutter. His evening coat was black, cut tight across his shoulders. Admirable shoulders they were.

He turned and she could not suppress her smile, despite knowing that Bella's watchful gaze was upon her. Sebastian's perfectly tied cravat, the impeccably white collar of his shirt, drew attention to the fact that he really ought to have shaved. The shadow of dark stubble gave him a raffish look. He was talking to Lady Innellan, who was looking up at him in a mixture of glee and astonishment.

Caro tried very hard to keep demurely still,

but as he made his way towards her, her feet of their own accord took several steps in his direction. His waistcoat was dark blue, with just the gold of his watch fob to detract from its plainness. His evening trousers were black and tightly fitted, strapped under black square-toed shoes. He had very long legs, which showed to excellent advantage in such trousers. Not that she should be looking at his legs, but really those trousers, they did draw one's eyes. It was like a woman's *décolleté*. She never could understand why evening gowns were cut so low as to put one's bosom on show, and yet when a man was discovered looking it was supposed to be the grossest of insults. Not that many people looked at her bosom, which was much too frugal. Cressie had a very nice figure, if only she would show it off. Sebastian had a perfect figure. He was smiling at her. No, she would not blush. She would not allow him to see how pleased she was to see him. He was certainly *not* the most handsome man in the room. His brow was too wide, his nose too strong, and his mouth...

'Lady Armstrong, you are acquainted with the Earl of Mosteyn, I know, for he is our country neighbour, the Marquis of Ardhallow's only son. Lord Sebastian wishes to dance with Lady

Caroline.' Lady Innellan did not say *quite insists upon it*, but it was obvious that was precisely what she was thinking.

Sebastian was bowing over Bella's hand. It was rather a perfunctory bow. Bella was frowning, obviously trying to think of a way of refusing Caro permission to dance. 'I have never had the honour of being invited to Crag Hall,' she said stiffly. 'Nor have I met your father, though he and my husband are well acquainted. Strange, that it is here in London and not the country that we are finally getting to know you so well.'

'Not so strange. It is common knowledge that my father is something of a recluse,' Sebastian replied stiffly.

'And very common knowledge indeed that his son is equally averse to keeping polite society,' Bella said, with a malicious smile. 'I was speculating just five minutes ago with Caroline here, as to the reasons for your rather sudden change in habits, my lord. In fact I am very sure it is quite a popular topic of conversation among Lady Innellan's guests.'

'I am sure that her ladyship's guests have far more interesting subjects upon which to converse.'

Sebastian's voice was cool, but Caro could

see, from the way his eyes glittered, that he was in a dangerous mood. 'Shall we?' she said, putting her arm through his and tugging him insistently in the direction of the dance floor.

'Caroline, you will not forget what I said, I trust,' Bella called after her.

'And what is it that you are not to forget?' Sebastian asked, putting his arm around her waist.

Caro shook her head. 'It's of no consequence.'

'Let me hazard a guess. Your stepmother has decided that I am not to be trusted with her virgin charge. She is afraid that being seen so often in my company is damaging your chances.' Sebastian spoke more bitterly than he intended, but the interview with his father which had just concluded, and was responsible for his late arrival, was still horribly fresh in his mind. For Lord Ardhallow to leave the sanctuary of Crag Hall was almost unprecedented. The lecture had been more painful than all the others he had received over the years. His father's cold fury, cutting sarcasm and icy hatred were just about bearable. It was his own lack of foresight, the self-delusion laid bare by his father, which pained Sebastian the most.

Since coming to London you have been unremitting in your efforts to bring shame and scandal to our family name. I believe you actually take pride in your reputation as a libertine. However, philandering with harlots and harpies is one thing, I will not stand by while a son of mine destroys an innocent, and especially not when she is my neighbour's daughter. Lady Caroline Armstrong deserves a far better suitor than a reprobate like you. This game of yours, for I am in no doubt it is a game, must end forthwith.

That the tirade was as a result of his having, for once, behaved with perfect propriety, made it all the more painful. *Have you not repeatedly suggested that I sample polite society?* he had thrown at Lord Ardhallow, only to be viciously laughed at. *Too late for that,* the old man had said, *you are too much the rake for any respectable man, far less someone as eminent as Lord Armstrong, to entrust with his daughter. His lordship was most insistent that I impress upon you his deep disquiet and disapproval of your dalliance with Lady Caroline.*

Too late. He was not yet twenty-five, but even his own father, the man who had spent the better part of the last four years urging him to reform, to settle down, to accept his responsibilities as heir to the ancient title, had given up on him. It should not have hurt so much. He was furious with himself that it did. Why the devil should he care what his father thought? He had never cared about that damned title, and it was not as if it would be his for decades, with the current incumbent as healthy as a horse.

But as he endured his father's haranguing, despite the show of indifference his pride maintained, the full scale of Sebastian's self-deception began to dawn on him. He had allowed himself to believe that Caro was merely indulging in a flirtation even though he knew she was far too innocent to know how to flirt. He had taken her protestations of indifference at face value because he wanted to. He had not allowed himself to wonder why such an innocent would have kissed him because he didn't want to confront the fact that she might be falling in love with him.

He didn't love her. He didn't love anyone. He was, however, by no means as indifferent as he thought he was. His father's contempt for his feelings forced him to admit, if only to himself, that he *had* feelings, and that is what confused him most. He had never felt like this before. He didn't want to feel like this. More importantly, he didn't want to hurt Caro. She deserved better. It pained him to agree with his father, but for once the marquis was right. He must break off contact with her before it was too late.

Becoming aware that she was studying him, that he had said almost nothing for two turns of the floor, Sebastian tried to smile. 'In short,' he said, 'your stepmother insists our acquaintance is inappropriate, and she is quite correct in that assertion.'

Caro flushed. 'No, she is not. I don't care if there's gossip about us, if I'm seen as your flirt, and...'

'You are *not* my flirt. Is that what they are saying?'

'Bella has a spiteful tongue. You are gripping my hand like a vice, Sebastian.'

'I beg your pardon. I should have realised there would inevitably be gossip. Even my own friends told me...' That he was turned soft in the head. That he was too young to be setting up his nursery. That he was a fool to be dancing with virgins when he could have his pick of women who offered more tangible pleasures. He should have realised that if people were talking about him, they'd be talking about Caro too. But he had not, curse it.

'What is it that your friends have been saying, Sebastian?'

'Merely that I have been deserting them of late,' he replied. 'They are right too. I have been most remiss in neglecting them. I must remedy that.'

Caro's flinch was barely perceptible. Had he not been holding her so closely, he may have missed it altogether. 'Then you must apologise to your friends on my behalf. It was not my intention to keep you from them, nor to monopolise your time, as I obviously have.'

Her smile was very determined. She did care. Oh God, he had been such a fool. He dreaded the coming confrontation, but it was best to make a clean break. The waltz was coming to an end. Their last ever dance, it would be, which would delight both his father and Lord Armstrong, whose interference in the matter he could not divulge to Caro. He had done enough damage already.

His thigh brushed against hers as he led her into a turn. Between them there were yards of silk brocade and petticoats, yet he could feel her body tingle against his, as though they were naked. Madness, to succumb to the temptation of holding her like this, far too close for propriety, but the devil fly away with propriety this one last time. The churning in his stomach, the tension in his body, which the interview with his father had initiated, which his self-flagellation following it had enhanced, now seemed to focus, forming a hard knot in his middle. *This one last time.* There was no alternative. 'Caroline…'

Her gloved fingers tightened on his. 'Why do you call me that? Oh please, Sebastian, don't pay any heed to Bella.'

The edge of panic in her voice entrenched his resolve. The dance ended. A quick glance reassured him that Lady Armstrong had succumbed to the appetising allure of the supper room. Tucking Caro's arm into his, Sebastian led the way out of the ballroom, through several increasingly less crowded ante-chambers, and into a small, deserted salon.

'How on earth did you know about this room?' Caro gazed about her, at the fire crackling in the grate, the decanter set out with glasses, the candles burning in their sconces above the mantel.

'It is the business of any rake worth his salt to know about secluded rooms when attending a party,' Sebastian replied, 'and the business of any hostess worth her salt to provide them.'

He was not exactly avoiding her eye, but he wasn't quite looking at her either. He wasn't angry, though he seemed extremely tense, and his tone, dripping sarcasm, was harsh. She had a horrible feeling in the pit of her stomach, but she ignored it valiantly, striving for a lightness she did not feel. 'I can't believe that of Lady Innellan. Do you really mean that she expects you—men to—to use rooms like this for...'

Sebastian lifted the decanter, sniffed the contents and put it back, wrinkling his nose in distaste. 'Dalliance. Seduction. Indecent proposals. Perhaps even the occasional decent one,' he quipped.

Caro was not fooled. She didn't like the way he was looking at her, as if he was about to tell her that someone had died. Sneaking a sidelong glance at him, she made a show of examining an ugly Chinese figurine of a greenish bullock which looked as sick as she felt. 'I am fairly certain that you would not offer me an indecent proposal, for you told me yourself you never seduce innocents.'

Her voice sounded peculiar to her own ears, but Sebastian didn't seem to notice. 'I am glad that you, at least, are confident of that,' he said.

There was a bitterness in his voice that she could not account for. Was he implying that someone *had* suggested he would make her an improper proposal? No, that was simply preposterous. 'I am also confident,' she said with a very, very false smile she was sure would not even fool Bella, 'that you are not about to make me a *decent* proposal either, for you have made your views on the subject of matrimony most clear. Once a rake, as my stepmother says, always a rake, isn't that so?'

She could have kicked herself for the pleading note in her voice, but Sebastian seemed oblivious. 'Your stepmother and my father agree on that too, it seems,' he said, removing the figurine from her hands.

'Your father? What has he to do with this? Has he been talking to Bella? But she said only tonight that they are not acquainted.' Caro shook her head impatiently, as if doing so would clear the confusion inside it. This was wrong, all wrong, but she didn't understand why.

'Caro, the point is, people are talking about us. If they knew we were here, alone, if we were discovered…'

'Then you would say we are betrothed, and everyone would be happy.'

She said it flippantly, without thinking. She said it because she hoped against hope that he would say something to *give* her hope, but Sebastian winced. 'It wouldn't make anyone happy, Caro. Your father wants a good match for you, he has no desire at all to see you married to a rake like me.'

'You are the heir to one of the oldest titles in the land, and your father is one of my father's oldest acquaintances. I should think Papa would be most pleased indeed at such an alliance.'

'Not if it meant taking on one such as I as a son-in-law,' Sebastian said with a sneer.

'How can you be so sure?'

'I have my reasons, believe me, but that is not the point. What matters is that I couldn't make you happy, Caro.'

The lump in her throat felt sharp, painful, like a stone with jagged edges. 'You mean you don't want to,' she replied. Tears welled up, but she refused, she absolutely refused to let a single one fall. She would not let him see how hurt she was. It was her own fault, after all, for allowing her emotions to slip off the leash. 'Don't worry, I should turn you down, in the very unlikely event of your being forced to propose.'

Sebastian looked at her for so long that she thought she was bound to give herself away. 'I never meant to hurt you,' he said heavily.

She clenched her fists tight in the folds of her gown, and kept her eyes wide to prevent them from filling. 'I am not hurt. Sebastian, there is no need for this. I *know* you have no intentions in that direction, why cannot you accept that and—and—*dammit,* why can't we just carry on as we are?'

'On top of all my other crimes, it seems I've taught you to swear. Please don't cry, Caro.'

'I'm not.' She dashed a hand across her eyes and sniffed. 'You really are—what is that expression—giving me my *congé*? You're actually yielding to the malicious tittle-tattle of my horrible stepmother and some gossipmongers. They don't matter.'

He pulled her towards him, kissing her eyelids, the tears that clung to her lashes. 'They do matter, Caro. I won't have them say I have ruined you. I won't ruin you. You deserve better.'

Anger came to her rescue. He felt sorry for her. She would not be pitied. 'Very noble. The truth is you are bored with me and so I am getting the brush off. I don't even merit a diamond bracelet, as Kitty Garrison did. Then again, I did not provide you with the kind of entertainment she did either. Perhaps if I had…'

'Caroline!'

'Oh, don't pretend you are shocked, Sebastian, when it was yourself who introduced us. Very well then, go back to your old haunts and your old lady loves and do whatever it is that the Heartless Heartbreaker does.'

His eyes flashed, but he bit back the angry retort he was about to make. 'I have decided to go abroad, as a matter of fact.'

'Abroad? You mean you are leaving London?' she asked stupidly. She could accept him avoiding her for a time, but if he was leaving London altogether… 'You can't mean it.'

Sebastian's mouth was set. 'When we met at the séance I recall telling you that I was thinking of doing just that.'

'You said you needed a change. But you've had a change, and…'

'I need a more substantial change. I need to get away.'

'No. Sebastian, please say you are teasing me.'

She had caught his hand between hers, was holding it as if she could keep him captive, which was exactly what she wanted to do. It was a mistake. A complete give-away, judging by the way he was looking at her. She could not bear his pity. She could not bear to be in this room, having this conversation, for a moment longer.

Caro flung herself free. 'Very well then, go and good riddance! In fact go with my blessing, because I see now that Bella was quite right. You have been a distraction. I am not here in London to have fun but to make a suitable match. Without you to call upon my time I am very sure I will make an excellent one and that will make my father happy and Bella happy and Cressie happy too, because then she won't have to worry so much about not having made a match herself.' She folded her arms across her chest and nodded firmly. 'I agree with you. It is absolutely for the best that you go. I cannot imagine why you have lingered so long. Please, do not let me keep you.'

She pushed him towards the door. Sebastian caught her hands, pulling her tight up against him with a groan. 'Oh God, Caro, I did not mean to cause you pain.' He ran his finger down the line of her cheek to rest on her lower lip before leaning in to her, brushing his lips to her cheek.

'No,' she exclaimed. One word, meaning nothing and everything to her. No, don't go.

No, you're not sorry. No, I do not want you. No, I do not love you. 'No,' she said again, meaning this time no, I will not give in. But desire, longing, and the ache of imminent loss washed over her. 'No,' she whispered, twining her arms around his neck, pressing herself against the hard wall of his chest. His mouth was just inches away from hers. His eyes were dark with desire. Heat seemed to smoulder from her skin. Or was it his? 'No,' she said, as his lips touched hers, and she thought only *yes*.

Gently, he nibbled the softness of her bottom lip, licking along its length, then into the corners of her mouth. His hands slid around her, one round her back to pull her into him, the other up to stroke her hair. With a tiny gasp, she kissed him back.

He traced the shape of her mouth with his tongue, kissing, the lightest of kisses, tantalisingly touching, brushing, tasting. She ran her fingers through the short silkiness of his hair, tracing the line of his neck above his neckcloth. Skin. Sebastian's skin.

His tongue brushed hers, her mouth opened wider, and his kiss changed. Deep, slow, an utterly satisfying kiss that left her ravenous for more. He kissed her again. Deeper. He tasted of fire. Their tongues touched, tasted. She arched against him, brushing the hard length of his manhood, and he moaned, digging his fingers into the soft flesh of her bottom to pull her tighter.

Her blood felt as if it were boiling, yet her fingers were icy. Inside her, low inside her belly, tension knotted. His mouth was feverish on hers, his breathing fast and shallow. She felt dizzy, light-headed, desperate, as they stumbled together, using the wall to brace themselves. His hands stroked her arms, the soft flesh at the top of her gloves, brushing the curve of her breast, then feathering over the edge of lace at her *décolleté*.

Her nipples hardened. Sebastian stilled, then released her abruptly. Breathing hard, his eyes heavy-lidded, a dark flush colouring his cheeks, he gazed at her with something akin to horror and swore under his breath, using a word she had never heard before. 'Forgive me.' He swore again, viciously. 'He was right. I am not fit to be in your company. What was it your stepmother said—once a rake. You have all the proof you need of that now. I am sorry, Caro. It is better for everyone that I leave London. I am fit only for my own company. I wish you—I wish you well.'

He was gone before she could stop him.

Stunned, she stumbled over to the fireplace and slumped down in a chair. What a fool she had been. She had almost convinced herself that she loved him. As well that she caught herself in time. No, she was not in love, she was in denial, living out a silly little fantasy, and it was time that she faced reality and got on with her life. Sebastian was no more her knight errant than she was his maiden in distress. She did not need rescuing. The time had come for her to play the role for which she was destined.

Caro reached for the decanter. Cheap brandy was better than no brandy, right now. She poured herself a glass and swallowed it in one bitter draught. It didn't help in the slightest.

Crag Hall—1830

Caro dreamt she was dancing, waltzing in a crowded ballroom with Sebastian's arm around her waist. Light filtered in through the bedchamber curtains causing her to slowly awaken. She squeezed her eyes tight shut. She didn't want to wake up, she wanted to stay for ever her younger, innocent self, safe in Sebastian's arms, the future awash with glittering possibilities, but the sun was persistent.

Donning a wrapper over her nightgown, she wandered through to the adjoining room. Like the bedroom, the boudoir was richly decorated, with rococo gilding on the cornicing and green damask hangings at the windows. The walls were covered with a number of portraits. A white-marble mantel was carved with cupids. It had once been a very beautiful room, but like every other part of the house was now in a sad state of neglect.

Sebastian had avoided her all day yesterday, leaving her to dine alone in that shabby little salon of his. She ought to apologise to him, but she would not. She was tired of apologising. Her whole life had been an apology. Sebastian, on the other hand, never apologised and never explained, he simply moved on. He had left Crag Hall for London to get away from his father. He'd swapped his rakish haunts for the *ton* because he was bored. He'd left England for the Continent when he'd become bored with her—for she never had believed that high-minded nonsense about protecting her reputation. And now Sebastian had come full circle, hiding himself away here at Crag Hall because...

Caro shook her head, exasperated. She had no idea why Sebastian was playing the recluse here, and she didn't care one whit. She had more than sufficient problems of her own to resolve, she reminded herself for the hundredth time. In fact, it was far better if she and Sebastian's paths crossed as seldom as possible while she was lodged here. Far better. She did not need his company and he obviously did not want hers.

She dressed herself in a gown of white muslin, with a triangular bibbed front edged in satin. Piped satin bordered the woollen embroidery around the hemline, which was worked in a design of ferns and acanthus leaves similar to an evening gown she had worn once on a most memorable occasion.

The bedchamber opened onto a long dark corridor panelled with wood. The window at the far end was shuttered. She made her way cautiously to the staircase, struck afresh by the neglect. The huge oriole window of stained glass which lit the corridor would filter the light spectacularly, but it was covered in leaves and moss on the outside. Below her, a large square atrium-like room, the doors all firmly closed, guarded the formal chambers which must lie beyond. *Why?* The question nagged her, despite her resolutions. Abandoning the elegant staircase, she made her way to the service stairwell, which was lit by oil lamps, and thence to Sebastian's room. As she suspected, it was empty, though the table had been freshly laid for breakfast. For one. The master of the house had obviously already eaten.

Caro buttered a bread roll and took it outside. Sunlight slanted across the stables and the paddock. Turning her face to the warmth, she breathed in the delightful smell of grass, fresh hay, horses and summer. The air was so sweet here, she had quite forgotten.

Sebastian was leaning against the paddock fence gazing off into the distance. He was dressed in what was obviously his habitual attire of breeches, riding boots and shirt, the sleeves rolled up to show off tanned forearms. The leather of his breeches stretched taut over his *derrière*. He still had a very nice *derrière*. Not that any lady should notice such things. Though Caro, according to the scandal sheets, was no lady. She continued to stare, and was still staring when Sebastian turned.

Surprise, the beginnings of a smile, then wariness, she noticed as she made her way over to him. 'Good morning. To what do I owe the privilege?'

'I wondered what became of Burkan,' she replied. 'And I wondered what had become of you too. You've been avoiding me.'

'Burkan is in the long meadow with some of the mares.'

'Lucky Burkan! A stallion after his master's heart. Can there be such a thing as a rakish horse?'

'Horses are far too noble to be rakes.'

'Unlike men, you mean?'

'Exactly. He is earning his oats, that's all. It's what I do now, in addition to playing the lord of the manor, I breed horses.'

'Which explains why you favour the garb of a stable hand. No, don't take offence, I like it. I remember the first time we met you were dressed just like this. I took you for a groom at first.'

Sebastian grinned. 'A groom with too much of a penchant for the whip, as I recall.'

'I thought you were going to use it on me,' she replied, smiling back at him.

'You are not serious. I would never...'

'Of course I'm not serious. I've never been afraid of you. Your anger always has just cause, even if that cause is frequently rather opaque. You can be extremely defensive when provoked, but you are never aggressive or malicious,' Caro broke off abruptly, staring at her finger, which still bore the indentation left by her wedding ring.

When she looked up, Sebastian was staring at her with an oddly arrested expression. Hiding her hand in her skirts, she summoned up a bright smile. 'Have you had much success? With your stud farm, I mean.'

Sebastian ignored her. 'Did he hurt you?'

Her mind went quite blank. She could feel the panic forming like a swarm of angry wasps in her stomach. 'Naturally,' she said, striving for a lightness she was far from feeling. 'The lies he told in those scandal sheets were really quite uninventive. If only he had asked me, I am sure I could have come up with something better than a boot boy.'

'That's not what I meant, Caro, as you know perfectly well.'

'Perhaps if he gets wind of the fact that I had to be carried unconscious from an opium den he will divorce me,' she said flippantly.

'If it's divorce you wish for, you merely have to inform him that you have taken up residence in the home of the notorious Heartless Heartbreaker.'

'Oh, but that sounds far too mundane. Now, if you were to invite some of your Paphians along, perhaps a few other rakehells, and throw a spectacular orgy, *that* would be something I doubt even my husband could forgive.'

'Does he want to forgive you, Caro?'

'He believes I have a lot to be forgiven for.'

'Enigmatic. That is not like you. Let me put it another way. Do you wish to be forgiven?'

'No.' She shook her head adamantly. 'I won't go back, Sebastian. I know it is what everyone wants, what everyone will say I ought to do. It is the law, after all, as his wife I am his property, but...'

He caught her hand, pulling her towards him. 'When have I ever urged you to do the right thing, Caro? None of that matters a damn, it is what you want that counts. I don't know what went on between you and have no wish to know, but you can rest assured, I'm on your side.'

He hadn't shaved this morning. His stubble gave him a raffish look. She was close enough to smell the familiar scent of him, soap and hay. There was a smattering of hairs at the opening of his shirt. His throat was tanned. His eyes, in the bright light of the summer morning, seemed more amber than brown. She could not doubt the sincerity she saw there, and found herself unexpectedly on the brink of tears. 'Thank you,' she said in a low whisper.

Sebastian touched her cheek, smoothing

away the single tear which had fallen with his thumb. 'I didn't mean to make you cry.'

'I know, it's silly, it's just that it's been so long since—it's just nice to know that there is someone on my side.'

'I said it because I meant it. If there is anything I can do, you need only ask.'

She managed a watery smile. 'I've already told you what you can do.'

'Hold an orgy in your name?' He smiled, pushing her hair back from her face. 'I have been hiding away here for so long, I'm not sure that I would know where to start. With the guest list I mean!' he added quickly, noting her sceptical look.

His arm was resting lightly on her waist. Her skirts were brushing against the leather of his buckskins. The very nearness of him was sending her pulses skittering. 'I can't believe that you are so out of touch. I do not expect diamonds of the first water nor even rakes in the first flush of—of rakedom,' Caro said. 'With only a boot boy and a few servants in my repertoire, I have not your exacting standards.'

His hand tightened on her waist. 'Indeed, it seems to me you are singularly lacking the experience to attend any orgy. Perhaps it would be better if we made the guest list more select. Restrict it to two, say.'

Sebastian's other hand was resting on her shoulder. His fingers stroked the bare skin at the nape of her neck, under the heavy fall of her hair. Did he know what he was doing? Did he know what it was doing to her? 'Can two people have an orgy?' Caro asked, trying to keep her voice level.

'Oh, I think so, if they are inventive enough. I may be out of practice, but I can assure you that my experience is second to none,' Sebastian replied, pulling her tight against him, and kissing her.

She was so shocked that she lay pliant in his arms for a few seconds. Then the heat of his mouth on hers, the heat of his body hard against hers, charged her senses. It had been such a long time since anyone had kissed her. And no one had ever kissed her as Sebastian kissed her. She wrapped her arms around his neck, pulling him towards her, feeling the soft silkiness of his short-cropped hair under her fingers. She was pressed against the paddock fence, she could feel the slats jabbing into her back. Sliding her hands down his back, she felt the ripple of his muscles under the soft linen of his shirt.

His kisses were like velvet, hot and soft and all-enveloping, so much more decadent here in the bright, bright sunlight. His tongue licked along her lips, touching the tip of hers, making her shiver. She gave a little moan, digging her fingers into the soft leather of his breeches, feeling the hard, taut muscle of his buttocks. His kiss deepened. The world darkened. Heat shivered through her veins. And then the kiss slowed, stopped. Reluctantly she opened her eyes.

Sebastian was breathing raggedly, looking, she was relieved to see, as stunned as she. 'I don't know about second to none, I have not your experience to compare with, but I will admit, Lord Ardhallow, that you have quite a talent for kissing.' She was pleased with that. The most important thing was that he didn't realise the effect he had on her, the memories that kiss had conjured. No, that was the second most important thing. The most important was that she did not allow it to conjure memories nor stupid fantasies about what that kiss might lead to because it could lead to nothing.

Sebastian made a mock bow. 'I am pleased to have been of service.'

'You can be of even more service to me now.'

'How?'

The wary look he gave her almost made her laugh. 'Take me to Burkan. I'd love to ride him again, for old times' sake.'

Chapter Five

Caro and Sebastian lay on the grass in a distant meadow beneath the welcome shade of a huge oak tree, their horses tethered by a small stream. She had ridden astride Burkan like a man, unwilling to take the time to change into her habit lest he change his mind, Sebastian realised. It had been exhilarating in a way he had forgotten, watching the ease with which she controlled the powerful Arabian stallion, the graceful way she sat in the saddle, her hair streaming out behind her, glinting like molten copper in the sunshine, her face alight with exhilaration. Her husband and family had stripped her of life. Seeing her vibrant, glowing, made his fists curl at the thought of what she must have suffered. Any reservations he had about bringing her to Crag Hall were dissipated in the pleasure he took in seeing her so restored.

He shouldn't have kissed her, but he hadn't been able to resist and he didn't regret it. *That night* two years ago had put an end to everything between them. For two years, he had hated her. Seeing her so pathetically fallen, his hatred had turned to pity. Seeing her now, restored to something like her old self, it was a relief to reject it all, and to simply enjoy her company as he had once done. It meant nothing. As he had said, they were two renegades, that was all, but it was nice, for a change, not to have to be a renegade alone.

'You know, you did once urge me to do the right thing,' Caro said, sitting up and wrapping her arms around her knees. 'Earlier, in the paddock,' she added, seeing his confused look, 'you said that you have never urged me to do the right thing, but years ago, during my first Season in London, you did just that when you advised me not to go to Crockford's.'

He laughed. 'As I recall, my urging you *not* to visit a gaming hell only made you more determined than ever to do so.'

Caro smiled. 'Last night, I dreamt we were dancing,' she said. 'Waltzing. When I woke I realised I was dreaming of the night of Lady Innellan's ball.' She turned to face him. 'Why did you leave England in such a hurry?'

Sebastian shrugged. 'I told you. I was tired of my life, I needed a change.'

'I remember. I also remember how angry you were that night. I never did understand that part of it.'

'You want the truth?' Sebastian rolled over on to his side, propping his head up with his elbow. 'My father informed me that I was ruining you. *Your* father informed him that he had other plans for his daughter and my attentions were unwelcome. I knew that even though I felt—oh, I don't know what I felt, Caro, but I knew they were right, the pair of them. You did deserve better.'

She stared at him in utter astonishment. '*My* father? What had he to do with it?'

'Lord Armstrong was the nearest thing my father had to a friend. When your friend asks you to ensure your profligate son doesn't spoil his matrimonial plans for his daughter, then you do what you can to remove said profligate son from the scene.' He spoke flippantly, but the pain of that last interview—that very last interview, as it turned out—was still amazingly raw even at a distance of over six years.

Caro looked aghast. 'I remember now, Bella told me that she'd spoken to Papa but I had no idea he would—I don't understand.' She plucked at a long stem of grass and began to shred it between her fingernails. 'It's not as if things between us were ever—you made it very clear you had no serious intentions. I told Bella that.' She cast the grass aside. 'All I have ever done is try to do what is expected of me and all I ever get for it is—it is so unfair! I did not once, not once give him a single moment's worry, yet it seemed he didn't even trust me enough to—to—he went off behind my back and plotted with your father rather than simply talk to me about it!'

She jumped to her feet, her fists clenched angrily at her sides. 'What if you had been serious?' she demanded. 'What if your intentions had been honourable? And why, now I come to think of it, assume that they were *dis*honourable?'

'To be fair, Caro, the evidence was rather stacked against me.'

She turned on him furiously. 'You told me yourself that you never seduce innocents, and though I scarcely knew you at all I believed you. I'd have thought your father would have realised—why did he not defend you?'

'Oh, by that time I had become so ingrained in my habits as to make it impossible for me to change, according to my father,' Sebastian said, unable to keep the sneer from his voice.

'You were four-and-twenty not four-and-fifty, for goodness' sake. And you might have been a rake, but you were also a gentleman.'

'Thank you, my lady, but it seems that was a matter of some dispute at the time.' Sebastian got to his feet. 'Much as it pains me to admit it, my father was in the right of it and I knew it. My reputation was such that your being in my company could only be detrimental. You deserved better.'

'I deserved better! Well, thank you kindly, my lord, I certainly got what I deserved.' She caught herself up on a sharp intake of breath. 'No. That is unfair of me. It was not your fault. You left. I did as I had always intended and made the match my father desired. I would have done so without his manipulating and scheming behind my back. He should have known that.' She smiled bitterly. 'Stupid Caro, of course he did not. He has proven quite conclusively not only that he doesn't love me but also that he doesn't know me at all.'

Relieved to see her smiling again, Sebastian held out his hand. 'Just think how mortified he will be when he discovers that you have been plotting an orgy on his very doorstep.'

'If only your father was still alive, we could kill two birds with one stone.'

'Holding orgies at Crag Hall would merely be confirming my father's expectations of me.'

'It seems we are both cursed with parents who don't understand us at all,' Caro said. 'But yours is dead now, Sebastian. Why not be rid of him once and for all, put your own stamp upon the Hall, claim it for your own, rather than shut it up like some sort of mausoleum to his memory?'

'Because ghosts belong in a mausoleum,' Sebastian said drily, 'and I intend to keep this one firmly closed.'

London—autumn 1828

The ripple of tepid applause which greeted the end of the first act roused Caro from her reverie. She'd come to the Theatre Royal hoping that, by immersing herself in Rosalind's travails in the latest production of Mr Shakespeare's *As You Like It*, she might divert herself from her own myriad problems. It hadn't worked. Instead of concentrating on the play, she had spent the last half-hour cudgelling her brain, going round and round in circles in an effort to decide what else, if anything, could be done to ascertain the whereabouts of her youngest sister.

It was very worrying. A few months ago Cordelia had eloped and simply disappeared off the face of the earth. Though she had twice written to reassure their sister Cressie that she was well, neither Cressie nor Aunt Sophia had any clue as to Cordelia's whereabouts, nor even whom she had eloped with! As if that wasn't enough, to everyone's astonishment Cressie herself—logical, sensible Cressie—had run off with an Italian painter, leaving Bella in a state of complete shock. With Papa detained in St Petersburg unable to do more than cast his diplomatic net by proxy and Aunt Sophia laid up in bed with the gout, Cordelia had been temporarily consigned to whatever fate she had chosen for herself. Unless Caro could find her, which, though she had been extremely glad of the excuse to escape to London, she had so far signally failed to do.

She fidgeted with her *brisé* fan, folding and unfolding it nervously. It was French, antique, made of ebony and beautifully carved. An expensive present from their trip to Paris three years ago when she'd thought, she really had believed, that finally she'd got her life back on a straight and narrow path. Alone in the theatre box Lord Armstrong maintained, though very rarely used, Caro got to her feet to stretch her legs, shaking out the skirts of her evening gown. Newly delivered by the modiste this afternoon, it was made of emerald-green velvet, fitted tight to the waist in the latest fashion, with a full skirt and very full puffed sleeves. The bodice and the hem of the gown were embroidered in silver, an intricate pattern of scrollwork and ferns which looked vaguely classical. The *décolleté* made the most of her modest cleavage and pale shoulders. Though she would never be described as voluptuous, she'd filled out these last two or three years and no longer had the coltish look of her first Season.

Returning with resignation to her seat in preparation for the beginning of the next act, Caro felt her skin prickle with awareness. Anxious to avoid having to make small talk with any acquaintance, she opened her fan again, shielding her face as she surveyed the other private boxes.

Oh, dear heaven.

Her heart skipped a beat. She forced herself to breathe deeply. So many times these last four years she'd thought she had caught sight of him. A tall figure with the same shade of hair, or build, or even just a similar gait, and her heart would jump and her mouth would go dry. A second glance invariably revealed that the hair was too light or too dark, that the shoulders were not broad enough, the legs were too short, or that there was not enough of an easy swing to the stride. It was never him.

She forced herself to take another look. The man who had caught her attention had turned away to address his male companion. He was tall, his broad frame straining the shoulders of his evening coat, which was unfashionably cut in the shape popular several Seasons ago, for the waist was not nipped tightly in, the sleeves were too fitted. This man was broader, surely, than Sebastian—though in four years he, like her, would have filled out. And his hair, it was a lighter shade of brown, more caramel than chocolate, and streaked with gold. A strong resemblance certainly, but that was all.

He swivelled round. His face was deeply tanned. The lines on his brow were deeper, but his mouth still turned down at the corners. And his eyes, dark brown and locked on hers, were exactly the same. Caro's fan slipped unnoticed to the ground as she clutched at her breast, for it really did feel as if her heart was trying to escape from her rib cage.

For several seconds, Sebastian could only stare. It was his first night back in London. Propriety dictated he should not even be here at the theatre under the circumstances, but spending the evening in the dark, familiar atmosphere of Limmer's coffee room held no appeal. He had arrived home—ha! What a misnomer—at Crag Hall just over a week ago, to find that his journey had been a futile one.

The letter which would have sped his return, which would have allowed him to reach England in time, had never reached him. He had not acknowledged even to himself how much he wished to try, not to forgive, never to forget, but at least to achieve some sort of *détente*, until fate took a hand and denied him the opportunity in the most brutal manner possible. Now there could never be any sort of reconciliation.

Save for the lawyer and the staff at the Hall, he had spoken to no one. Holed up in the shuttered, gloomy house, he had been unable to face the mountainous pile of post, nor even to read the newspaper. He'd grown accustomed to thinking that this momentous event, when it finally came, would signal freedom. He had not for a moment considered the possibility that he would for ever be burdened with the weight of the questions he had never asked, for ever locked on the other side of some door beyond which lay understanding.

At times, he was so angry with his father that it was almost physical, alleviated only when he had exhausted himself riding, walking, or practising alone with the rapier he had bought in Italy. For four years, he had travelled the world, wandering further and further afield, losing himself in the anonymity of new cultures, strange places, with no other responsibility than simply to experience. He had no reason to return to England. Indeed, his father had given him every reason not to.

He had not been aware that the desire to reassess and reappraise, the wish to effect a fresh start, had been growing until it was too late. The turmoil caused by his father's death had unleashed such a vortex of emotion, Sebastian wondered if he would ever know for certain how he felt or who he was again. Every fixed point in his life had moved, cleaving away the foundations of his world. Who'd have thought that the old man's ghost would cast even more of a shadow than his presence?

In the old days, a visit to the theatre would have been the prelude to a raucous night on the town. It would have been easy to join the throng in the pit, to renew old acquaintances with fellows who would know the latest fashionable places to see and be seen. Afterwards, they would fill him in on the latest gossip and scandal, introduce him to the latest toasts. But upon arriving at the brightly lit theatre, Sebastian had taken one look at the crowded pit with its crush of ogling beaus and preening dandies and recoiled in horror. Four years, most of it spent roaming far beyond the reaches of what these people termed civilisation, had changed him so much that he couldn't believe he'd ever taken pleasure in such pastimes.

Upon the brink of turning tail, he'd bumped into his cousin, and could not, given recent events, decline Bernard's invitation to join him in his box, 'for the first act, at least old chap, just to take your mind off recent events.' One interminable act had proved more than sufficient. By the time it drew to a close, Sebastian was longing for solitude. Nothing, it seemed, could distract him from the whirl of his thoughts, the endless circles of questions and regrets, so he may as well be alone with them.

As he was bidding his cousin farewell, the hairs on the back of his neck had stood on end. Someone was watching him. He had turned, and her presence hit him like a blow to the stomach, quite literally depriving him of his breath.

She had changed. She'd lost the angular look of youth and the extreme slenderness too. She was still slim, but there was a softness about her now, and more defined curves. Her hair was as vibrant as ever, shimmering in the flame of the candlelight, and her eyes were still that remarkable shade of summer blue. Four years. He thought he had forgotten her. He was mistaken. Sebastian quit his cousin's box and was rapping on the door of hers in seconds, pushing it open before she could respond. 'Caro?'

She was clutching the back of a gilded chair, staring at him as if he were an apparition. 'Sebastian?'

He pulled her into the dark recesses of the box, well away from prying eyes. She was the only touchstone left in his life. Right at this moment, she felt like sanctuary. 'Caro. I can't believe it's really you.'

He took her hands in his, and would have pulled her closer, but she resisted. 'I heard about Lord Ardhallow,' she said stiffly, 'please accept my sincere…'

'Thank you.' He cut her short, having no wish to discuss his late father. His emotions, already in turmoil, now felt completely scrambled. She was the last person he'd expected to see. The silence hung between them like a void as they each recalled the last time they had spoken, that fateful night at Lady Innellan's ball.

'I've missed you.' He was as surprised as she, when he blurted the words out. Even more surprised by the truth of them.

'Don't.' She was staring at him, her expression stricken, her eyes over-bright. Caro hated to cry, yet a tear tracked its way down her pale cheek and she made no effort to stop it.

'Are you here alone?' he asked in surprise.

'I—yes. This is my father's box. He is in Russia with Wellington, and Bella is at Killellan.'

'Your sister Lady Cressida is not available to accompany you? Forgive me, I know nothing of what has transpired in London since I left, I have made rather a point of not keeping in touch.'

'Nothing? You mean nothing at all?'

She was chalk white. There were lines

around her eyes that had not been there before, and dark shadows too. Her features seemed more finely etched, and despite her more rounded shape, her appearance seemed more fragile, brittle even. Sebastian shook his head. 'Most of the places I've been in latterly don't receive post.'

'And besides, you were not interested, were you? As I recall, you could not wait to kick the dust of London from your feet.'

He was nonplussed by her apparent lack of emotion. The elation of seeing her again, the sudden shaft of light which was the realisation that she was the only person he wanted to see, both faded in the face of her reserve. 'I beg your pardon, I see I have misjudged the situation. I should not have intruded.' He sketched a bow. It was not that he wanted to leave, but he had no idea what else to do.

'Don't go.' Caro reached for him as he made for the door, then faltered. 'I mean, there is no need to go just yet. I was just thinking of leaving myself. I find the play does not hold my interest.'

'Nor mine. May I—would you like me to escort you to…?'

'Cavendish Square. I have my father's carriage, but—yes. Yes, yes, you may escort me. We are old friends, after all, why not?'

The time it took to summon her father's town coach from the long queue of carriages lined up outside the theatre seemed like an eon, the short journey to Cavendish Square an eternity. Caro had chosen to stay in her father's town house rather than her own, which she never thought of as hers in any case. Being in Cavendish Square made her feel closer to Cordelia, most of whose clothes and possessions had been left there when she ran off.

She sat beside Sebastian in silence. He was, she assumed, as confused as she by the atmosphere between them, a tension that both pulled and repelled at the same time. She could hardly believe they were sitting in a carriage together as if nothing had changed. Everything had changed. Except what she felt for him, that had remained unchanged. No, that was not at all true. Four years had passed. She was no longer a naïve young girl in love with the idea of being in love with a rake. Something precious had been lost along the way.

Her father's house was shuttered, the knocker removed, for her youngest sister's elopement earlier in the Season had forced

Aunt Sophia, who had been acting as Cordelia's chaperon since Bella was indisposed, to
close the place up. Caro inserted her key in the
lock of the front door, and turned it with some
difficulty. 'There is only a skeleton staff here,
and I have asked them not to wait up,' she said
to Sebastian, leading him to the small salon at
the rear of the house which had always been
the Armstrong sisters' domain. On the wall
above the sewing table was the drawing Cassie
had sketched of Caro astride her favourite pony
as a child. Atop the mantelpiece was the shell
owl which Celia had made following a trip to
Brighton. A battered and well-thumbed copy
of *One Thousand and One Nights* lay hidden
in the secret drawer of the escritoire.

Caro was nervous. Her hand wavered as she
applied a taper to the fire and lit the branch of
candles on a side-table. The house was eerily
quiet. Her father would be appalled if he ever
found out she was here alone with a man other
than her husband. Good! It was not that she
blamed him for her choice, which had been
entirely her own decision, albeit one he had
previously approved, but she did blame him
for the relentless ambition which had forced
her into the yoke which he made for her in the
name of duty.

She unfastened the clasp at the neck of her evening cloak and cast it over the back of a wingback chair by the fireside. The buttons of her left glove were too stiff for her shaking fingers to undo.

'Here, let me.'

Remembering too late why she should have kept her gloves on, she tried to snatch her hand away. 'No. It's fine, I'll manage.'

'Don't be silly.' She flinched as he caught her fingers, stifling a cry of pain. 'You're hurt,' Sebastian said.

'It's nothing.'

But he was already unbuttoning her left glove, carefully unrolling it down her arm and easing the soft kid material over her fingers. An ugly bruise, purple fading into yellow and brown, covered most of her hand. Her fourth finger and the little one next to it were swollen. 'What happened?'

'I fell.'

'Fell?' He looked at her incredulously.

'I was—a door closed on me. It was an accident. Please give me back my glove.'

'Have you consulted a physician?'

'No! For heaven's sake, Sebastian, it's just a bruise.' She snatched the glove back but made no attempt to put it back on.

'What's wrong, Caro? Would you prefer it if I left? I would understand if you did.'

'No! Don't go. Not yet.' She removed her other glove, throwing them both down on top of her cloak. 'So, you are the Marquis of Ardhallow now,' she said in an attempt to make conversation, though what conversation she imagined they could possibly have...

Sebastian nodded.

'That must be—difficult for you. You never did wish to walk in your father's shoes.'

He nodded again, more tersely this time. Stupid! She should have known better than to mention his father. Caro smoothed out a crease in the skirt of her gown. They had neither of them sat down, but were facing each other across the hearth, as if they were both afraid of making a wrong move. Was there such a thing as a right move? She should not be thinking of any sort of move. She should not have invited him in but neither did she want him to leave. She smoothed out another crease in her gown. 'Things are not particularly easy for me either at present. There are things relating to—my sisters, my family. I went to the theatre tonight thinking to escape for a few hours.'

Sebastian made a sound which might have

passed for a laugh. 'Indeed, so did I, and failed miserably.'

The sheer weight of all she had left unsaid at their last meeting grew too heavy for Caro to bear. There were enough regrets in her life without adding another. 'I thought I was in love with you, you know,' she said abruptly. 'I pretended I didn't care when you said good-bye, but I did. Anyway, it doesn't matter now.'

Sebastian swore under his breath. He had suspected as much, which in a way validated his decision to leave. But he could not reveal the prominent role their respective fathers had played in helping him arrive at his decision.

'I thought my eyes were deceiving me tonight,' he said instead. 'I couldn't believe it really was you.'

'Nor I. You, I mean. I thought—I've seen you before, or thought I had, but it never was you. Am I making any sense at all?'

He laughed. 'No more than I.'

His smile faded as he stared at her. 'What's wrong, Caro?'

She made a helpless gesture. 'Nothing. Everything.' She wouldn't cry. 'If only you knew the half of it. I am so glad you don't.'

'I really have missed you, you know.'

'No. It's too late for that. I wish—I wish—

oh, what is the point in wishing! I wish it would all go away, just for a few moments.'

'Solace,' Sebastian said bitterly. 'No, oblivion. *That* is a very attractive prospect.'

'We always were of like mind.' Caro gave a sad little shrug. 'Let us not dwell on the past. In fact, I'm not sure I want to talk about the present either, and I'm absolutely certain that I don't want to think about the future.'

'Which leaves us at a bit of an impasse,' Sebastian replied. 'Perhaps it really would be best if I go.'

'Yes. That would be the sensible thing.'

Yet she made no move to see him out and as their eyes met, the air seemed to crackle with awareness. Trance-like, she closed the gap between them. She had no idea who made the first move, but when his lips met hers, she realised that it was this she'd wanted from the moment she first set eyes on him tonight. Just this once, she wanted not the harsh reality of her life but the dream she had once dreamed.

He kissed her, and she felt as if she were drowning. Or perhaps she was dead, and this was heaven. Such heaven. Sebastian's mouth, his hands, the smell of him, the intoxicating maleness of him, all felt so much better in the flesh. It was not a dream. She was no longer the naïve young girl who had kissed him four years ago. How innocent she had been, how worldly-wise she had thought herself, and how utterly disillusioning the intervening years had proved to be.

But she would not think of that. Though she ought. This was so wrong. She should not be kissing him. She should not be touching him. She should tell him—tell him the stark truth— and she would, she would, but not now. Not now, when this felt so right, making the harsh reality of her life feel, in contrast, so very, very wrong. Later she would return to her senses, allow duty and propriety to rule her actions, but for now, all she sought was exactly what she knew he wanted too.

Oblivion. She squeezed her eyes tight shut and balled her hands into fists, making her broken finger throb with pain. Remembering how it looked, ring-less and swollen, this latest bruise spreading purple and yellow over her hand, she felt a spark of rebellion. She had tried so hard to do what she was told was right, tried so hard to please everyone by doing as she was bid, but it was slowly destroying her.

Sebastian didn't want her to be someone else. She had always been truly herself when she was with him, and only with him. It was too late, but all the same, here he was, flesh and blood, kissing her, crushing her to him as if she would save him. As if he could save her. If only.

Wanting to stop her stream of thoughts, to quiet her conscience, she burrowed more closely into his embrace. Bathed in the soft glow of the firelight, he looked older and more world-weary than the self-assured young man she remembered. Changed but no less attractive. If anything more so. More human, more vulnerable. She reached up to trace the shape of his face, smoothing her palm over the roughness of the day's growth on his cheek. There were not just lines around his eyes, but shadows under them. He had the look of someone to whom sleep was a stranger. She knew all about that. She wanted him so much. The intensity of this wanting made of her youthful desire a meagre flame compared to the fire which burned inside the woman she had become. In contrast, what she had been taught of intimacy by that other seemed a sham. It frightened her, and it reassured her, the strength of that knowledge. This was right in a way *that* never had been.

'Caro, we should not.' Sebastian kissed her forehead. Her eyes. Her cheeks.

'Sebastian.' She meant to agree with him, but was distracted by the silkiness of his sun-bleached hair.

His fingers plucked at the pins which held her coiffure, spreading her tresses out over her back. He lifted the weight of her hair to kiss the nape of her neck, the hollow at her throat. 'Fire,' he said, 'you set me alight.'

His mouth found hers, his lips hungry on hers, his tongue stroking along the soft inside of her mouth, making her moan. His hands were feverish now, as were hers, struggling with his coat, his waistcoat, in the urgent need to feel skin on skin.

'We really should not be doing this,' he muttered as he shrugged impatiently out of his evening coat, dropping it onto the floor.

'No. We should not.' She tugged his shirt free of his trousers, running her palms up his back, relishing the ripple of his muscles in response.

'Caro.' His voice was rough, his breathing hard. 'Wait. Stop. We have to stop.'

But she could not. She could not leave any room for rational thought. Besides, she was still fully clad. 'Yes. We will. But not yet. Take it off. I want to see you.'

He hesitated, his eyes clouded with confusion and desire. Then he laughed. A throaty, utterly masculine sound, quite different from anything she had heard before, it made the muscles in her belly tighten. His movements cast shadows on the walls as he tugged the garment over his head, revealing his body from the waist up. Concave belly. Rib cage. The musculature of his chest. A spattering of hair. Nipples flat, dark brown. His skin was tanned, a golden brown all over. He was much broader than she had imagined. So different. A body used to sunshine and exercise. Where had he been, what had he been doing, to have acquired such a colour?

His laughter stopped when he saw the way she was looking at him. She reached out, running the flat of her palm tentatively over his skin. The muscles of his stomach tautened. 'Caro.'

There was a warning note in his voice. The effect it had on her was quite the opposite from what he intended. It had been so long since she had indulged her rebellious spirit. It was roused now, just by the way he looked at her. *I dare you,* she thought. And dared, spreading both her palms over his chest, feeling the friction of his hair, the smoothness of his skin, the hardness of his nipples.

'Caro.' Not a warning now. Anguish. Desire. She was playing with fire. She'd forgotten how much she enjoyed it. She splayed her hands over his back and kissed his throat. His shoulder.

The muscles of his chest tensed. He swore a short guttural oath. Then he swept her into his arms, laying her down on the hearth rug, kissing her wildly. His fingers struggled with the fastening of her gown. His hands were shaking which she found strangely reassuring. He was in the same uncharted waters as she. She was shivering. Finally, the laces gave. He eased her robe over her arms, running his hands down her sides, her waist, her thighs, as he removed it. Her corsets fastened at the front. She loosened them herself. The soft cambric of her chemise was no barrier. It grazed her nipples deliciously as he pushed it aside.

For a long moment she gazed up at him as he lay over her, the pair of them half-naked. His eyes were dark, hungry with desire. Like her, he seemed to be torn by the need to resist and the irresistible urge to continue. Like her, he seemed to be assuring himself that they would stop after this, after this, after this. And they would, but not yet.

Not when he was looking at her with such desire as she had never experienced. Not yet, when her desire matched his. Not yet, when he was cupping her breast in his hands. The hard length of his erection nudged at her belly. She reached around him to stroke his buttocks through his trousers, revelling in the way his muscles flexed, contracting and expanding as she ran her fingers over him, thrilling in the way her lightest touch made him moan.

He bent his head to take one of her nipples in his mouth. His tongue was warm, licking slowly over the aching bud before he sucked, jolting her to a new level of wanting. He licked again, then sucked again, while his other hand stroked languorously.

She writhed with pleasure under his expert caress. Her hands slid under the waistband of his trousers. He shuddered. 'Caro. God, Caro, I have never felt—and you feel so—oh God.'

She knew they were reaching the point of no return. She knew she should stop. She *wanted* to stop. Or at least she wanted to want to stop. Or at least she wanted. She wanted. She wanted so much.

His hand was on her bottom now, tilting her

up towards him. She fumbled for the fastenings of his trousers. He kicked off his shoes. All the time she told herself she would stop. She knew he was thinking the same, but every time he hesitated she drew him on. As he did her. Or that was how it felt.

She tugged at his trousers, encouraging him to slip them off. She undid the ties of her pantalettes. 'Caro.' His breathing was harsh. 'If we do not stop now...'

'Do you want to?'

'That's not the point.'

She closed her eyes momentarily. For the last four years she had done what she ought and not what she wanted. Not once. Opening her eyes again, she met his gaze unwaveringly. 'Yes it is, Sebastian. It is. It is exactly the point.'

His hand swept up her back, pulling her hard against him. The shock of his shaft nudging against her thighs made her gasp. She arched her back, wrapping her arms around him, pressing her breasts against the soft hair, the hard muscle of his chest.

Sebastian moaned. 'You have no idea what you do to me.'

'I know exactly what I do to you, because

you do it to me. Fire,' she said, 'you set me on fire.'

He kissed her hard. She kissed him back harder. His tongue thrust into her mouth. She dug her fingers into his back. He nudged her legs apart. She thrust herself up at him shamelessly, wanting him inside her now.

His kisses deepened. He rolled over to lie beside her on the floor, his hand splayed across her breast, travelling down her belly, fingers trailing fire over the soft flesh at the top of her thighs, teasing her open then sliding inside her, making her cry out with the delight of it.

She reached for him blindly, her fingers circling the unfamiliar girth of him, satiny skin, hard muscle, throbbing in her hand. Her mouth was dry. He was so—so—potent. Caro closed her mind to the cruel connotations of that particular word. Hard. He was so hard. And she was so—she had never been so—yielding?

His fingers move further inside her, gently, so gently, then out, then over, stroking, circling, making her squirm as the tension inside her tightened, knotted. She couldn't bear it, but she didn't want it to stop. She tensed as he touched her, stroked her, so wet that his finger slid over the hard nub of her arousal. She tried to focus, not on this, but on him. On the thickness of him. On the way he pulsed in response to her strokes. On the tightening she could feel at the base of his shaft, heavy with his need for her.

'Caro, Caro, oh God, Caro, I've never...'

His kiss, the plunge of his tongue into her mouth, set her over the edge. She climaxed with a shudder and a hoarse, guttural cry. Wave after wave sent her spinning out of control, her muscles contracting and tensing. She released her hold on his manhood, desperate for the final oblivion of having him inside her, hands tugging at his back, his buttocks, pulling him on top of her. 'Please, please, please,' she moaned, hardly recognising herself in the wild creature and not caring, desperate to give him the release, share the pleasure he had given her.

He hovered over her, his shaft nudging at her sex. 'I'll be careful. Are you sure?'

He thought her an innocent. If only. It would break her heart when she thought about it later, how honourable he had been. So she resolved not to think about it. 'I am certain.' She wrapped her legs around him, pulling him to her.

He watched her intently, his eyes dark, focused entirely on her face, as he slid inside her.

Slowly. Carefully, though there was no need. She wished there was.

He stilled. It felt so right. He felt so right, the thickness of him buried deep inside her. Just this once, she thought, closing her eyes on the sudden rush of tears. Just this once. Then she dug her nails into his buttocks, and thrust up under him, tightening around him, making him shudder in response.

He thrust deeper into her. He withdrew slowly, then thrust again. His eyes were focused on hers. She could feel the strength of his gaze through her closed lids. She opened her eyes, blinking away the tears. He thrust again, sending ripples through her. And again. She held onto him, tightening around him, as the surge of her climax renewed with each thrust, building quickly, making him thrust more urgently, until she broke and he came in unison, crying out, withdrawing at the last moment, spilling on to the rug.

Oblivion. She curled herself around him, closing her eyes tight shut. Oblivion. And also, right at this moment, paradise.

Chapter Six

Oblivion. Save that oblivion was the state of feeling nothing and Sebastian felt as if he had been turned upside down and inside out. Love-making for him was usually a pleasant release. There had been times when it had amused him and times when he had been bored. There had been women whose performance and imagination intrigued him, women whose gymnastics exhausted him or made him feel slightly ridiculous. But always, he retained an innate sense of self, a detachment which made a mockery of the notion love-making was anything other than the pleasurable and temporary coupling of bodies.

He felt strange. Empty yet replete. It bothered him that he had lost control, that there had been moments when he hadn't been thinking at all, had lost himself in sensation. He felt—nervous?—no, not that, but as if he was missing some crucial point. Tense. Edgy. This wasn't right, though nothing about it had felt wrong. In fact there were aspects of it that hadn't ever felt so good. Which wasn't right either. In short, he didn't know what the devil to think.

And Caro? The full enormity of what they had done, of what *he* had done to *her*, hit him with appalling force. He rolled away from her, scrabbling for his trousers which had landed under a side table. Pulling them on, he grabbed a large embroidered shawl from the faded damask sofa and held it out for her.

She wrapped it around herself, though she remained curled up on the floor, leaning back against a footstool, saying nothing, her face a blank. With a growing sense of foreboding, Sebastian found his shirt and put it on before sitting down in the wingback chair across from her. 'I don't know what to say.'

'Whatever you do, don't apologise. I was as much to blame as you.'

'I should have known better.'

She smiled wanly, shivering. 'My maxim.'

Part of the problem was that he was still caught up in the dizzying aftermath. His body

was still tingling, while his mind struggled
with the consequences of what had caused him
to tingle. It was a small consolation that he'd
had the presence of mind to prevent the most
drastic consequence of all.

Sebastian swore under his breath. It was
a lie, telling her he didn't know what to say.
There was only possible one thing to say. He
pressed his knuckles so hard into his eyes
that he saw stars. For a fleeting moment the
idea had actually seemed attractive. He swore
again, and got to his feet. 'Caroline. Obviously,
we'll get married.'

She looked aghast. Granted, it was a very
poor proposal, but then he had never proposed
marriage before. Sebastian cleared his throat.
'What I meant to say was, will you do me the
honour of marrying me?'

Caro mouthed one of his own more colour-
ful expletives. Jumping to her feet, she dropped
the shawl and stood before him in just her chemise. 'Sebastian, I beg of you, don't continue
in this vein.'

'Don't—you must see I have to. Having
taken your innocence, it is the only honourable course of action. I should not have allowed
things to go so far. I don't know what possessed me.'

'Oblivion,' she snapped. 'That's what we both wanted, wasn't it? That's *all* we wanted.'

Her response, the aggressive tone in which it was delivered, quite unsettled him. 'I am trying to do the right thing by you.'

'Yes, just as you claimed you were doing when you left four years ago.' She threw out her hand. 'No. No, you don't deserve that.'

Turning her back on him, she drew several deep breaths, obviously struggling for calm. The firelight made her chemise transparent. Through the fine cambric, he thought he saw the shadow of a bruise on her left buttock. Had he done that? Surely not. Another fall? He had not thought her clumsy. Sebastian frowned, running his hands through his hair. It had grown too long. He must visit a barber before returning to the country. Devil take it, what was he doing, thinking of barbers at the moment. His mind was as dishevelled as his hair.

'You have to go,' Caro said, whirling round on him suddenly, cutting through his jumble of thoughts.

Sebastian nodded. 'You're right. We're both somewhat overwrought. It's not the time to discuss something as important as this. I shall call on you in the morning when we can talk calmly and rationally.'

'No!'

The first seeds of doubt began to push their way into his conscience. His stomach knotted. 'The afternoon then? For Heaven's sake, we can't just ignore what has happened. Caroline?'

'Don't call me that. You never call me that.'

'Why are you so angry?'

'You don't want to marry me. You don't love me. I don't want your pity.'

It was the way she ticked off each reason that threw him, as if she were critiquing a play. 'It has nothing to do with pity. I have compromised you, therefore we have no option but to get married.'

She picked up the shawl and threw it over her shoulders, wrapping her arms tight around her waist, holding herself as if she might shatter into a thousand pieces. 'Compromised me! Trust me, my innocence is not at stake. That, I am afraid, is long gone.'

He had not noticed, in the heat of passion, but then to his knowledge he had no experience of virgins. It was not always painful or difficult, that was surely the stuff of male mythology. 'Do you mean that someone else...' Cold sweat broke out on his brow. 'Caro, oh dear heaven, Caro, do you mean that some other man seduced you? Took advantage of you? Is that what you meant when you said that things had been difficult for you?'

She put out her hands defensively in front of her when he made to cross the room. He stopped in his tracks, utterly confused. The very thought of Caro with another man was unpalatable to say the least, but he was extremely conscious of the fact that she was very far from his first woman. Most men would say the cases were not the same, but he was not most men, and Caro was most certainly not most women. On the other hand, if she had been forced—the very idea made him cold with fury.

What to say? He had to say something, because though his instincts were to comfort her, he thought she would very likely scream if he touched her. 'Caro,' Sebastian said carefully, 'whatever is the truth, you can trust me to understand.'

For a moment, he thought she would cry. Her mouth wobbled, but she drew herself up, tightening her grip on herself so that the skin was stretched tight across her knuckles. 'The truth is that there is no need for you to marry me. In fact, you can't marry me, because I am already married.'

'Married!' The word came out as a gasp. Sebastian stared at her in utter incomprehension. 'You can't be married.' But her stricken face told him otherwise. He snatched at her left hand. 'Devil take it woman, you can't be. You're not wearing a ring. You're staying here alone, you said you were alone, here in your father's house. You never mentioned a husband. A more than trivial oversight you'll agree.'

He had forgotten her injury until she winced, making him release his hold immediately. 'My finger was too swollen,' she said, rubbing her hand gingerly. 'I had to have the ring cut off.'

'When you caught it in the door?'

'I—yes.'

'And the other bruise? This one, on your behind. I suppose you'll tell me that was caused by a door too.'

'I will tell you it is none of your business.'

Sebastian flung himself from her. 'Married! For how long? Who to?'

'Three years. Sir Grahame Rider. You would have known, had you taken the least bit of interest in me, but you washed your hands of me the minute you left me that night in Lady Innellan's,' she snapped in return.

Her cheeks were bright with temper. She was no longer holding herself rigid but was trembling. It was a relief to give vent to his own fury, for it prevented him from confront-

ing the sense of betrayal her revelation had
evoked. A part of him should be relieved, he
had never had any desire to marry, but though
he stopped momentarily to search his conscience, he could find no trace of this. There
was, however, a large and most unjustifiable
dose of jealousy, he was mortified to discover.
'Three years! You told me just tonight that you
were in love with me four years ago, yet you
must have married within a year.'

'As I told you I would when you left. It was
always my intention to make a good match,
and I did.'

'If your marriage is so good, why were you
hiding out in the theatre quite alone and patently miserable? You deceived me,' Sebastian
threw at her, resorting to righteous indignation
as he scooped up his waistcoat from the floor.
'What the *hell* were you playing at? Why didn't
you tell me?'

'Why didn't you ask? It's been four years,
Sebastian. You knew it was my intention to
marry. Why did you assume I hadn't? Just because you avoided all news of England doesn't
mean there was no news. Life here carried
on without you. *I* carried on. Did you really
think you would come back and find nothing
changed? Were you really arrogant enough to

think the world would stop turning and wait patiently for your return?'

She was right, Sebastian realised with sickening clarity. His father was dead. Caro was married. The only thing that hadn't changed was that he was quite alone. Which was exactly what he preferred, and how he would make damned sure to keep it from now on. Ignoring the sense of crushing disappointment, he finished dressing. 'Are there any children?' he asked as he struggled into his coat.

Caro shook her head. 'No.'

Her voice was barely a whisper. She looked just as shattered as he felt. And so she ought, for this was as much her doing as his. If he had not asked, she had certainly omitted telling him.

He was making for the door when her voice halted him. 'You have no right to judge me, Sebastian.'

'I did not...'

'Don't bother to deny it.' She began to pick up her clothes, moving slowly. 'Tonight constituted what we agreed upon, oblivion. A temporary escape from the real world, in which no questions are asked or answered on either side.'

'I am not married, if that is what you are alluding to.'

'I wasn't,' Caro said after a long moment, 'but I am not surprised that you are not.'

He desperately wanted to ask her what she meant by that, but was equally determined to bring this débâcle to a swift conclusion. She was shutting him out. He should be relieved to be absolved of all responsibility, but the more she excused him the more he wished not to be excused.

'Just one more thing, Sebastian,' Caro said as she held open the door for him. 'I did not say I was in love with you, I said I thought I was. When you left, I realised that I didn't know you. How can you be truly in love with someone you know nothing about?'

What she meant was that he meant nothing to her. 'I no longer understand you,' Sebastian said bitterly. The Caro he thought he knew would never have lied to him. She would never have dismissed such an intimate act as meaningless. That it was the first time he had ever found it to have meaning made this fact even more painful, made him even more determined not to allow her to wound him. He didn't know her, he never had, and moreover he didn't want to.

His anger returned, surging like a spring tide, washing away his hurt. 'I had planned to spend this evening alone at Limmer's with only a decanter of brandy for company. I wish now that I had.'

He waited for her to say something, anything, but her expression remained frozen, her eyes wide, her skin mottled with tears. No explanations, no excuses, nothing to mitigate the damage she had done. Oblivion.

Sebastian picked up his hat and gloves from the writing desk by the door. 'If I never see you again, it will be too soon.' He quit the room without a backwards glance.

Alone, Caro listened to this muffled footsteps crossing the reception hall. She counted to one hundred as he unlocked the front door, pulling it firmly closed behind him. Then two hundred. At three hundred, she let loose her grip on the back of the chair and sank on to the hearth rug. She was still there, engulfed in her broken dreams and bitter regrets, when dawn broke.

Crag Hall—1830

'So you see, it is imperative that, as landlords, we present a united front on this issue.'

Sir Timothy Innellan had been pontificating for over an hour now and showed little sign of flagging. *How* the man liked the sound of his own voice, Sebastian thought wearily. To listen to him, one would think he had been ploughing the fields himself for the last decade, when in fact he had inherited only two years ago, at about the same time as Sebastian himself had done.

'If one of us starts paying over the odds for labour, then it will cause great unrest when others do not follow suit. Do you not agree, my lord?'

The question was purely rhetorical. Sir Timothy continued without a pause for breath. Patience, Sebastian told himself. He strolled over to his desk and selected a book at random. *Contributions towards the Improvement of Agriculture with Practical Suggestions on the Management and Improvement of Livestock.* As good a topic as any. He cleared his throat. 'As a matter of fact, Sir Timothy...'

The parlour door was suddenly thrown wide open. 'Sebastian, did you know...' Caro stopped in her tracks. 'Oh, I beg your pardon, I did not know you had a visitor. I will leave you to complete your business.' She hurriedly made to withdraw from the room.

Sebastian dropped the worthy tome back on the desk and strode over to the door. 'No, please join us, your presence is most welcome,' he said, casting Caro a pleading look. 'Sir Timothy, may I introducc…'

'Lady Caroline.' She filled the awkward gap herself, giving Sebastian an almost undetectable shrug before stepping forwards with a very fair imitation of polite diffidence. 'How do you do?'

Sir Timothy, who had automatically begun to get to his feet, had now paused midway, his breeched behind hovering over the chair upon which he had been sitting. *Lady* Caroline? What would any respectable lady be doing in the home of a notorious bachelor? The question may as well have been writ large on the man's forehead, so obviously was he thinking it, but Caro's calculated assumption that manners would dictate that he would acknowledge her proved to be accurate. Sir Timothy made a small bow and briefly touched his fingers to hers. 'My lady,' he said, though his tone was frankly questioning.

'Sir Timothy.' Caro dropped a small curtsy. 'I am pleased to make your acquaintance but if you will excuse me, I have interrupted your visit long enough.'

The look of relief on his visitor's face as she began to back out of the room riled Sebastian. The man may already have drawn his own dubious conclusions, but allowing Caro to beat the polite retreat she so obviously desired would only reinforce them. Besides, he was damned if he'd allow her to be forced out of the room.

'There is no need to leave us,' Sebastian said, catching her at the door and ushering her into a chair, managing to give her hand a reassuring squeeze as he did so. 'Sir Timothy has been most—er—passionate upon the subject of agricultural labour, but I fear his erudition is somewhat wasted on me, since our views are rather diametrically opposite. In fact, your intervention has prevented us from coming to blows on the matter, has it not, my good sir?'

His neighbour, still eyeing Caro with some suspicion, managed a distracted smile. 'Oh, as to that, my lord, I am not a violent man,' he said, tugging at his beard. 'I am sure there is a middle ground to be found. My point is,' he continued, obviously having decided that the best policy would be to ignore Caro's presence, 'we currently have rather a glut of labourers and rather a scarcity of work for them. They are proud men, they will see the payment of a higher hourly rate as an insult. "An honest penny for honest sweat", my father always used to say.'

'Indeed,' Sebastian said shortly, struggling to hide his irritation. As Sir Timothy continued with his lecture and continued to ignore Caro, he could see that while she appeared on the surface to be amused by the pompous prig, the awkwardness of the situation was making her most uncomfortable. She was lacing and unlacing her fingers together in her lap. There was the slightest of flushes on her cheeks. While it was one thing to jest about courting scandal, Sebastian realised that it was, for her at least, quite another thing to suit actions to words. Her response to the vile things her husband had said of her had been to hide, not brazen it out. Though she claimed she was happy to embrace the freedom which her ejection from polite society gave her, Sebastian was beginning to get an inkling of what her notoriety would cost her.

And now he had placed her in the unenviable position of having to endure the man's tedious sermon or risk a snubbing. *Dammit*, he should not have forced her to remain in the room, yet her leaving could only draw attention to her presence. How the devil was he now to be rid of the man?

Blissfully unaware of his host's displeasure, Sir Timothy, had settled into what was obviously a well-rehearsed speech. 'As to this notion that we landowners should provide employment for the customary numbers despite the quality of the harvest—well!' He gave a hearty guffaw. 'Ridiculous idea. One is not a charity.'

'But if you do not provide them with the employment they expect what do you think will happen to them? They will have no wages, no money to feed and clothe their families.' Caro's sudden entrance into the conversation startled them both.

Sir Timothy's eyes boggled. 'Why, that is what the parish is for,' he said disdainfully. 'And the workhouse. An honest penny for honest sweat, my—er, lady. And if they do not take to such work—well, there is a natural cycle of things, I believe.'

'You mean they will die,' Caro exclaimed indignantly, earning herself a baleful stare.

'I mean that a poor harvest yields poor peasants,' Sir Timothy said. 'I cannot be doing with poor peasants. I require strong, hearty men.'

Caro gave something which very much resembled a snort. 'I am very sure you do.'

Sebastian bit back a smile, but his guest, no longer able to deny Caro's existence, was not amused. 'I am afraid that the finer nuances of agricultural practice are lost on ladies—and the weaker sex in general,' he said, making it clear that he had decided she did not belong to the former category.

Caro, obviously equally aware of the implied insult, refused to be cowed. 'Indeed,' she enquired with a tight smile, 'what then, I wonder, would you consider a fit topic for us to discuss?'

'That is a difficult question to answer since I am unclear as to your—ahem—status here at Crag Hall.'

This blatant insult sent the colour flooding to Caro's cheeks and made Sebastian's fists clench automatically. 'Whatever conclusions your provincial mind has come to with regards to Lady Caroline's presence here,' he said through gritted teeth, 'let me assure you, they are likely to be far off the mark.'

'I came here merely to discuss our common interest in these itinerant labourers. I have no interest in your personal circumstances,' Sir Timothy said haughtily. 'Since we have now concluded that discussion, I will take my leave.'

'But we have not concluded that discussion at all, for you have given me no chance to express my own opinion. You will, I am sure, wish to do me the courtesy of hearing it before you leave.' Sebastian leaned casually against the parlour door, giving his guest no option but to resume his seat, albeit with extreme reluctance.

'I will be brief, since you are so eager to be on your way,' Sebastian continued. 'The salient point, and one you yourself made, is that these labourers are proud men. Many would rather die than throw themselves on the parish.'

'Many forced to live on the parish, *do* die,' Caro interjected before casting him an apologetic glance.

Sebastian grimaced. 'Lady Caroline is in the right of it. Come, Sir Timothy, these same families have been employed at harvest time on our estates for generations. Don't you think we have an obligation to support them through difficult times?'

His guest, however, was unwilling to surrender an inch of his entrenched position. 'We are experiencing difficult times ourselves, my lord, if I may remind you. Labourers are not the only ones affected by a poor harvest.'

'We can, however, weather the storm rather better, can we not? We are not faced with eviction because we can't pay our rents. Our families are not going to starve.'

'It seems to me that you are already tightening your belt,' Sir Timothy said, eyeing the parlour askance. 'Your predecessor left his affairs in a tangle, I take it? Understandable that you have shut the place up. Houses this size are a huge overhead. I thank my good fortune that my own establishment is somewhat more modest. Although one still has the burden of responsibility. My mother was saying to me only the other day that it was about time I took a wife. Obligation to the title, and all that,' he added, looking suddenly unhappy. 'Have to confess, it's a burden, sometimes—the title, the land. In fact there are times when I would be very happy to hole up in a little bachelor apartment like this and...' He broke off with an embarrassed laugh.

'I met your mother in London,' Sebastian said. 'A most enterprising woman, I thought. I would imagine she has her own views on a bride for you.'

'Oh, my mother has many plans for me. Point of fact, at one time she was quite set upon making a match with one of the Armstrong girls over at Killellan Manor—egad!' He stared at Caro with almost comical incredulity then leapt to his feet. 'Just remembered, urgent appointment. I must go.'

More likely he was anxious to hotfoot back to share his juicy gossip with his mother, Sebastian surmised. Even if Sir Timothy hadn't recognised Caro as an Armstrong, just the mention of her Christian name would have ensured that Lady Innellan put two and two together.

As if reading his thoughts, Sir Timothy coloured as he addressed himself to Sebastian. 'I came here merely to discuss agriculture,' he reiterated. 'How you choose to conduct your personal affairs is none of my business. You may rely on my discretion. Now, *if* you will permit me, I will take my leave. Of you both,' he said, finally nodding curtly at Caro.

Realising that he had slightly misjudged the man, Sebastian held out his hand. 'Come, let us not end this visit on an unpleasant note. When the harvest begins in earnest I intend to do my best by the men who have served my family faithfully for years. I won't have them forced on to the parish. I will be employing the usual number, at an increased rate. Upon one matter we are, I hope, in complete agreement. It is imperative that we landlords present a united front. Between us, you and I wield considerable influence. I trust I can count on your support?'

The compliment had an immediate effect on Sir Timothy, who almost visibly puffed up. 'Well.' Torn between pride and a sneaking suspicion that he had been manipulated, he nodded, shook his head, and nodded again before shaking Sebastian's hand. 'Well,' he said again, 'it's been most interesting talking to you. And—er...' He nodded at Caro. 'Good day.'

Sebastian gratefully closed the parlour door behind his guest and let out a sigh.

'I am so sorry,' Caro said. 'I had no idea he was here or I would have stayed well out of his way.'

Sebastian took her hands in his. 'He may be a pompous prig but I believe him when he says he will not blab.'

Caro shook her head. 'Perhaps not, but it is only a matter of time before word gets out.'

'Does it bother you so much?'

Caro frowned. In truth, she had been taken aback at how strongly the conclusions Sir Timothy leapt to had affected her. 'The other things—the things that were printed in the scandal sheets, they were not true,' she said.

'Nor is it true that you are my mistress.'

'No, but my being here—Sebastian, it isn't

right. The truth is, I do not think I am cut out for notoriety. Seeing Sir Timothy's reaction to my presence here brought that uncomfortable fact home to roost.'

'Does your being here feel wrong?'

She was forced to laugh. 'Sophistry.'

He did not smile. 'You cannot possibly be worried about my reputation.'

'Once a rake?' She lifted his hand to her lips and pressed a quick kiss to his fingers. 'I sometimes think you use that as a convenient cloak to mask who you really are. Sir Timothy might not talk, but you know it is inevitable that who I am and my presence here will become common knowledge regardless.'

He ran his hand lightly over her hair. 'Foolish Caro, there is really no need to worry about my reputation. I don't give a damn.'

'But you obviously do give a damn about your estates, and in order to do your best by them—Sebastian, you can't live the life of an outcast for ever.'

'Caro, if living a respectable life means cultivating Sir Timothy the matter will not arise. I will die of boredom before I am forty. In fact, if you had not come into the parlour as you did, I suspect I would even now be slowly desiccating while he propounded his theories.'

'*I require strong, hearty men,*' Caro said, laughing. 'Cressie suspected as much with regard to his proclivities. Perhaps that is why he was so particularly intent on ignoring me.'

'I doubt Sir Timothy would have been interested if you'd rolled about the hearth naked.'

'Sebastian! I have no intentions of rolling around naked on your hearth.'

'That is a pity, for unlike Sir Timothy, it is a sight which would interest me greatly. Don't you think you could try it,' he teased, 'just in order to prove to yourself that you can behave outrageously if you wish?'

He slid his hand down the curve of her spine. Her unease receded, replaced by a shiver of desire. 'If we are to talk of the outrageous,' Caro said, 'I must mention Sir Timothy's beard.'

'I have no desire at all to talk about Sir Timothy. Let us talk instead of you.'

'But I have no interesting personal quirks to discuss.'

Sebastian grinned. 'What about your penchant for pink?'

'What penchant for pink?'

'You told me once that it is your favourite colour. You told me that you never wear it, for it clashes with your hair, but I know you lied about that.'

'How do you know?' she demanded, flustered.

'Because you wear pink stockings. At least you used to, when I knew you in London.'

'That is a most improper thing to say. You should not have been looking at my stockings.'

Sebastian's smile turned wolfish. 'I was looking at your ankles, not your stockings. Something which any man, gentleman or not, would do, given the opportunity. You have very beautiful ankles. Am I right about your predilection for pink, or is it a habit you have broken?'

'Oh, for goodness' sake, you are incorrigible.' She held out her foot, lifting just enough of her gown to expose a slim ankle sheathed in a pink stocking. 'There, are you satisfied now?'

She remembered, suddenly, that she had been wearing pink stockings that night, when they had met at the theatre. In fact at one point she was wearing nothing but pink stockings. Their gazes locked, and she knew he was recalling exactly the same thing. Her hands untying the strings which held her pantalettes. His palms cupping the curve of her bottom as he slid them down, his fingers trailing over her thighs, the way he had gasped when she wriggled, brushing against the solid heft of his erection, her pink-stockinged legs curling around his waist.

She should not be thinking such things. Caro licked her lips, and Sebastian ran his thumb along her mouth. His eyes were riveted on hers. His fingers fluttered over her jaw, trailing down her throat to her collar bone, to the scooped neck of her gown. His palm brushed her breast. Her nipple responded immediately, peaking against her chemise.

'Remember?' he murmured.

His words broke the spell. Caro twisted free of him. 'It would be better if we did not.'

Another memory, of the vicious words he had thrown at her, of the confusion and hurt she had felt when he left her that night, made her flinch.

'Oblivion,' Sebastian said, obviously still attuned to her thoughts. 'I said some terribly hurtful things. I was very angry.'

'I never did quite understand why.'

He threw himself down on one of the chairs by the empty grate. 'Why didn't you tell me you were married before things got out of hand?'

'I don't know.' Caro began to distractedly tidy the desk, stacking books and papers anyhow. 'I suppose I just wanted to forget that I was married, even for a little while. I wanted exactly what you said, oblivion.'

'But you returned to your husband and you stayed with him for another two years.'

'Duty is a very difficult habit to break, especially when it has been inculcated in one.' Caro sank on to the seat opposite him. 'I knew after seeing you at the theatre that night that my marriage was over. I would not have allowed myself to become so—so carried away—elsewise. But it is one thing to think such things, quite another to act upon them when the consequences are so very dreadful.'

'He hurt you. Don't deny it, Caro, I saw the evidence with my own eyes that night.'

She looked at her twisted ring finger. 'One of his few enduring gifts,' she admitted quietly. 'It wasn't often and it was never life-threatening, and I could never understand what triggered it. But that's not the only reason I left.'

Sebastian's brow quirked. 'So Rider did not cast you out as he claimed. To quit the marital home, with the law of the land and the weight of the world against you, you must have been desperate indeed. What happened, Caro?' he asked.

His tone was gentle, obviously afraid that she may be simply unable to answer him, but she discovered that for some reason she was finally ready to talk about it. 'I left because I no longer cared for him, and I knew that whatever happened, even if I ever conceived the child he so longed for, it would not change things between us. In fact, the very thought of bringing a child into that relationship appalled me. To put it simply, I left because I realised I deserved better, and so did he.'

'He deserves to be whipped by the cart's tail,' Sebastian said viciously.

'No. I didn't make him any more happy than he made me.'

'You didn't beat him for failing to do so, however.'

'That is—you know, I hadn't thought of that.'

Sebastian swore. 'Think about it now. He deserves to be thrashed for what he did to you.'

'Do you really think there is going to be trouble if there is a poor harvest?'

He accepted the abrupt change of subject after a brief silence.

'The signs are all there, my bailiff tells me. The workhouses will be full at the end of the year, and believe me, the workhouse is not a place to spend the winter. I visited the local one, my father was on the board. It was appalling.'

'What are you going to do about it?'

'Do? I doubt the good ladies and gentlemen of the board will allow me to do anything.'

'Can't you take up your seat in the House then, influence things there?'

'What, would you have me a reformer?'

'Why not? You must do something with your time, and since you claim you are already hugely unpopular, why not make yourself even more so and do some good at the same time?'

Sebastian burst into hearty laughter. 'You always did see things from a decidedly different perspective, Caro.'

She dropped a mock curtsy. 'Thank you, I think. If you opened up the Hall you could employ an army of servants. You said yourself that times are hard in the countryside. Don't you have an obligation to employ as many people as possible?'

'I don't want to open up the house, and I don't want to be waited on hand and foot by an army of servants in powdered wigs and livery.'

'Then don't have them wear powdered wigs and livery. This is your home, Sebastian, you may run it any way you see fit.'

'I am doing so.'

Caro laughed. He was so stubborn, but she had noticed how uncomfortable he had looked when Sir Timothy eyed the shabby little parlour with such disdain. 'Of course you are,' she said, 'if you choose to hide away here, that is no one's business but your own.' Without allowing him time to react to this barbed remark, she immediately changed tack. 'Do you know, in all the years I lived at Killellan, I never once was inside Crag Hall. My sisters and I used to spin such tales about this place. We called your father the Marquis of Ardhellow.'

'So you told me,' Sebastian said shortly.

Caro touched his arm, looking up at him with fluttering lashes. 'I would very much like to see around the house, Sebastian. Perhaps viewing it with a fresh pair of eyes might help to change your mind about the Hall.'

'I planned to sell the place when I inherited,' he admitted, surprising her. 'It's not entailed.'

'But you could not bring yourself to do so?'

'Perhaps in time—no. No,' he sighed, 'I don't think I will ever sell. I don't think I want to.'

'Then what is to be done, for you can hardly spend the rest of your life in this parlour.'

She knew she was treading a fine line. She longed to say more, but she bit her tongue, knowing that beyond a certain point he would dig his heels in.

And her silence was rewarded. Sebastian pulled off the neckcloth he had obviously donned to receive Sir Timothy, and held out his hand to her. 'So, you would like to see the Marquis of Ardhellow's lair? Come then, let us see how well your girlish imagination matched reality before I think better of it.'

Chapter Seven

They started in the picture gallery, a long room leading directly off the Romanesque reception hall. The gallery was located in one of the original sections of the house, with a Jacobean ceiling and a polished wooded floor of dark oak, which now echoed with their footsteps. 'My father, as you know,' Sebastian said, pausing in front of a large portrait in a gilt frame. The marquis was standing in full heraldic robes, under which he wore a full-skirted coat and breeches of gold brocade. Behind him, through the window, could be seen the formal gardens stretching towards the first of the estate farms. On the table before him was a sheaf of paper depicting the family tree. He wore a grey wig, the curls tightly rolled. His narrow mouth was unsmiling. His eyes were pale blue.

'He looks just as I remember him,' Caro said with a shiver. 'Cold. Intimidating. The Marquis of Ardhellow. You could never inherit that particular title.'

'I confess I had assumed that I had.'

'Oh no,' Caro said, 'you are not nearly old enough. My sisters and I decided that the Marquis of Ardhellow was at least a hundred years old. His skin is as pale and dry as parchment. He has to stay cooped up indoors else he would crumple and turn to dust in the sunshine. *You*, on the other hand, are positively tanned.' She touched Sebastian's cheek. Her fingers were cool on his skin. 'And as usual,' she said, running her thumb over his jaw, 'you need to shave. And you need to learn to dress like a gentleman too,' she said, touching the open neck of his shirt. 'Ardhellow now—well, just look at him.' She frowned, staring intently at the portrait. 'You will never be Ardhellow. I find it difficult to think of you even as Ard*hal-low*. You really look nothing like your father.'

'I thank God that I do not resemble him in any way.' He led the way out of the gallery through a door and into the Tribune, the square room which acted as the central axis for the piano nobile and all the state rooms. Above their heads was the trussed gallery, and above that, the domed roof soared. Caro was looking up in astonishment. The dome had apparently been designed to emulate the interior of the dome of St Paul's. Sebastian had always thought it unnecessarily ostentatious. 'I know, it's dammed pretentious,' he said.

She looked at him in astonishment. 'Perhaps, but there's no denying it's absolutely beautiful. It makes one feel quite dizzy, looking up at it, all those different tiers of plasterwork, like stairs climbing towards heaven.'

Caro's expression was rapt. As she examined the dome, he in turn examined her. The long line of her throat. The hollows at the base of her neck. The fall of her hair down her back as she tilted her head to look up. Her hair was darker in colour now than it had been two years ago, six years ago, ten years ago. Burnished copper. He remembered it loose, trailing over the creaminess of her skin in the firelight. Fire and earth. They had always been the elements he associated with her.

Dragging his eyes away, Sebastian looked up at the dome. He still thought it far too overwrought, but Caro was right, it was also beautiful and actually perfectly fitting for the house itself, which was more palace than hall. 'My father loved this place,' he said. 'The original building was a much more modest manor house, dating back to the seventeenth century. It has been a tradition for every earl to find some way of adding to it, to put his own mark on the place.'

'What was your father's contribution?'

'The library. I do not intend to keep up the tradition.'

'You don't feel you have the moral right to this house, is that it? Because your father hated you. Because you hated him.'

'It is not a question of morals,' he said, 'I simply think it's far too big for one person.'

'Yet you can't bring yourself to sell it. Whatever it is that came between you and your father, it started here, in this house. And now it belongs to you, you don't feel entitled to it. That much is obvious,' Caro continued inexorably. 'What I don't understand is why.'

'And what I don't understand is why you think I'd want to discuss it with you or anyone else,' Sebastian snapped.

He regretted his outburst immediately. He rubbed a weary hand over his eyes. He had camped out in the old kitchen wing the first day he arrived back to find his father not only dead but already buried. Aside from the necessary papers, which he had the lawyer remove from Lord Ardhallow's desk, and a selection of favourite books from the library, almost the first thing he had done, as the new lord and master, was to order the closing up of every state room—and there were many. Not once had he felt inclined to visit them, far less inhabit them. Mrs Keith had orders not to clean them. It had seemed like a good idea, to throw open the doors and shutters, to prove to Caro and more importantly himself, that he was not afraid of ghosts. But it was a far more painful experience than he had expected, and they had barely started. 'It has nothing to do with whether I feel entitled to live here or not, I have simply never wanted to.'

'Perhaps we should abandon this tour, I did not intend it to be detrimental.'

'I am perfectly capable of opening a few shutters without falling into a melancholy. I'm doing this for you, Caro. You asked me to and I am obliging you. What more do you want from me?'

'I want you to do it for yourself! To rid yourself of this—what did you call it?—mausoleum full of ghosts.'

Had he said that? Surely he would not have said anything so melodramatic.

'Yes, those were your exact words, more or less,' Caro said, as if she had read his mind. She glared at him, refusing to back down. 'Now, do you wish to carry on or not?'

'Oh, for heaven's sake! Pick a door.'

Caro swivelled round, looking at each door in turn. The Tribune was perfectly symmetrical. Two huge stone fireplaces carved with all sorts of mythological creatures faced each other from either end of the room. There were eight huge pedimented doors, two in every corner, all exactly the same, giving her no clue as to what lay behind them. 'That one,' she said, taking Sebastian's hand and leading the way with a confidence she did not feel.

Through a gloomy ante-chamber which was almost in darkness, she could just about make out a set of double doors which she flung open, enjoying the sense of theatre. Light seeped in through the cracks in the shutters. She could make out shapes, mounds of furniture huddled in holland covers, but was too afraid of bumping into one of them and knocking something over to move from the doorway. Sebastian however, strode towards the windows without hesitation, and wrenched back the shutters of one long window.

The vista revealed was of the manicured formal gardens at the rear of the Hall. The window, one of three set into the same wall, gave out onto a small balcony. Dust motes danced in the sunlight. There was a smell of mothballs, what Celia amusingly used to call stour—a term she had learned from their Scottish kitchen maid—and also the faint scent of dried flowers which Caro traced to a huge bowl of dusty petals sitting on the hearth under the white-marble mantel.

'The tapestry room,' Sebastian said. 'A homage to Versailles created by my great-grandfather.' He pulled back the cover from a huge sofa. 'As you can see, he took the tapestry theme to extremes. The design on the back of this is a detail from one of the main tapestries which hang on the walls. They're all rolled up over there in the corner. There's a clock somewhere, with a mechanical swan at the base, which I remember fascinated me as a child, though I was never permitted to wind the mechanism myself, naturally.'

Naturally? Sebastian sounded so matter of fact, as if he was reciting from a guidebook, but there was a bitterness in that one word that betrayed him. Pretending not to notice, Caro tried to remove the cover from an intriguing object which sat atop a massive marble sideboard with cupids carved into the legs which matched the cupids on the fireplace. The cover snagged on something underneath which was out of her reach. Sebastian was staring out of the window, as if trying to detach himself from the room. Caro found a footstool, which she used to help her clamber on to the sideboard. Whatever was underneath the cover was bronze. She could see a pair of bare feet. She reached under the heavy drab cotton to try to free it.

'What the devil are you about!'

Startled, Caro wavered, caught at the cover to steady herself only to discover that she had, unfortunately, managed to free it. For a moment, as she swayed, she thought she would right herself. Then the cover slipped loose, she slipped backwards and fell off the sideboard landing not, as she expected, heavily on to the bare floorboards, but in Sebastian's arms.

He staggered back, cursing as dust floated down over them. Caro sneezed. Then she laughed. Then she sneezed again. Sebastian caught his foot on the edge of a rolled-up rug. He fell heavily, taking her with him.

For a few long seconds, there was silence. Sebastian groaned, and Caro opened her eyes. 'Oh, are you hurt?' He was winded, most likely. And crushed by her weight too, for she was lying on top of him. She tried to move, but her skirts were tangled up in his legs. She wriggled. He groaned again. 'You *are* hurt. I am sorry, but I seem to be caught. If you could just move…'

A large hand clamped firmly over her bottom stilled her. 'Stop wriggling, Caro, you're making matters much worse.'

'My skirts are caught.' She craned her neck sideways. Her skirts had ridden up revealing her bare legs up to her thigh. 'If you could just move your left leg a little, then I could…'

'For the love of God, Caro, will you stop wriggling!'

'But I'm crushing you.'

'You weigh almost nothing. That is not the problem.'

'Then what—oh.' Heat flooded her face. The problem, now that she had stopped wriggling, was pressing insistently into her right thigh. She knew that any lady would politely pretend that it wasn't even there, and wait patiently on it subsiding. Perhaps she should concentrate on the sheer ugliness of the bronze statue of Diana the Huntress and her horribly realistic collection of her prey that had caused them to get into this compromising position. Diana was gazing down at Caro and Sebastian disdainfully, as if she, a goddess, was not to blame one little bit for the situation that they, mere mortals, had got themselves into.

Diana was bare-breasted. For such a statuesque female, her breasts were quite small. Caro's breasts were pressed against Sebastian's chest. Sebastian had a very broad chest. 'Do you think we've shocked her?'

'Who?'

'Diana. She looks shocked. Do you think this is the first time she has seen two mere mortals in such a compromising position?'

'In this house, certainly.'

'Your father would be shocked to find us like this in full daylight in one of his formal rooms, wouldn't he? Especially since he and my father went to such pains to ensure that we never would,' Caro said. 'I wish they could see us now.'

Sebastian laughed. 'What would they say if they walked in?'

'I think it would test my father's diplomatic skills to the limit,' Caro said, smiling wickedly.

'Then let us test him a little further.'

* * *

Sebastian groaned and wrapped his arms around her, pulling her tightly against him. Her mouth was hot and sweet, her kisses teasing, tantalising, somehow wickedly smiling, just as she had been. Ever since she had walked into the parlour, he had wanted to kiss her. All that talk of rolling about on the hearth naked had sent such images firing into his brain, he had barely been able to think of anything else.

The way she nipped at his earlobe made him shiver. He hated that sort of thing, usually. The way her fingers splayed across his chest, the way she flattened her palms over his nipples, the faintest of touches through his shirt, sent the blood coursing to his shaft. He was unbelievably hard. If she did not stop that little rocking motion—no, he didn't want her to stop—but if she didn't stop…

He closed his eyes, clutching at the soft mound of her bottom. Her tongue flitted over his lips, another of those most fleeting of touches that sent his pulse racing. She was almost astride him now, if it wasn't for those damned skirts of hers, he would feel her thighs enveloping his own. He tugged at her petticoats but they were too tangled up. He rolled her over on to her back, taking her by surprise, and pushed her skirts up.

'Pink stockings,' she said, stretching her leg up, pointing her toes like a ballet dancer.

He ran his hand up her calf, fascinated by the way his touch was reflected in her eyes, in the way her skin flushed. 'Lovely pink stockings, and lovely Caro,' he said, kissing the delicate skin behind her knee. She smelt divine. Her skin was hot to the touch beneath the silk.

'And look,' she said, pointing her other leg up into the air, 'I have two of them.'

Laughing, he kissed her other calf, the skin behind her other knee. He was fascinated by her in this mood, teasing, fun, teetering on the edge of outrageousness. He remembered that feeling, of being tangled in a net he didn't want to escape from, that night at Crockford's. It was the same, but not the same now. She was no longer a naïve young girl. She had been unhappy, hurt and very much alone. She had suffered, but perhaps it was this determination not to suffer again which lent her this edge, a need to grab at life with both hands? Whatever it was, it was infectious.

Releasing her pink-stockinged leg very reluctantly, Sebastian planted a final swift kiss to her swollen lips, then jumped to his feet, scooping her up into his arms.

'What are you doing?'

Sebastian headed for the door of the Tapestry Room. 'You're quite right, my father would be spinning in his grave if he could see us here.'

'Then why are we leaving?'

He smiled wolfishly down at her. 'Because there are a hundred other rooms in need of the same treatment. Do you think you're up to it?'

'I'm not sure I have either the repertoire or the stamina for a hundred rooms, but if it helps exorcise your demons I suppose I must try.'

Sebastian threw back his head and roared with laughter. 'How very obliging of you indeed, my lady.'

They arrived in the library by way of the Great Dining Room, the Gold Drawing Room, the Lesser Dining Room and the Crimson Drawing Room. They kissed on top of Jacobean oak chests, under gilded rococo tables, on sofas and *chaise longues*, and on one occasion they kissed while embracing a statue of Hermes between them. They danced from one end of the polished dining table to the other. They threw open shutters, cast holland covers to the floors, and unrolled carpets, sneezing on the dust they cast up.

Caro's stomach ached with laughing. She felt edgy, exhilarated, so tightly wound she thought she might explode. Sebastian's kisses were driving her frantic. 'How many more rooms are there?' she asked.

He caught her to him, pulling closed the door, which was fitted into the arcade of book-cases which lined the wall, giving the impression that the room itself was sealed. 'Are you weary of my kisses?'

She wondered what he would say if she told him the truth, that she was not tired but on fire. Each time he dragged his mouth away from hers, she wanted to scream in frustration. A crystal chandelier hung low from a trabeated ceiling extravagantly gilded in gold leaf. Glass-fronted bookcases lined three of the four walls, separated on one by a porphyry mantelpiece carved in the Egyptian style. Pulling a cover off a sofa covered in red damask, Caro sank down with a sigh. 'I think you have exhausted my kissing repertoire.'

Sebastian sat down beside her. 'It is a very impressive repertoire,' he said, nipping her earlobe.

She shivered. 'Considering my lack of experience, you mean?'

'No, I don't mean. You kiss beautifully, Lady Caroline. My compliments. In fact you kiss so beautifully I'm not sure how many more of your kisses I can take.'

'I am very relieved to hear you say so, my lord. Allow me to return the compliment.'

'Do you mean that?'

She twined her arms around his neck, sliding down the sofa and pulling him on top of her. 'Sebastian, would it be very wicked of me to suggest that we indulge in something other than kissing?'

'Wicked, wanton and utterly—music to my ears,' he said with a groan, rolling away from her on to his feet. 'Not here, though.'

Caro's senses were swimming. She wanted him now! 'But you told me this was the room your father had refurbished when he inherited. You told me it was his sanctuary, surely there is no more appropriate place.'

But Sebastian was already pulling her to her feet. 'Trust me, there is another room far more sacred.'

'Not his bedchamber,' she exclaimed, appalled.

'Lord no, not his. The Queen's.'

Laughing, he caught her hand and dragged her across to the bookcases, counting round the wall adjacent to the fireplace, then counting carefully along the volumes on the first shelf and to her astonishment withdrawing a large iron key from the hollowed centre of a book. 'Come on.'

She tripped after him, back out through the Tribune, up to the galleried first floor, past her own bedchamber and on to a door at the very end of the corridor. 'It was created for Queen Anne, for a visit that never materialised in the end, and has never been used,' Sebastian said. 'Tradition has it in the family that only a monarch can occupy it, so naturally it became an objective for me to discover the location of the key and to make this place my own secret kingdom.'

He turned the lock and pushed open the heavy door. Crossing the room, he pulled back the stiff wooden shutters, flooding the bedchamber with late afternoon sunshine. The corniced ceiling was brightly painted rather than gilded, in vivid greens, reds and shades of gold. A lion and a unicorn adorned the pediment of the door frame. 'The tapestries have been taken down, and the carpet, which is woven with gold crowns, is rolled up over there somewhere,' Sebastian said, pulling the covering from a huge walnut armoire taller than Caro. 'I used to hide in here when I was very small and didn't want to be found,' he said.

The bed itself was placed in the centre of the room. The covers came away easily, Sebastian casting them carelessly on to the bare boards of the floor. Once the dust had settled, Caro stared, awestruck. The four bedposts were set upon large plinths, each bearing the Stuart coat of arms. The posts themselves, wood painted gold, were elaborately carved with vine leaves from which both lions and unicorns peeped. The same design was carved along the tester from which hung a tasselled canopy.

'I've never seen such a magnificent bed,' Caro exclaimed, tracing the design of one pillar with her fingers. The mattress came up to her waist. 'It is truly fit for a queen.'

Sebastian pulled the final protective cover from the bed itself, revealing a bedcover of crimson embroidered with gold. He reached under the valance, and produced a wooden step. 'They thought of everything. Try it.'

'Isn't there some curse which will fall upon anyone not of royal blood who lies here?'

'As far as I am aware, no one save me ever has lain there,' Sebastian replied. He made a flourishing bow, and held out his hand. 'And in any event, are we both not already thoroughly cursed? Will you, my lady?'

Wholly entranced, Caro swept a curtsy. 'Indeed, I rather think I shall, my lord.' Taking his hand, she mounted the wooden step and sank on to the bed. The headboard was adorned with a tapestry, a hunting scene with a royal stag. Gathering her skirts around her, she lay back. 'Good gracious!'

The inner canopy was of blood-red silk, gathered and pleated. In the centre of the tester was fitted a large oval mirror. It was mottled, some of the silvering worn, but it still gave out a perfectly adequate reflection. There she was, her hair spread out on the bolster, her hands folded across her stomach, her ankles clad in their pink stockings on display. 'Good grief, I have never seen anything so extraordinary in my life.'

The mattress dipped as Sebastian joined her. He lay on his back, keeping a few inches between them. 'When I first discovered it, I had no idea why anyone would want to put a mirror in such a location.'

'I can only imagine that the queen was a very vain woman,' Caro said. 'Though from what I recall of her portrait, I don't think she had much cause to be.'

'I don't think the mirror was intended to indulge her vanity, Caro,' Sebastian said. 'I rather think its function was to reflect the other person occupying the bed with her.'

'What do you—oh, surely not! You cannot mean that it is for—you mean to watch themselves? While they were—but that is shocking!'

They were not touching. They were not looking at each other, talking instead to their reflections in the overhead mirror. It was as if they were watching two strangers. It was not Sebastian and Caro, lying here together on this vast, ostentatious bed, but two others, whose behaviour they could not control. Sebastian had kicked off his boots and stockings. He had very elegant feet. His lower legs were covered in fine, dark brown hair, the same colour as the hair on his chest, which she could see where his shirt lay open at his throat.

Sebastian's laughter was a low rumble. 'Shocking, but extremely arousing.'

'Really?' Her reflection was blushing.

'Try it.' Sebastian's reflection had rolled a little closer. His leg was lying against hers. His bare leg. Hers protected by a stocking and the skirts of her gown. His forearm brushed hers. Both were bare. In the mirror, her bosom rose and fell visibly as her breathing quickened.

She put her hand experimentally over the soft mounds of her breasts, feeling them rise and fall, watching her reflected hand touching them. Her littlest finger touched her nipple. A frisson of pleasure made her shiver. In the mirror, she could clearly see the outline of its hard peak, unrestrained by her corset, through the thin cotton of her chemise and gown. In the mirror, she saw the sharp intake of the other Sebastian's breath under his shirt as she moved her hand, letting it fall over her breast, lightly cupping it.

The woman in the mirror was flushed. Her eyes were heavy. Her lips seemed to be fuller, redder, than Caro's. Her other hand drifted down, tracing the line of her rib cage, the soft dent of her belly. She could feel the sharp rise and fall of Sebastian breathing, quicker, shallower, alongside her. She was conscious of the tension in him. The Sebastian in the mirror had his dark eyes fixed on her.

Was this her, the sensual being with her hair spread out over the pillow, whose feet were pressed into the gold damask coverlet? Feet which were, now free of her slippers, covered in pale pink silk stockings. She lifted one leg, pulling the skirts of her gown up to display her ankle, the curve of her calf, the dark cerise ribbons of her garters. Her skirts fell higher, above her knee, to reveal the whitework trim of her pantalettes.

Beside her, Sebastian groaned. In the mirror, he rolled on to his side and caught her leg, cupping her heel in his hand, then running his palm up her ankle, her calf, the back of her knee. His fingers slipped in between the top of her garters, the border of her pantalettes, to trace delicate patterns on the sensitive skin there. The woman in the mirror slid her hand beneath the cotton of her gown to touch the bare flesh of her breasts. The man in the mirror let her leg slide back on to the gold counterpane. He rolled over, the top of his body covering hers. Their limbs tangled. Male legs, bare to the knee. Pink-stockinged legs, somehow distinctively female compared to his muscled limbs. Leather stretched taut over male thighs, male buttocks. The instinctive arch, the parting of female legs to accommodate him. The back of his head dipped into the curve of her breast. His hand gently removing a female hand from the *décolleté* of the gown. The feel of his tongue, his lips, kissing over the mounds of flesh she could no longer see, covered by the shape of a male head with close-cut dark brown hair.

She closed her eyes. His mouth was like velvet on her skin, kissing along the line of her gown, his hands on her shoulders, her arms, pushing the sleeves down and with it the bodice. A shudder ran through him as he took her nipple in his mouth. A shudder ran through her as he sucked, slowly, sending her blood fizzing, making her belly clench and tighten.

She touched his back, pulling his shirt free of his breeches to run her hands over his skin, the knot of his spine, the ripple of his shoulders. Gently, he removed her hands. Her eyes flew open, questioning. 'Watch,' he said, 'just watch.'

So she watched, fascinated, enthralled, transported, feeling everything twice, what he did to her, and what she saw him do to the woman in the mirror, shifting to kneel between her legs so that she could see as he kissed her breasts, licked her nipples, circled them with his thumbs. In the mirror they were dark pink against the pearl-white of her breasts. Her eyes drifted shut with the pleasure of what he was doing, for he seemed to be connecting up every part of her body, every nerve and sensitive little spot, with his languorous caress.

'Watch,' he whispered. She watched as he kneeled before her, between her, lifting her leg, rubbing his face against the silk of her stocking, then kissing, her toes, her ankle, her calf, the back of her knee. His mouth burned hot through the sheer silk fabric. In the mirror, the other leg received similar attention. Her skirts pushed up. His hands under her bottom, tilting her to remove her pantalettes. In the mirror, her thighs were not white but cream. The skin on his face seemed stretched tighter. Slashes of colour on his cheekbones. Eyes dark, heavy, smouldering. Watching her. Giving her time to say stop, to call a halt. Watching her intently. The woman in the mirror smiled. A sleepy, sensual smile that could never belong to Caro. 'I'm still watching,' she said huskily.

He kissed her mouth, a brief, passionate kiss she missed for her eyes were closed. When she opened them, he was tilting her up again, his mouth on her thigh, the soft inner flesh of her thigh, first one then the other. Then his mouth was not on her thigh, but between her thighs, in the most intimate kiss imaginable.

She cried out, not in protest but in surprise. In the mirror there was a jumble of images. His head, her skirts, his hands on her legs. White flesh. Pink stockings. Feet curled into the coverlet. Hands, fingers, plucking at it. His mouth, his lips, his tongue, kissing, licking, making her squirm, making her tense, making her hot, then cold. Licking. Sucking. Kissing. His fingers inside her. Was it his fingers? She could not see. She did not care.

She closed her eyes and gave herself up to sensation. Slippery kisses. Languid licking. His mouth, his tongue teasing and tormenting her at her very core. Every part of her was focused, concentrated. A hand on her breast, her nipple tightening with unbearable pleasure. Tension. Heat. She cried out, arching her back and thrusting up against his mouth as her climax took her.

Sebastian's heart was racing. His erection throbbed. In the mirror above, a man lay with a beautiful woman splayed over his chest. Her hair streamed over the gold counterpane. Caro opened her eyes, gave a little sigh and smiled at him, a sated, sensual smile that filled him with an absurd pride. 'I have never been kissed like that before,' she murmured.

'I know.'

'It made me wonder,' she said, wriggling

from his embrace and pushing him on to his back, 'if a man can kiss a woman in such a way, then surely a woman can return the favour?'

He was so stunned, he could think of nothing to say for several seconds as she unfastened the buttons on his breeches.

'Sebastian? Have I got it wrong? Would you not like me to...'

'Like!' His mouth had gone quite dry. His shaft was straining inside his breeches. 'Caro, I can think of few things I would desire more, but...'

'But this is not something a lady should be offering?' She smiled, that newly wicked smile of hers that heated his blood. 'Since I am no longer a lady but a wanton-in-waiting, and since you have been so very, very obliging as to introduce me to something I find so very, very pleasurable, I think it only fair that I offer to return the favour.'

As she spoke, she pulled his shirt free from his breeches, planting little nipping kisses on his belly, at the same time tugging at his breeches, easing them down his legs. His erection sprang free, jutting up, taut and engorged. It was ridiculous, but the way she looked at him, the tip of her tongue pink on her lips, her eyes wide, reaching out to trail one rosy-tipped finger along his length, it did strange things to his gut.

She was kneeling between his legs now. In the mirror he could see her, cupping him in one hand, the other circling his erection, her face intent, flushed, her glorious hair trailing over his thighs. He had never wanted something so much in his life as this, but he had to be sure. 'Caro, you do not have to...'

'Sebastian, believe me, I do.' She leaned over him, and took him gently in her mouth and he surrendered all thoughts to feeling.

Sebastian dragged open his eyes. The sun had moved round. The light in the Queen's Bedchamber was softly golden. His body felt leaden, utterly sated, glowing like the sunshine. What Caro had just done was hardly a new experience, but it felt like it. It was her very lack of experience that made it so, he realised. She had none of the practised art, the clever tricks to prolong and to induce, that the courtesan deployed. Her touch had been tentative, explorative, instinctive. Watching her in the mirror, he had seen the pleasure in her expression as she pleasured him, and that had only added to the experience. Just thinking about it was making him stir.

He had never felt like this. Except once. The memory made him uncomfortable. Seeing Caro in the mirror, draped over him, his arm almost protective around her, made him more uncomfortable still. He was about to carefully disentangle himself when Caro sat up, pushing her hair back from her eyes. 'It's late,' she said.

She did not meet his gaze, but edged herself away from him and off the bed. That she seemed as dazed, as unsure of what to make of this encounter as he did should have been reassuring, but it merely set him on edge. He began to pull his clothes on, watching her as she trailed aimlessly around the room, pushing open the window to gaze out, picking up one of the discarded holland covers, folding it roughly then casting it back on to the floor. 'You are regretting this,' Sebastian said, pulling his boots on.

'No. At least—are you?'

'No.' He smiled. 'You have a hidden talent for wantonness. I had not expected—that.'

'Do you think we have exorcised enough ghosts for you to open the house up now?'

'Not if it means we won't be doing this again.' She flushed, but declined to answer.

Was she regretting it despite her denial? 'I was only teasing,' Sebastian said.

'I know. It's not that. I am still married, Sebastian. We cannot ignore that fact for ever.'

'I am perfectly well aware of that.'

'I am much restored. You have given me exactly what I needed here, sanctuary, and I will be eternally grateful to you, but it's time I stood on my own two feet.'

'You're going to confront your husband?'

'No, not yet.'

'Contact your family, then?'

'No. I'm not ready to face them yet either.'

'So, you are going to stand on your own two feet how, exactly?'

'I don't know, but I can't stay here indefinitely. Besides, you will want to be getting on with your own life, now that the ghosts are banished.'

'Caro, of course you cannot remain here for ever, but you are not ready to leave yet. Until you can come to some sort of terms with your husband, you are still married. That— that man, he has the right to do with you as he wishes. He can bed you. He can beat you. He can slander you and he can cut you off from your family.' His hands formed into fists, quickly unfurled. 'I have not the right to defend you, but I can keep you safe here until you are more capable of defending yourself. To leave here without any sort of plan, without even the confidence to have discussed matters with your family—it would be foolish, especially since there is no urgent need for you to go. It is not as if I am anxious to evict you.'

He waited while she pursed her lips, thinking over his words, trying not to think about how much he would miss her. He had been perfectly content without her, hadn't he? And while it was true he hadn't laughed in a while, it was also true that he didn't really seek company. Sebastian pulled on his other boot and got to his feet. 'Whatever you decide, I am damned if I will simply stand back and watch as you fall back into the clutches of that man who calls himself your husband.'

She sighed, shrugging her shoulders as if to be rid of whatever doubts were plaguing her. 'You are quite right,' she said with a resigned smile, 'I need to think it through properly. It is too important, it would be wrong to act hastily. But act I must.'

Sebastian nodded. 'Good. The timing of your leaving is a decision best left to another day.'

Wandering over to the large armoire which

took up most of one wall, she ran her fingers over the heavy carving distractedly. 'Did you say you hid here, when you were a child? It is absolutely huge, do you think it would take me?'

As she pulled open the door, Sebastian had a horrible premonition. 'No.'

'You think I'm too big?' She peered into the cupboard and began to climb in. 'There's something in the way.'

'Caro…'

She emerged, holding a box. 'What can this be?'

Sebastian said nothing. He had forgotten. How could he have forgotten?

'A box of toys. And—oh, look at this, it's a miniature. Who is it, Sebastian?'

He had no need to look at the portrait she held up. 'It's my mother,' he said flatly.

Chapter Eight

'A portrait of your mother! May I?' Assuming Sebastian's shrug indicated consent, Caro took the miniature over to the window to examine it in better light. Lady Ardhallow's hair was a rich auburn tinted with flecks of gold. Her eyes were dark brown, almost chocolate-coloured. And her smile turned down at the corners in a way that hinted at both sensuality and melancholy. 'You are very like her,' she said to Sebastian, who was still standing motionless in front of the armoire. 'I can understand why you kept those toys. I've still got the birthday gifts Mama gave me before she died. It is nothing to be ashamed of.'

'Except my mother is not, to the best of my knowledge, dead.'

Caro's jaw dropped. 'Not dead,' she repeated stupidly. 'You mean she's alive?'

'Unless an imposter is claiming her jointure from the bank each quarter.'

Caro frowned, trying to recall what, if anything, she had heard of the mysterious countess. 'I had always assumed—but you never mentioned her.'

'Why should I, she is nothing to me, she may as well be dead as far as I am concerned.'

'Sebastian!' Caro dropped on to the floor beside the box, carefully turning out the contents. A spinning top. A set of lead toy soldiers. A shabby little stuffed dog. A carved wooden pony and cart. All showed signs of wear and tear. All had obviously been well used and well loved. She remembered a peg doll she had had, every bit as shabby as this stuffed dog. Peggy, she had called it, and had been devastated when the cloth had worn so thin that not even Celia's clever stitching could fix her. Celia had made her a new doll, but it hadn't been the same, because it had been Mama who had made Peggy.

Sebastian was staring determinedly out of the window, his shoulders set, refusing to look at her—or the box. 'My mother did not die, she left.' He gave a heavy sigh and turned around.

'She ran off when I was four years old. My father told me that she didn't love me, didn't love either of us. He told me she was never coming back. I didn't believe him, didn't believe any of it, until enough time had passed as to make it impossible for me to believe anything else and since then I have put her from my mind.'

'You mean she just disappeared off the face of the earth? She didn't write or visit?'

Sebastian laughed bitterly. 'Oh, she made sure we knew her whereabouts. I told you, the one thing that has remained consistent is her claiming of her allowance.'

Caro scrambled to her feet. 'You have never made any attempt to track her down, make contact with her?'

'Why should I, when her years of silence speak volumes of her complete indifference towards me?'

'But she is your mother.' Caro clutched at her forehead. 'I lost my mother when I was five years old, almost the same age as you were when yours ran away. I would give anything—*anything*—to be able to talk to her, to ask her questions, to know her. Good God, I even went to that ridiculous séance all those years ago in the vain hope that I might make contact, however brief, with her. Yet your mother is alive, she is living—where?'

'Italy, I believe. Where she lives is irrelevant. The one place she does not live is here.' He tapped the area over his heart. 'She forfeited the right to that when she abandoned us so callously.'

'But—but you do care. I saw the way you looked at those toys, as if you had seen a ghost.'

'If I saw anything it was the ghost of my own, childish self, stupidly hoping against the odds. I was embarrassed by my gullibility.'

'Dear heavens, Sebastian, you have nothing to be embarrassed about. You were a child. Of course you believed she would come back for you. Any child would. Of course it must have hurt, it must have been agony for you to finally realise that she was never coming back.'

'You make too much of this. I admit it was upsetting at the time but I have been quite reconciled to it for many years.'

Beneath his tan, his face was pale. His mouth was set in a rigid line, the frown lines so deep that his brows almost met over his nose. She was not making too much of it, he was not making enough of it. 'Aren't you curious to know why she didn't get in touch? Could your father have prevented her? After all, he was a very proud man and her leaving must have caused a deuce of a scandal. You were all he had left, it makes sense that he wouldn't want to risk losing you too.'

Sebastian sighed heavily, and ran his fingers through his hair. 'Caro, it's ancient history.'

'So she is dead to you, just as she was to your father? I am surprised, I thought it pained you to walk in his shoes.'

'You go too far.'

'Your father died while you were abroad, with goodness knows how many questions left unanswered, how many matters left unsettled between you. I know you regret it, though you can't bring yourself to admit it. Don't make the same mistake twice. There is still time to remedy matters with your mother. I beg you, take the opportunity while you still can or you will have further cause for regret.'

'Enough!' he roared. 'I have had more than a sufficient amount of your home-spun philosophy. You would do better to reflect on your own situation, my lady. There are ample matters for you to resolve in your own life without your involving yourself in mine. A mutually pleasurable afternoon in bed together doesn't give you the right to dictate my actions.'

She felt the blood draining from her face.

'I see. For you, that is all it was, a mere afternoon's pleasure?'

'What did it signify for you, if not that?'

A very good question, Caro realised with alarm. 'I thought it was most educational,' she said with a creditable attempt at carelessness, 'and for that I must thank you. As to my interfering, rest assured, I have no desire whatsoever to embroil myself in your life, my lord. Apart from the fact that I am already married, you will understand it is very much a case of once bitten twice shy. My own affairs, as you rightly point out, are in dire need of attention. If you would inform Mrs Keith I will not require dinner this evening, I would appreciate it.'

He took a step towards her, then stopped. She made her way out of the Queen's Bedchamber, closing the door swiftly behind her. Then she picked up her skirts and fled for the sanctuary of her bedchamber.

Caro slipped down the stairs and out of the side door as the clock above the stable yard struck six. The sun was only just rising, the sky a pale blue canvas streaked with pink. Almost exactly the same shade of the stockings she had been wearing yesterday.

She had barely slept. Making her way around the paddock, where the morning dew clung to her skirts, she entered the rose garden. The scent was heady, the large blooms at their extravagant best after the spell of hot August days. Kneeling down to sniff a particularly strong perfume, idly running her fingers over the velvety petals of a large crimson flower, Caro closed her eyes. Yesterday, in the Queen's Bed, had been a revelation. It was not just what Sebastian had done to her, it was what she had discovered about herself. Seeing herself as a sensual being, that lush, passionate woman in the mirror, was—enlightening.

Only now did she realise the degree to which she had detached herself from her body. Making love to her husband had at first been pleasant enough. Never passionate, never more than mildly exciting, but she would not lie to herself, it had been—nice. Later, when the novelty had worn off, when it had become less and less likely that doing her marital duty was going to produce the much-desired heir, she had tried to recapture that pleasant feeling, to pretend to her husband and to herself, that it was still—nice. She had failed on both counts, and that failure had resulted in—well, that too was her own fault. Perhaps if she had been a better wife…

No, that was the old Caro who thought that way! She got to her feet and made for the other end of the rose garden, to the meadow which led to the boundary wall. If she had failed as a wife, then Sir Grahame had also failed as a husband. The simple fact was, she should not have married him. She had known from the start that she didn't love him, and *that night* had proven to her that she no longer even cared for him. Not that she loved Sebastian. She'd been infatuated with him once, had thought that she could love him once, but she'd been in love with a dream. She hadn't known the real man. She was only just beginning to know him now, and if ever there was a man she should run a hundred miles from, it was he.

Though it was usually Sebastian who ran away. Not that she could blame him, after yesterday's revelations. It made her feel quite sick, thinking of how miserable he must have been as a child, abandoned by his mother, bearing the brunt of his father's anger and shame. Had the countess made a failed attempt to contact her son? Surely, surely she would have. Yet there were parents who didn't care for their children. She had one herself, for goodness' sake. Perhaps Sebastian was right, it was better not to know. Or was it? Wouldn't it be better to be certain? Or would that hurt even more?

He had been so angry yesterday, quite furious with her, yet she had not once felt threatened. It hadn't taken much, of late, for her husband to turn his anger upon her. She had learnt to detect the signs, and had become adept at smoothing the waters, diffusing the threat. She could see now that such behaviour only made things worse, enhanced her feelings of being a helpless victim, trapped in a loveless marriage. She was getting stronger now. Feeling much better about herself. Thanks in no small part to Sebastian. Though trying to picture herself confronting Sir Grahame—her mind baulked at the notion. Not yet. Perhaps she should tackle her father first. But even that thought made her stomach knot.

Sebastian was right. She had far better focus her energy on her own problems without interfering in his. But his were so much more interesting. She didn't love him of course, but she did care for him. It was her duty, really, to help him, when he had helped her so much.

She had reached the boundary wall. Through those woods, across the rustic bridge, lay the formal gardens of Killellan Manor. She had come here by that route ten years ago. She'd thought herself miserable at the time. How young and how very naïve she had been. Looking back, she realised Bella must have been younger than Caro was now. Not much older than Celia, in fact. It's true, Bella could have made more of an effort, but really, they had made it so clear that they considered her an interloper—little wonder she was so uppity with them.

Caro propped her chin on her hands, leaning on the cool stone of the wall. No one could ever accuse Bella of having failed to do her duty. Four healthy boys, and when last they had met, she had been increasing again—a surprise to all, since it had been six years since the twins were born.

A melancholic mood stole over her. She knew her father well enough. Once he had made a decision, he would stick to it. Given time, a great deal of time, spent in whatever obscurity she could manage, her father may soften his stance enough to allow her to call upon him, but she doubted very much that he would allow such a wayward daughter to contaminate the air breathed by any of his precious sons. She did not see her brothers often, but she loved them wholeheartedly, and it pained her a great deal to think about how long it might be before she was permitted to see them again.

It was pointless even to contemplate changing her father's mind. In fact, it was wrong of her to think about doing so, when it was obvious she would fail. She was done with bending to his will, and she would not return to her husband. Which left the tricky question of what she proposed to do instead. She was not at all confident she could persuade her husband to provide her with an adequate allowance upon which to survive. While living in London, her lack of funds meant she had no option but to run up debts in Sir Grahame's name. Meagre debts, for necessities, but even those he had held against her, exaggerating both the amounts and the nature of the purchases. If she could live independently she would, but how to do that, when he would not even return her dowry?

It was so unfair. The marriage she had made to make her father happy was the cause of their estrangement. She had paid a high price for her mistake, physically and mentally. She had failed, but it hadn't been wholly her fault. She wasn't so conceited as to think she was entitled to an easy life, but surely she didn't deserve this?

Suddenly exhausted, she sank down on the daisy-strewn grass. What with dead mothers who weren't dead, and fathers who didn't deserve their daughter's love and husbands whom she wished were dead, she had barely thought about yesterday afternoon. Sebastian's kisses. Sebastian's touch. The mirror over the Queen's bed. Who would have thought there could be such pleasure in doing such wicked things. She smiled and closed her eyes, remembering. Within minutes, she was asleep.

Sebastian finished tying his cravat and slipped into a striped waistcoat. Frowning, he picked up the calling card from the silver tray, but the flowing script gave him no more clue as to his visitor's purpose than when Mrs Keith had delivered it fifteen minutes earlier. There was still no sign of Caro, who had missed breakfast as well as last night's dinner. He had spent a sleepless night wrestling with his conscience. All very well to tell himself that Caro was as much to blame as he for what had happened in the Queen's bed. All very well to tell himself that it was exactly what he had told her, a pleasurable way of spending the afternoon and nothing more. All very well, but it was Caro and not some courtesan who had been in that bed with him, and no woman, courtesan or mistress, had ever made him feel that way.

But Caro was not the sort of woman who had *affaires*, and he was not the sort of man who had anything else. Yet he struggled to convince himself that it was wrong. Which was the thing that worried him most, because it *was* wrong.

He picked up his coat of dark blue superfine and pulled it on. He had lied to her, deliberately understating what she had made him feel because he didn't like admitting that he felt anything. Other than pleasure, of course. Pleasure was perfectly acceptable, provided that was all he felt but the truth was with Caro, that wasn't all he felt. He liked Caro. He admired her. He enjoyed her company. What he didn't like was the way she got under his skin. He didn't like the unpalatable truths she told. He didn't like the way she challenged him, forced him to look anew at long-established facts. His mother, for example. Ancient history. Dead and buried.

Until yesterday, dammit! Now the questions she had thrown at him went round and round in his head demanding answers. Which was rich, considering how many questions of her own she was avoiding. Most likely in fact, that she was managing to avoid them by distracting herself with his problems. Damned if he would let her!

Now fate had unexpectedly dealt him a wildcard. He smiled, eyeing the visitor's missive. It would be interesting to see how this particular hand played out. Giving his reflection a final check in the mirror, he quit his bedchamber.

Throwing open the doors of the Gold Drawing Room, Sebastian made a sweeping bow. 'Lady Armstrong,' he said to his visitor, 'this is an unexpected pleasure.'

He remembered Caro's stepmother as a large, full-bosomed woman with a raddled face. The woman who held her hand out to him now was substantially slimmer, rather pretty in the manner of a faded English rose, and dressed in the height of fashion, if rather over-elaborately for a country call, in a violet gown with a silk underdress and a tiered tulle skirt embroidered with white cotton lace in a floral design. 'How do you do, Lord Ardhallow.'

He brushed her gloved hand with his fingers, and sat down in the chair opposite, banishing the image that flashed into his mind of himself and Caro kissing on the window seat.

'It has been some years since I had the pleasure of your acquaintance.'

A tight little smile greeted this remark. 'Indeed.'

'I think it was in London, wasn't it, the last time our paths crossed? At a ball hosted by one of our neighbours in fact. Lady Innellan. I had the pleasure of meeting her son only the other day. I wonder if her ladyship mentioned it to you?'

Another tight little smile, but he noticed the tell-tale blush on her cheeks. Naturally Lady Innellan would have interrogated her son about his visit to Crag Hall, for the rumours of Caro's presence would have been bound to percolate through by now. Even if Sir Timothy had tried, as he had promised, to be discreet, Sebastian doubted he'd have lied. Caro's name, or even the colour of her hair would have been enough to alert Lady Innellan who would, of course, have been anxious to alert Lady Armstrong. It was clear Lady Armstrong's curiosity exceeded her scruples, given her unexpected and not coincidental decision to come calling.

'This room is in need of some radical refurbishment,' she was saying, eyeing the drawing room with disdain. 'I hope you will not think me rude, Lord Ardhallow, but I must inform you that your housekeeper deserves her notice. This place has not been swept for months.'

'You must not blame Mrs Keith. She has not the staff to maintain the estate adequately.'

Lady Armstrong fidgeted with the strings of her reticule. 'I have heard—you must be aware—in short, my lord, it has come to my attention that you have a—a female residing here who is not of the servant class.'

'Come to your attention via Lady Innellan,' Sebastian replied, earning himself a sharp look.

'A female whom I suspect is not unknown to me, my lord.'

'One who should, in fact, be a lot more dear to you than she is. Did Lady Innellan, for I have no doubt it was she, also speculate as to the intimacy of my relationship with this lady? No doubt she put the most scurrilous slant on it. I trust, since you are marginally better acquainted with this lady than our neighbour, that you had no hesitation in contradicting her?'

A dark flush stained Lady Armstrong's throat. Her mouth pursed as she wrestled with the need to demonstrate her outrage by quitting his depraved lair at once and her desire to discover whether the rumours were true. Her inquisitiveness won. It was, in truth, a routine victory. 'Since I have had no communication with Caroline for months, it is impossible for me to make any comment whatsoever on her various—behaviours,' she said, twitching her skirts.

'I believe that to be rather your fault than hers. Or should I say, it is rather attributable to the decree Lord Armstrong issued.'

'My husband only ever wants what is best for his daughters.'

'It would appear he signally failed in the case of Caro.'

Lady Armstrong flinched. 'It is a mistake to interfere between man and wife, Lord Ardhallow. One must not judge what goes on behind closed doors.'

In the face of such determined indifference, which bordered on the callous, Sebastian could hardly control his anger. The woman must know what type of a man Rider was, she could not possibly be ignorant of what Caro had suffered. Her own stepdaughter! 'You advocate a reconciliation?'

'My husband believes that Sir Grahame would be most forgiving.'

He jumped to his feet. 'It is not for that bastard to forgive. Dammit, have you any idea…'

He forced himself to bite his tongue. 'I beg your pardon.'

'I see Lady Innellan was right in her suppositions as to Caroline's presence here,' Lady Armstrong said tightly. 'And *I* was right when I warned Caroline about you all these years ago.'

'Once a rake, eh? You were wrong, you know. I never had any intentions of ruining her.'

'One can only assume that like is attracted to like, however. She is quite ruined now, and will be beyond rescue if she continues to reside under your roof.'

'But if she returns to the man who beat her all will be forgiven and she will be welcomed back into the family fold, is that that?'

'She is his wife. My husband assures me that...'

'Your husband would call black white if it suited his purposes. Caro won't go back.'

'Not while you are providing her with an alternative, Lord Ardhallow. But what will happen to her when you grow bored with her as you do with all your mistresses?' Lady Armstrong got to her feet. 'You see, I am not so ill informed as you might think, for one who spends most of her life in the country.'

'Caro is perfectly capable of making a life for herself.'

Lady Armstrong snorted. 'From which I must assume that her residence here, under your protection, is indeed temporary. I confess I am relieved, it is somewhat embarrassing for my husband to have her so near at hand.'

'He would prefer she took her disgrace abroad?'

'He would prefer she repented. Be assured, I will keep Caroline's presence here to myself. I see no point in inflaming the situation even further.' Lady Armstrong opened her reticule and handed him an embossed card. 'I did not come here solely to discuss Caroline. The other reason for my visit is to deliver an invitation to my daughter's forthcoming christening.'

Sebastian took the card with some surprise. 'You want to invite me to Killellan Manor, even though...'

'You are the Marquis of Ardhallow.' Lady Armstrong interrupted him with one of her tight smiles. 'Whatever I may think of your person or your habits, your title is one of the oldest in the county and your lands the most extensive. I freely confess it would be quite a social coup for me to have you attend Isabel-

la's introduction to the world, given your re-
clusive reputation.'

He was about to throw the invitation dismissively at her feet, when a most devilish thought
occurred to him, giving him pause. Sebastian
made a small bow. 'Since it would be most
ungallant of me to deny you your social tri-
umph, Lady Armstrong,' he said, 'I look forward to seeing both you and Lord Armstrong
on the day.'

'Bella was here at Crag Hall!' Caro put a
hand to her mouth in horror.

'I received her in the Gold Drawing Room,
to be precise,' Sebastian said. 'She is gone now,
so you need not look so spooked.'

Caro sank down into her customary chair in
the small cluttered salon. 'I can't believe she
was actually here. Goodness, if I had not fallen
asleep in the meadow, I might have bumped
right into her.'

'So that's where you were.'

'I had a somewhat disturbed night.' She
flushed, suddenly remembering the terms
upon which they had parted yesterday. 'You
were right,' she said, quickly turning the subject, 'it is time I put my own house in order, so
to speak, without attempting to order yours.'

'Good. As to that I think you should start sooner, rather than later.'

Caro felt her heart sink. To her surprise, Sebastian smiled. 'Did you think I meant…? No, a perfect opportunity for you to make a start has fallen into our lap, right here.'

'Here?' She wasn't relieved, Caro told herself. It wasn't that she *wanted* to stay, or that she would have any reason to object if Sebastian wished her to leave sooner rather than later. Not at all. 'How so?'

'Your stepmother came to invite me to her daughter's christening.'

'So Bella has finally had a daughter,' Caro replied, momentarily distracted. 'She will be delighted.' Her face fell. 'My stepsister will probably be making her come-out by the time I meet her.'

'On the contrary, you will see her in two days. You are coming with me to the christening.'

'Good grief, Sebastian, how can you even suggest such a thing!' Caro jumped to her feet and began to pace the very small amount of available floor space anxiously. 'My father will be there. My father who, in case it has slipped your mind, has utterly disowned me. And Bella too, you are not going to tell me that she included me in the invitation. No, of course not, how could she when she doesn't even know that I am here at Crag Hall.' She stopped in her tracks as a sudden appalling thought occurred to her. 'She doesn't know I'm here, does she?'

'Lady Innellan put two and two together following her son's visit, and made short work of informing her bosom bow. I'm sorry, but you said yourself it was inevitable.'

Caro nodded, feeling slightly sick. Bella knew. Bella would assume exactly what Sir Timothy had assumed and judge her accordingly. Leaving her husband's protection, Caro had at least felt herself to be morally in the right. Living at Crag Hall with Sebastian, no matter how innocent—and there was nothing at all innocent about what had occurred between them yesterday—she had placed herself firmly in the wrong. 'Do you think my father knows?' she asked faintly.

'Your stepmother swore she would not tell him, but—Caro, your father is not a man who keeps his head buried in the sand. If he is not aware of your presence here now, he most certainly will be when you turn up on his doorstep.'

She shuddered. 'I intend to do no such thing.'

'Dammit, Caro, I thought you'd be pleased,'

Sebastian exclaimed. 'This is a golden opportunity to send a message to your family and the world that you are not prepared to hide yourself away like some common criminal. You will attend as my companion and I for one will be proud to have you on my arm. You expressed a desire to be scandalous, since that is how you have been unfairly labelled. What better opportunity to demonstrate it?

'I *can't*! Sebastian, it is one thing to behave scandalously, it is quite another to be notorious, I think. Besides, I have no wish to disrupt or ruin the christening of an innocent child. That would be wrong.'

'Which is why I suggest we forgo the church service and save our grand entrance for the party.'

'Sebastian, I not sure I could carry it off. My father…'

'Lady Armstrong made it very clear that you have burnt your bridges, Caro. Your father will not forgive you unless you return to your husband. Why are you concerning yourself with your father's sensibilities? He has forfeited the right to such consideration.'

Caro nodded. 'I know, but it is a very difficult habit to break,' she said, managing a weak smile. 'One thing is for certain, however, I am categorically not going back to my husband, regardless of what my father wishes. Did Bella— was she really so plain on that matter?'

'I'm afraid so,' Sebastian said, pulling her into his arms.

She knew she should resist, but she was feeling decidedly unnerved and his embrace was distinctly comforting. Caro leaned her cheek against his chest. She could hear his heart beating, slow, steady, reassuring. 'I married the man of his choice—at least, one of the selection he gave me.'

'Perhaps that's why he's taken it so badly. You've proved his judgement flawed. Even worse, from what you've told me, all your other sisters who have married men not of your father's choosing are blissfully happy.'

'And the great diplomat cannot bear to be wrong. Which is why he's being so intransigent with me.' She nestled closer, enjoying the smell of him, that delightful mixture of soap and outdoors and something peculiarly Sebastian. 'I hadn't thought of it like that.'

'So you see, you don't owe him anything.'

She disentangled herself from his embrace and began to pace the floor again, wringing her hands. 'Yes, but to turn up uninvited, in front of half the county! What if I lose my nerve and can't go through with it? I'm terrified just thinking about it.'

'Have a little faith in yourself. I believe in you.'

'Do you?' She searched his face for signs of mockery, but could find none.

'I'll be with you, remember, right by your side. Polite society has been more than happy to accept the lies your husband disseminated at face value, now is your chance to show society just how little you care of their opinions.'

'By attending my stepsister's christening with my rakish lover,' Caro said slowly.

'Precisely. So you'll do it?'

She smiled. 'I rather think I will.'

'That's the spirit!' Sebastian was smiling his upside-down smile. Her heart gave a funny little kick. Nerves, she told herself. Anticipation. Nothing to do with Sebastian at all. 'I'll do it on one condition,' she said.

Sebastian's smile faded. 'Which is what?'

'You are right. My father is selfish, ambitious, pompous, single-minded and above all utterly self-centred. He doesn't love me, he doesn't even know me well enough to like or dislike me. Cressie put it perfectly all those years ago, his only interest in any of his gals is as pawns in his game of matrimonial chess.

Well, I'm done with playing that game, and I'm done with trying to please him.'

'I am extremely pleased to hear that, but…'

'My point is, Sebastian, that you need to do the same. I am happy to confront my father, but only if you confront yours.'

'My father, in case it has slipped your attention, is dead.'

'But your mother is very much alive. Don't you see, she could help you to understand why things were so difficult between you and your father.'

'It's quite simple, Caro. He couldn't abide the sight of me.'

'No, it's not simple. Speaking from experience, relationships between parents and children are never so.'

'My relationship with my mother is so simple as to be non-existent. She ran off when I was four years old. I barely remember her, and she has shown no interest in me at all since then.'

'Aren't you even a little bit curious?'

'Why should I be?'

'Because she is your mother!' Caro stared at him, aghast. 'You can't pretend she never existed, though it sounds to me as if that's exactly what you and your father did. Didn't he ever mention her?'

'Why should he?'

It was like throwing a ball against an unforgiving surface. He bounced everything back to her, determined not to allow even a sliver of a crack to appear in his armour. She tried, but could not think of one single occasion when he had mentioned his mother before she had found that box of memories. The extent of his self-deception took her breath away. 'He encouraged you to think of your mother as dead. He removed her portrait from the gallery—for there must have been one there when they were married. In fact now I think about it, there is not a single trace of the woman anywhere in this house.'

'Devil take it, you are like a dog with a bone. My mother's rooms are in the East Wing. Apparently my father ordered that they be closed up the day after she left.'

'You inherited two years ago. Are you really telling me that you have not once thought to look?'

'Once and for all, I am not interested.'

'Prove it then,' Caro said. 'Prove to me that you don't give a damn.'

'What do you mean?'

'Take me to these rooms. The East Wing, I want to see it.'

He hesitated. She thought she had pushed him too far, but she had underestimated his strength of will. 'Very well,' Sebastian said, holding out his hand, 'no time like the present.'

Chapter Nine

The East Wing was accessed through a door concealed in the panelling next to the late marquis's suite of rooms. Once it was pointed out to her, Caro was astonished she had had failed to notice it previously.

'You can see the traces here of where her crest was once displayed,' Sebastian said, pointing above the door. 'I have no idea what condition we'll find the rooms in.'

He selected a key from a large bunch on a metal ring. 'My father kept this with him at all times, so there was no possibility of anyone gaining access, especially me.' His fingers shook very slightly as he turned the lock, she noted. He was not nearly as indifferent as he claimed. She wanted only what was best for him. She hoped she would not regret pushing him into confronting his past like this.

'Of course, I have only my father's word that my mother ran off. We could be about to discover her incarcerated corpse,' he said with a twisted smile.

Caro shuddered. 'You don't really mean that.'

'Of course I don't,' Sebastian said impatiently. 'That would constitute a crime of passion and my father was incapable of passion of any sort. The only skeletons we're likely to encounter will be of the rodent variety.'

Holding an oil lamp high above his head, he led the way uncertainly through the antechamber and then through another door. Once opened, a large room was dimly revealed. Sebastian hurried to undo the shutters, struggling with the stiff latches. The windows themselves were so dirty that the daylight was filtered, casting shadows across the furniture when he threw two of them open.

There was an extraordinary amount of dust. Covering her nose with her handkerchief, Caro looked around her with dismay. 'Nothing has been covered up,' she said. 'It looks as if it has been left quite untouched.'

Her voice was no more than a whisper.

There was something about the atmosphere in the room which was making her shiver. It was clearly designed to be a boudoir and was about twice the size of the one Sebastian had given her for her own use, and more ornately decorated. At least it had been once. The carpet, powder blue woven with roses, was motheaten. When she touched the damask window hangings, a golden tassel crumbled in her hand. Cobwebs hung from the crystal chandelier. Everything, the white-marble fireplace carved with cupids, the beautiful array of Sèvres figurines on the mantel, the rosewood escritoire, the side tables, all were covered in a thick layer of dust. A tall lacquered cabinet was inlaid with a Japanese scene, a young woman holding a lotus flower, an ornate pagoda, doves holding up garlands flying overhead. Behind the doors, what seemed like a hundred little drawers, each engraved with a different flower or animal.

'A cabinet of curiosities, I think is what it is known as,' Sebastian said. 'Traditionally used to store artefacts. I cannot imagine...' He pulled open a drawer at random to reveal, not an artefact, but a brooch in the form of a butterfly, encrusted with diamond chips, turquoise and emeralds. The next drawer contained another brooch in the form of a golden hummingbird, the next a hatpin formed from a silver rose.

Dumbfounded, he jerked open drawer after drawer, spilling glittering jewellery, each one an animal, a bird or a flower. 'What the devil!' He ran his hand through his hair, leaving a streak of dust on his forehead.

The paintings on the wall of the boudoir were all classically rendered, mostly in the French style, many so stained and damaged that the subject matter was almost impossible to make out. Aphrodite rising from the waves—or Venus, Caro could never be sure which was which. A woman on a swing that was either an original Fragonard or a very good copy. Another, rather shocking, of a semi-naked woman surrounded by cherubs, and another even more shocking, depicting a woman, completely nude save for the blue ribbon in her hair, lying on a gold-velvet *chaise longue*, the pink and white pillows echoing the pink and white tones of her skin. The woman was lying on her front, barely concealing her breasts. The artist had concentrated instead on the curve of her spine, dipping down to her bottom, then the curve from her buttocks down her thigh to the curve of her knee. It was a singularly sensual painting, the likes of which Caro had never seen before. It reminded her of seeing her own reflection in the ceiling mirror, the contrast of her own skin against the gold bed-covering, the surprising softness of her flesh, the flush of rosy pink on her skin afterwards.

Sebastian, who had been obsessively opening and closing every drawer in the curiosity cabinet, now joined her at the portrait, standing just behind her. He stared at the naked woman for a long moment. 'These rooms are decorated like an up-market bawdy house. My father would have considered himself tainted just by crossing the threshold.'

'I suppose you would know, since your experience of up-market bawdy houses is no doubt extensive,' Caro said, looking around her somewhat dazedly. Roses were carved into the frame around the bedchamber door, and roses, garlands of them, were carved in swags on the cornicing of the ceiling, which was painted like a sky, pale blue with fluffy clouds, and cherubs. The bed curtains, like the window hangings, were motheaten and crumbled to the touch. Blue and gold, varying shades of pink, and everywhere, on the mantelpiece, painted on the doors, carved and inlaid into the furnishings, embroidered on the bed hangings and the curtains, cherubs and roses. 'It certainly has a very feminine, almost carnal exuberance. Your mother must have been a fascinating personality.'

'My mother must have been the antithesis of everything my father valued. This room speaks of everything he disapproved of.'

'They say that opposites attract,' Caro said.

'Scientifically speaking, as your sister Cressie would tell you, opposites repel. Judging from this evidence, my parents were singularly mismatched.'

The bed was still made up, with satin sheets, lace-edged pillows. Across the bottom of it lay a lace peignoir. There was a dried-up tablet of rose-scented soap beside the basin on the nightstand. On the dressing table, a set of brushes, a tangle of tortoiseshell comb, ribbons and hairpins. Pulling open a drawer, Caro found it full of delicate lace and silk undergarments, stockings with elaborate clocks, petticoats of finest lawn, all motheaten and mildewed. In the dressing room were her dresses. Day gowns, promenade gowns, tea gowns, evening gowns, all high-waisted with the straight skirts and fitted sleeves popular in the early days of the Regent's rule. Pelisses and evening cloaks jostled for space. Furs, smelling of camphor lay on a shelf, slippers, boots and sandals lined the floor. They all looked sad, old-fashioned and slightly eerie, as if they had been waiting a long time to be reclaimed.

Which indeed they had, twenty long years. 'She must have left with only the clothes on her back,' Caro said.

'I know she didn't take any of the family jewels, for they are kept in a vault at the bank, but I assumed she would at least have taken her own wardrobe.' Sebastian was trying to force the lock on a large leather case without success. 'Her lover must have been rich for her to leave all this behind.'

'You don't think that perhaps your father did not allow her to pack?' Caro said tentatively.

'You mean he threw her out?' Sebastian grimaced. 'Which implies he discovered her *in flagrante.* It is a possibility I suppose but not something I have any desire to conjecture about.'

'How awful it must have been for him.'

'Again, you imply he cared, Caro. More likely that he was mortified or shamed, rather than heartbroken.'

'Does it matter? Either way, it explains why he tried to eradicate her from both of your lives.'

Sebastian pulled the heavy damask window curtain to one side. 'And this, I think, explains why he could not bring himself to look at me.'

The portrait he was referring to was resting on the window seat. The countess was not beautiful, Caro thought, studying the life-size image, but there was indeed something extremely attractive about her, and extraordinarily familiar. It was not just the hair colouring, nor the eyes, nor even the mouth, but the shape of the face. Though on Sebastian's face the lines were much harder, the chin decidedly stronger, there could be no doubt, looking from one to the other, that they were mother and son.

'The resemblance is striking,' she said quietly.

Sebastian shrugged, but his face was set. 'I must have been a constant reminder of his shame.' His smile was twisted. 'That is why he hated me.'

'How can you say that!' Caro exclaimed. 'Look around you. For goodness' sake, Sebastian, can't you see this is a shrine? He couldn't bear even to have the bed linen changed. He did not hate you, he hated being reminded of her because she didn't just bruise his pride by leaving, she bruised his heart.'

'I find it difficult to accept that he had a

heart at all.' Sebastian was still studying the portrait intently. 'I remember this hanging in the portrait gallery. And then one day it suddenly disappeared, just like my mother.'

'Sebastian...'

'I was the youngest boy in my school, you know. He couldn't wait to send me away.' His eyes were blank, unfocused, lost in the past. 'I hated school at first. I begged him to let me stay here, but he wouldn't hear of it. I responded by breaking every rule in the book. It was the only thing guaranteed to get his attention.'

'My brothers are always in trouble at Harrow, but my father is rather proud of what he calls their high spirits.'

'While propriety was my father's creed.'

'You certainly could not be accused of worshipping at that particular shrine,' Caro said, attempting a lightness she did not feel.

'No,' he said with another of those strange twisted smiles, 'unlike you, I have made scandal my life's work because scandal was the one thing he could not abide.'

'Perhaps he was afraid.'

'To face society? You think that is why he became a recluse?'

'No.' Caro frowned. 'Partly, I suppose, but

that's not what I meant. Perhaps he was afraid of losing you.'

'What the devil are you talking about! I asked you yesterday to spare me any more of your homespun philosophy.'

'Your mother's elopement must have caused an enormous scandal at the time,' she continued doggedly. 'Your father kept the details quite secret, we don't know the circumstances but we do know that you bear an extremely strong resemblance to her. And you said it yourself, you have dedicated your life to scandal, just as she did. Don't you think that it is possible that your father assumed you would reject him too? Don't you think that his determination to reform you was driven by fear of history repeating itself?'

He stared at her for a long moment, then he burst into a horrible, harsh laugh. 'Your desire to constantly repaint history in more palatable colours is breathtaking.'

'I'm trying to show you that you're wrong. You're angry because it's too late to do anything about it, because your father is dead, but for heaven's sake, Sebastian, he did care, else he would have given up on trying to reform you. You know how difficult is it to obtain an Arabian horse. Lord Ardhallow must have gone to extraordinary lengths to secure Burkan as a birthday present.' Caro sighed. 'I know what it feels like to discover that your actions have been based on a set of false assumptions. All my life I have tried to do what was expected of me on the assumption that my father loved me, ignoring the fact that the harder I tried the more miserable I became.'

'It's not the same, Caro.'

She bit her lip. Why did it hurt so much? It was not just that she wanted to help him. She wanted him to be happy. She wanted him to realise that he had been loved. She wanted— oh, no, not that. Fear clutched at her, sending an icy draught coursing over her skin. No point wanting the impossible. 'I think it is, but I know that you have to make your own mind up,' she said, trying not to panic at the realisation that was slowly dawning. How could she have been so blind!

'What is wrong? You have turned quite pale, Caro.'

'Have I? I am anxious about the christening tomorrow. It must be that,' she managed. 'Talking of which, I have a big day ahead of me. I think it would be best if I got myself organised—decide what to wear and so forth and then have an early night. I will see you tomorrow, Sebastian.' Without giving him a chance to answer, she made her way back out through the dust and cobwebs, through the musty scent, to the sanctuary of her room.

She could not possibly be so stupid as to have fallen in love with Sebastian. Caro sat on the window seat, hugging her knees, looking out at the moonlit paddock where they had first met, ten years ago. How young she had been, and how naïve. She'd thought herself miserable too, what with Bella's arrival at Killellan and Celia's recent departure. If she had only known then what lay ahead…

She made a face at her reflection in the window. It was done, and there was nothing she could do to change it. What mattered was the future, whatever that may be. One thing was certain, it would not include Sebastian.

A lump rose in her throat, but she refused to cry. The thought was unbearable, but she had borne the unbearable before. She may love him—very well, she probably did love him—but she had enough complications in her life without adding another so potentially catastrophic. Today, in the countess's rooms, it had become horribly clear just how deep-rooted was the damage inflicted upon him by his father. It made her heart contract, thinking of the pain he must have endured as a child, at the slow estrangement between father and son which had petrified into a permanent barrier. Would he ever be able to see the truth? She would never know.

She gave herself a little shake and got up from the window seat to stretch her cramped legs. Whether or not Sebastian could ever love her was rather beside the point. She remembered how she had felt, desperately trying to hold together her vision of her marriage as it disintegrated around her. So deeply ingrained was her sense of duty that it had been incredibly difficult to accept she had failed. It had been a slow process too, the falling apart of her dream, making it easy, so easy, to ignore it, to pretend it was not really happening, to hope against the odds that it would somehow un-happen.

Only now, with the nadir of her opium overdose behind her, could she see how very far she had fallen in her efforts to contain, to shore up something she had known was irretrievably broken. She had spent much of the last two years trying to work up the courage to leave her husband. Her independence, such as it was, had been too hard won for her to contemplate surrendering it to any man, and especially not a man whose history categorically proved his determination not to commit to any woman for more than a few months. Besides, she was not truly independent. She was still married. If Sebastian ever did decide to reform his way of life, the last thing he would wish to be saddled with would be a married mistress.

It was all very well to laugh about scandal and provocative behaviour, to speculate about thumbing one's nose at society, but she suspected the reality of life as a social pariah would be anything but glamorous. Sebastian was a rake, but he was also an extremely eligible bachelor. She could not continue to contaminate Crag Hall with her socially toxic presence for much longer.

Especially not after tomorrow. Just thinking about it made her feel quite sick. She doubted very much whether she would go through it, left to her own devices, for there was a tiny, shameful part of her that still hoped for some sort of reconciliation with her father. She hadn't been able to bring herself to admit this to Sebastian. If she was honest, painfully honest, she knew it was a very forlorn hope indeed. One thing her father most abhorred was being backed into a corner. Tomorrow, she was going to do exactly that, and the consequences...

She didn't want to think about the consequences. She didn't want to think about what happened afterwards either, because that entailed leaving Crag Hall and leaving Sebastian for ever. Oh God, she loved him so much.

She threw herself down on her bed, but her mind would not cease whirling. Images of Sebastian, of their days here, kept playing over and over in her mind, interspersed with moments of frozen panic when she turned her mind to the morrow. She couldn't sleep. If only she could stop thinking. She jumped out of bed again, and returned to the window.

She thought he was a spectre at first, leaning against the paddock fence, his white shirt gleaming, his face a pale profile.

He looked so lost and lonely standing there. She was lost and lonely too. Clad only in her nightgown, Caro made her way barefoot downstairs before she changed her mind.

He thought she was a ghost, flitting across the cobblestones to the paddock. Through the long white gown, he could clearly see the outline of her body. Her hair floated out behind her, a cloud of fire. Not a ghost, but perhaps a dream.

'Sebastian.'

Not a dream. Her face was pale in the moonlight, her eyes were dark pools. Since she had left him, alone in his mother's mausoleum, he had been awash with feelings he could not understand, drowning in confusion as the certainties of his life buckled underneath him. 'What if it was all a lie?' he asked. 'If what you say is true, then I have made myself in an image which—what if it was all a lie, Caro?'

She slipped her hand into his. 'Then you must do as I must do,' she said softly. 'You must start anew.'

He slipped his arm around her waist and pulled her to him. 'You put me to shame. All I have to deal with are ghosts, while you…'

'While I resorted to overdosing with opium. And I am so terrified about tomorrow that I can't sleep.'

'I'll be right by your side.'

'I know, and I won't let you down, but—Sebastian, you don't have to compromise yourself with the county in this way. I am fallen irretrievably from grace, but you…'

'You know what they say. Once a rake.'

'The Heartless Heartbreaker who never broke a single heart.'

'Save perhaps his father's,' Sebastian said bitterly.

'Don't say that.'

'And your father? Are you reconciled to being un-reconciled? For tomorrow will force him to nail his colours to the mast, you know that?'

'Tomorrow.' She sighed heavily and tightened her arms around his waist. 'Let us not talk of tomorrow. When I saw you from my window, I thought you were a spectre.'

He ran his hand down the curve of her spine, resting the flat of his palm on the curve of her bottom. 'Flesh and blood,' he whispered, 'Just like you.'

She shivered. 'I know.' She ran her hands up his back, twined them around his neck. 'Flesh and blood,' she murmured, so close he could feel the caress of her breath on his cheek. 'Make it stop, Sebastian. I'm so tired of thinking.'

'Oblivion. We tried that once before and look what happened.' *Why now?* he wondered fleetingly. But her lips were too close to his. Her breasts brushed against his chest. He could feel her nipples harden through the thin cotton of her nightgown, and he realised he wanted it too. 'Oblivion,' he murmured, closing his eyes gratefully.

Her kiss was different from before. No uncertainty, no waiting for him, she claimed him, her tongue sweeping along his lower lip, her mouth opening for him, passionate and utterly sensual. She drank from him, she ran her hands through his hair, urging him to a deeper, more possessive angle, her body pressed, pliant against his.

He was immediately, throbbingly hard. She shuddered in response, her body arching against him, a tiny low moan escaping from her. He ran his hands down her back, up her sides, sweeping over the pert mounds of her breasts. She shuddered again, and tugged at his shirt. He needed no encouragement. They were already past the point of no return.

Picking her up, he carried her swiftly to an empty stable. Setting her down, he summarily ripped his shirt off. Her hands were already on him. His mouth found hers once more, devouring the sweet, heady taste of her, his hands caressing her breasts, stroking the hard buds of her nipples, his erection stiffening, his blood singing.

Her hands fluttered over his back, down his

sides, back up to his nipples, in an echo of his touch, her tongue flicking, tasting, driving him into a frenzy of desire. He kicked off his boots, still kissing her, stroking her. She tugged at the waistband of his breeches, gave a sigh of exasperation then released him, not to undress him but to pull her nightgown over her head.

The sight of her in the moonlight, a pale white goddess with a flame of hair, took his breath away. He would have folded her into his arms, only she was struggling with the buttons of his breeches. He had never, ever, wanted anything so much as to be naked beside her. Everything, every sense, every inch of skin, every nerve, was on fire. This was no oblivion. He felt completely and utterly alive, stretched tight, his entire body attuned to the woman beside him, wanting only to be inside her.

There were no words. Their eyes spoke eloquently of their needs. And their hands. Tracing shapes, stroking, licking, touching. Her breasts. The dark pink of her nipples. The softness of her belly. The way she shuddered when he touched her. The way he shuddered in response.

When she cupped him, where he was achingly heavy, when she held him, he thought he would come. The way her fingers circled his shaft, her touch so delicate and yet so sure. Her eyes on his, watching him, sensing his response. His on hers as he slid his fingers between her legs, into the hot, tight, wetness of her. Her eyes widened. Her fingers tightened around him. His thumb stroked the hard nub of her sex, and she stroked him in return, making him pulse, throb, clench with the effort of holding back.

She brushed her breasts across his chest. His fingers quickened. Her strokes quickened. If they did not stop, it would be too late, and he could not bear for it to be too late. 'Caro,' he said desperately.

Caro put her fingers over his mouth, keeping her other hand on his manhood. Velvet skin, solid muscle. She stroked him slowly, feeling his potency, relishing her power. He sucked hard on her finger, holding it in his mouth, his tongue flicking over her fingertip. Her senses were singing, screaming. Inside, where he thrust and slid and stroked, she was tightening.

His eyes pleaded with her. She did not want it to end, but she could not stop it. She urged him backwards on to a bale of hay. When he would have rolled her under him, she straddled him, laughing, a low, husky laugh, at the surprise, at the delight on his face.

He kissed her, hard and swiftly. She kissed him back, passionately, pouring all her love, all her longings, everything, into her kiss. His shaft was nudging between her thighs. She was throbbing inside, pulsing, tight, aching. She kissed him again, bracing herself by holding on to his shoulders. He lifted her, his hands on her bottom, and finally, slowly, deliciously, he entered her.

She came as he filled her, clenching around him, fingernails digging into his skin, crying out over and over. He thrust as she came, and her climax intensified. Then he thrust again, and she twisted, clenched, arched back, so that he could thrust higher. He buried his face between her breasts, his hands cupped over her bottom, as she lifted herself again and he thrust again. Her nipple in his mouth. His lips tugging, sensation spiralling down, to the heat, the damp pulsing of her sex. Lift and thrust. Hands. Mouths. Lift and thrust, until she had no idea whether her climax had ended and begun again, or simply ebbed temporarily, and she did not care.

Perspiration trickled between her breasts. Sebastian's face was etched pale and taut in the moonlight. She felt him thicken inside her, heard the harsh cry drawn from his depths as he came, lifting her clear of him at the last moment. His kiss was ragged, his breathing fast and shallow. *I love you,* she thought, kissing him back, screwing shut her eyes to avoid the hot sting of tears.

Sebastian woke with a start from a heavy sleep, his heart racing. Pushing the damp sheets away from him, he staggered to the window and, not for the first time, cursed the broken catch which kept it permanently closed. Why did he persist in sleeping in this cramped and stultifying cubbyhole of a room, when he had a hundred others to choose from!

His head felt as if it were stuffed with cotton. Hastily pulling on a shirt, breeches and boots, he made his way out to the stables. A gallop in the early morning air would clear his head. The overturned hay bale pulled him up short.

Caro. Sebastian groaned. These past two years, he felt as if he had been living underground, burrowed away in a cave, living a sort of twilight life, existing but not truly alive. So many emotions he had endured since her arrival, he ought to feel wrung out, but instead he felt—invigorated. She was not just fire, she was earth. Real. She made him realise how stultifying his life had become. She made him remember that he was flesh and blood. She had, quite literally, brought light and life back to Crag Hall.

She had forced him into opening those damned rooms. It had been like lifting stones in a pool to discover what lurked beneath. He still had no clear idea what to make of it all. He was aware of the past reshaping itself, but as to the final shape it would take—he had no idea, but he realised, with some surprise, that he had already accepted that it would change. Quitting the stables, he made his way back to his room.

Last night, there had been a new dimension to their passion. Their hunger for each other had been feverish. What had changed between them? Outside, the clock on the stable tower chimed the hour. Sebastian checked his watch. He realised had been sitting here for hours and resolved nothing. He had no idea what he thought or felt.

Cursing, Sebastian resolved to have his things moved to another suite just as soon as it could be made ready. This cramped little space was smothering him.

Chapter Ten

Caro stepped down from the gig on to the gravel driveway. A manservant she didn't recognise stood to attention in all-too-familiar livery at the open doorway of the gatehouse. She had dressed with care in a cream-silk day dress with leg-of-mutton sleeves. The tiny flowers which embellished the silk were the same cornflower blue as the lining of her bonnet. Her hair was ruthlessly pinned, her gloves spotless, and her heart quaking. Beside her, Sebastian was immaculate in a coat of dark blue with a dove-grey waistcoat. His black trousers fitted his long, muscled legs like a second skin. His shoes were buffed to a high shine.

'You look so different,' she said, trying gamely to smile.

'I thought that my usual stable-hand garb might find disfavour with Lady Armstrong, given the importance of the occasion.'

Caro paled. 'I doubt very much that either my stepmother or my father will be too concerned with what you are wearing when they see who your companion is.'

Sebastian tucked her arm into his. 'You look perfectly ravishing and I am proud to have you on my arm.'

'It is good of you to say so, but I know perfectly well that I have never in my life been ravishing.'

'You are quite wrong, you know.' He lifted her hand to his lips, and brushed a kiss on her gloved palm. 'Of course, I think you look most ravishing with your hair down and your pink stockings on display, but even a hardened rake such as myself would admit that it would be inappropriate to attend a christening party in such attire.'

'Sebastian! You must not say such things when I am about to confront my father.'

He gave her a wicked smile. 'That is precisely why I said those very things. Aside from the fact that they are true, they have given you the most delightful flush. Now you look like a woman who has just been complimented in the most intimate way by her lover. Let us enter the lion's den before my handiwork fades.'

She still wore the remnants of her smile as they entered the drawing room on the first floor. Her father's butler was halfway through announcing the arrival of Lord Ardhallow and companion when he recognised her, and broke off in mid-sentence.

'Egad! Is there no end to the fellow's brazenness!' Sir Timothy Innellan's shocked exclamation drew the attention of the very few people in the room who had not been alerted by the butler's actions.

Caro's knees began to shake. Were it not for Sebastian holding her firmly by his side, ushering her just as firmly forwards, she would almost certainly have turned tail and fled.

Sebastian paused in front of his neighbour. 'Allow me to present Lady Caroline Armstrong,' he said with a polished smile.

'Lady Caroline Rider,' Sir Timothy's mother hissed, making her son drop Caro's hand with some haste. 'I confess,' Lady Innellan continued, 'I am surprised that even you have the nerve to bring that woman into polite company.'

'Oh, we rakes have the nerve for anything,' Sebastian said icily. 'As I recall, there was a time when you were happy to welcome Lady Caroline into polite society. In fact, the last time we three were together, it was at a ball hosted by your good self.'

'Lady Caroline's circumstances, as I am sure you are perfectly well aware, my lord, have changed significantly since then.'

'Indeed, I am perfectly well aware, and would have thought that polite society would rather credit her for having had the good sense to escape those circumstances than turn their backs on her. But then, as you have already pointed out, I am not a member of polite society myself. I trust, if one must forfeit common decency to be admitted into such hallowed portals, that I never shall be.'

'Common decency should prohibit your flaunting your mistress at a family function,' her ladyship said waspishly.

'I wonder, is it common decency that motivates you when you provide those cosy little rooms at your own parties,' Caro said with a smile every bit as sweet as Sebastian's. 'Rooms where guests may conduct their liaisons shielded from the beady eyes of society. How ill mannered of me to have failed to sweep my indiscretions under the carpet.'

'I think your crimes go far beyond indiscretions. In any event you would be better served directing your apology to your father.'

'Oh, I'm not apologising, Lady Innellan.'

'Lady Caroline has nothing to apologise for,' Sebastian said tightly. 'You will excuse us now, I'm sure. We wish to pay our compliments to the new arrival. My felicitations,' he added for Caro's ears alone, 'you set her down beautifully. You see, you can face down such small-minded hypocrites with ease.'

'Not with anything approaching ease, Sebastian. I feel sick.'

'Remember, you are not at fault or on trial here, and I am right by your side. Courage, *ma belle*, your father is approaching. Lord Armstrong, may I congratulate you upon your new arrival. As you see, I have brought your daughter to meet her new sister.'

Sebastian made his bow. Caro was incapable of moving. Her father was as immaculately turned out as ever. He had always looked younger than his years, with a full head of grey hair and a distinguished countenance. His eyes, which were the same colour as her own, met hers for the briefest of moments. She flinched at the iciness apparent there. He was far too much the diplomat to make his outrage apparent, but she had no doubt that he was none the less utterly livid.

'Lord Ardhallow.' Her father made the stiffest of bows, taking great care not to look at her. 'I do not hesitate to tell you that your father would have been appalled by your presumption.'

'Why, it was your own wife who delivered my invitation,' Sebastian said. 'She was however, quite unaware that I would ask your daughter to do me the honour of accompanying me,' he added hastily, seeing Lady Armstrong's horrified look.

'I so wanted to meet my new sister.' Caro was unable to keep the tremble from her voice.

'And now you have achieved your objective, you are free to go. I bid you good day.'

'Papa!' She took a step towards him, and froze as he recoiled. 'Father, I would be obliged if you would grant me a word in private.' Seeing that he was about to refuse her, Caro garnered her courage. 'I know you would not wish me to say what I have to in front of your assembled guests,' she said, relieved that her voice sounded firmer.

He gave a curt nod. 'I will give you precisely five minutes. Let me make myself clear, I do this not because I wish to hear what you have to say, but because I do not wish you to spoil my wife's day. She has waited a long time for the gratification of a daughter. Not that daughters are, in my painful experience, remotely gratifying. Let us get this over with.'

Watching Caro follow in her father's wake, Sebastian had to force himself not to follow suit. Much as he was desperate to be by her side, a small shake of her head told him that she wished to manage the interview unaided. Knowing how much she had dreaded this encounter, he was filled with admiration at her courage.

Beside him, Lady Armstrong cleared her throat. 'I must thank you for your discretion,' she said *sotto voce*, 'my husband would have viewed my failure to inform him of Caroline's presence at Crag Hall very dimly indeed. He is a man who values loyalty above almost everything else.'

Sebastian raised a brow. 'Does he then consider Caro has been disloyal?'

Lady Armstrong grimaced. 'She is the only one of his daughters to marry the man he had chosen for her, apart from Celia, and that hardly counts as her husband had the ill manners to get himself killed after a matter of months. My husband views Caroline's desertion of Sir Grahame as a personal insult. I don't know what it is she expects from this interview, but believe me, reconciliation is absolutely out of the question at present.'

'And in the future?'

Lady Armstrong shrugged. 'That is not for me to say, but it is unlikely unless Caroline does the decent thing.'

It was the answer he had expected, but it was a blow none the less. 'Return to her husband. He is aware of the reasons for her leaving, I take it?' Sebastian asked carefully, trying to disguise the anger in his voice.

'The circumstances are of no concern to my husband, Lord Ardhallow. What matters to my husband is the *fact* of her leaving.'

Lady Armstrong leaned over the cradle to pick up the swathed bundle of lace which was her baby daughter. 'My little Isabella.' Her expression softened. 'A very easy confinement, if you will forgive the indelicacy of my mentioning it. I had a midwife to attend me this time, a most sensible woman, I must say, who believed firmly in allowing nature to take its course, and had none of Sir Gilbert Mountjoy's more intrusive methods.' She shuddered. 'Sir Gilbert attended when I had my boys, Lord Ardhallow, at my husband's insistence. Though he is the most respected physician in the country, I must say that I think in these matters, a woman always knows best. My husband would have been very much against it, but fortunately my husband was abroad at the time.'

She put the baby gently back into the cradle, and turned back to Sebastian, her smile fading. 'You are no doubt wondering what my point is. Let me enlighten you. Caroline has quite publicly flaunted her father's authority. She has, by leaving her husband, declared to the world that she believes her marriage a mistake, and that is what my husband has taken so personally. What he does not know, Lord Ardhallow, cannot harm him. But when one rubs his nose in it, he will neither forgive nor forget. I trust I am making myself clear?'

'Extremely.'

'Then let me be even more clear. When he finds out that Caroline has not only fled her marital home but is living under your roof, my husband is likely to take offence so great that she will be for ever beyond the pale. An errant wife is one thing, a woman who publicly flaunts her lack of morals quite another.'

Bella sighed. 'You do not like what you hear but you would do well to heed my advice upon this matter, my lord. You are a man of excellent sense, excellent title and ample means. In short, you are the most eligible bachelor in the county, and could, if you chose, hold a position of some considerable influence. But if you continue to allow my stepdaughter to taint Crag Hall with her presence, you will find yourself ostracised along with her. Society will close ranks against you both, which is like to make your life very uncomfortable. The hiring of servants and tradesmen for example, you could find most—taxing.'

'Are you threatening me, Lady Armstrong?'

'I am, I hope, merely putting you straight for your own good, Lord Ardhallow. We would hate to lose you as a neighbour just as you have rejoined society.'

He was acutely aware that the eyes and ears of the entire drawing room were discreetly upon them. 'I am grateful for your concern for my welfare,' Sebastian said icily, 'but be assured, my lady, that until Lady Caroline is given the welcome here she descrves, I will never again darken your doorstep, nor any of these other spineless sheep.' Taking a purse of gold coins from his coat pocket, he bent over the cradle to tuck it behind the baby's pillow. 'I believe it is traditional to make a wish,' he

said. 'Mine shall be that this daughter, unlike
the others, is blessed with her father's love.
And that she will be the one to break his heart.'

Nodding curtly, he left the drawing room
and waited, pacing anxiously up and down the
gravel driveway, for Caro to emerge.

Lord Armstrong's study was on the ground
floor. A room redolent with childhood memories for Caro, few of them pleasant, it was
small and dominated by the enormous desk
which faced out from the window bay. The
walls were lined with ledgers, quarter books
and dockets of scrolls tied with red ribbon. In
this austere space, Lord Armstrong admin-
istered his estate and meted out his punish-
ments. It was here that he had informed Caro
and her sisters that Mama had died, and here
too he had announced his betrothal to Bella.
Defiantly, she pulled a chair over and sat down,
refusing to stand shame-faced before the desk
as she had as a child. 'Papa, do not think ill of
Lord Ardhallow. He has merely been providing me with—sanctuary—while I decide what
course of action to take.'

'Sanctuary.' Now that they were alone, her
father dropped his icy reserve. 'Do not be

melodramatic daughter, you make it sound as if you live in fear of your life.'

She stiffened. 'My husband was very careful to ensure that the injuries he inflicted upon me were not life-threatening.'

Her father looked distinctly uncomfortable. 'Sir Grahame has given me his assurance that you will be perfectly safe if you return to him. I insisted I had his word on that. I would not have you think me utterly indifferent to your well-being.'

'Sir Grahame,' Caro said, 'assured me each time he assaulted me that it would be the last time.'

'Then you must have provoked him, Caroline. As indeed, you provoke me with your intransigence.'

'You have many faults as a parent, Papa, but you have never once raised a hand to me.'

Had she been in the mood to be amused, she would have found his astonished expression comical. 'You dare criticise me,' Lord Armstrong exclaimed, 'you actually dare criticise me, when you have been cast out by your husband, when the most scurrilous of rumours pertaining to your behaviour are being bandied about, and rather than hide your head in shame, you are positively flaunting your new-found aptitude for scandal by setting up home with one of the most notorious rakes in England.'

'I have not set up home with Sebastian, and he is not a rake,' Caro riposted. 'He is the kindest, most honourable man I have ever met. In fact he's the *only* person of my entire acquaintance to take my side in this affair.'

'And more fool him for doing so.' Her father shook his head impatiently. 'Conway is bringing shame on one of the oldest titles in the county, to say nothing of the fact that he's laying himself wide open to a crim. con. suit.'

'Sir Grahame would not dare.'

'You really are extraordinarily naïve for an adulteress, Caroline,' Lord Armstrong said with a condescending smile.

The word stung like the lash of a whip. *Adulteress.* It cheapened what she and Sebastian had shared, but Caro realised now, with jolting clarity, that it was nonetheless accurate. In the eyes of the world her behaviour was not scandalous but sordid.

'Your husband has most generously offered to forgive you,' Lord Armstrong continued, oblivious, 'an exceedingly generous offer in the circumstances, when your behaviour is already proving detrimental to Rider's political career, which I may add is something in which

I have invested a significant amount of effort. I strongly advocate your return to the marital home. The consequences of your failure to do so will be dire indeed. However, you need not take my word for it. I suggest you take the matter up with your husband.'

Her father was a diplomat, Caro reminded herself, and an extremely skilled one. There was no one more adept at turning circumstances to his own advantage. She would not allow him to manoeuvre her into doing what she knew was wrong. Not again. Anger came to her rescue, staving off the hurt. 'What a—a damned hypocrite the law is. No one could doubt that it was written by men, for men! To put it crudely—for us fallen women have no need to respect the proprieties, you know, Papa—if I fail to return to the man who beats me—the man *you* chose for me—you will punish me by disowning me.'

'You must take responsibility for your own actions, Caroline, I have made my position very clear.'

'Extremely. All my life I have tried to please you, but nothing I've ever done has been good enough. I'm done with it, Father. No more. I have a right to be happy.'

Lord Armstrong drummed his fingers on

the blotter. It was one of the few tell-tale signs that he was angry, Caro remembered of old. 'I have often wondered if it was a misjudgement on my part,' he said, 'sabotaging your youthful dalliance with Lord Ardhallow—the Earl of Mosteyn as Conway was then—but notwithstanding his excellent pedigree his reputation was, frankly, appalling. I had other, more circumspect irons in the fire for you.'

'Sebastian told me that you and his father were in cahoots. May I know whether it was yourself or Lord Ardhallow who was most set against our acquaintance?'

Her father shrugged. 'I would say on balance it was I. Ardhallow was of the opinion that marriage might encourage his son to mend his ways, but I was not prepared to take the risk.'

'Had you taken the trouble to consult me you would have discovered there was no risk. Sebastian had no intentions of marrying me.'

'As I suspected. I am relieved to know that my judgement was as sound as ever,' Lord Armstrong said with a thin smile. 'It is still sound, Caroline. You are married, whatever your feelings for Ardhallow—and you need not trouble to deny that you have feelings, for I know you better than you think. Regardless of the gossip, I am perfectly well aware that you are not of loose morals,' he continued in a more mollifying tone. 'Only feelings of a sentimental nature can explain your consorting so publicly with that man. You will no doubt tell me that you are following in the footsteps of your sisters by considering the world well sacrificed for love. But you are not like your sisters, Caroline. Despite recent evidence to the contrary, I have every faith in the sense of duty which I have been at pains to inculcate in you. You will return to your husband because it pleases me, and because it is the right thing to do.'

'Even though it will make me miserable?'

Lord Armstrong sighed. 'Why must you girls always be so dramatic? Of course you will be miserable if you set your mind to it, just as you will be perfectly content if you choose to be so. Society will never acknowledge an unrepentant sinner. Do you have any idea what life will be like for you on the fringes of society? Misery does not even begin to describe it. Why stubbornly choose that path? Repent and everything can be put to rights. What do you say?'

Caro got to her feet. 'The only thing I repent is marrying Sir Grahame in the first place. I

won't go back to him. I can't believe you expect it of me. If you loved me...'

The pencil which Lord Armstrong had been
toying with snapped in two. 'Enough. I have
been more than patient, I have even taken the
trouble to point out the reality of the situation
to you, but I will not listen to any more of your
hysterical outpourings. I do not know why you
chose to flaunt your disgrace in my face by
coming here with your paramour...'

'Don't call him that,' Caro interrupted indignantly.

Her father held up his hand. 'That is precisely what he is in the eyes of the world, and
will be in the eyes of the law too, if you do not
extricate yourself from his company with immediate effect.' Lord Armstrong paused, closing his eyes in silent meditation, then leaned
forwards over the desk, fixing his daughter
with a stern and most determined eye. 'Return to your husband and no more will be said
of the matter. If you decide, after searching
your conscience, that you are unable to do as
I ask, then I entreat you to at least agree terms
with Rider. Heaven knows, a separation will
be a slur enough, but in time—a great deal of
time—and with exemplary behaviour on your

part, we too may be able to come to some sort
of compromise.'

Caro narrowed her eyes, for she could almost see the workings of her father's devious
diplomatic brain. 'What sort of compromise?'

'I make no promises, but it may be that rela-
tions between yourself and your siblings could
be resumed. Not in public, you understand, we
can never again acknowledge you, but perhaps
visits—letters—we will have to see.'

'And when you say exemplary behaviour,
what precisely do you mean?'

His lordship sighed heavily. 'You know perfectly well what I mean.'

'I wonder that you do not demand I wear a
chastity belt! What about my husband?' Caro
demanded. 'Is he too required to live the celi-
bate life?'

'Your husband is not the one at fault.'

'Have you discussed any of this with him?'

'I have not, but if you are imagining he will
remain long in ignorance of your liaison with
Ardhallow, then you are very much mistaken.
If he does not already know, I will inform him
myself rather than allow him the indignity of
being informed of the *affaire* by some gossip-
monger. As I have already suggested several

times now, you must resolve matters with him yourself.'

Caro's fists were clenching and unclenching, but she was far too angry to be anywhere near tears. 'My sisters will not follow your line in disowning me.'

'Two of your sisters live at the other ends of the earth in Arabia. One is roaming the Continent with a dissolute artist. And the other's whereabouts have been unknown for two years. Your sisters are hardly in a position to be of much comfort to you.'

'What about my brothers? You cannot mean to prevent me…'

Lord Armstrong got to his feet. 'I was under the impression that I had made myself very clear,' he said, pointedly holding open the door.

It was with an extraordinary effort that she bit back her words. She would not allow him to see how much he had hurt her and she would certainly not beg. 'I would have you know that if ever you softened your stance I would be happy to renew our—acquaintance, my lord.'

She held out her hand. Lord Armstrong ignored it. 'I never change my mind. You will oblige me by leaving without further contact with my guests. I have had your brothers removed to the nursery until you have vacated the premises.'

She was not even to be permitted to say farewell. Tears welled in her eyes at this cruel act, but she held them from falling with a supreme act of will. 'Please inform Lord Ardhallow I shall await him at the front door. Goodbye, Lord Armstrong.' Caro made her way across the marble reception hall and through the gatehouse without looking back. She was surprised to see Sebastian already waiting for her, his expression stormy. He had obviously found the whole experience just as unrewarding as she.

'I knew that there was little prospect of my father having changed his mind, but I couldn't help hoping all the same. It was stupid of me.'

They were sitting in the sunshine, on the steps of the ruined orangery. Sebastian watched as Caro dabbed frantically at her eyes. Aside from a few stray tears in the gig on the return journey to Crag Hall, she had stoically refused to cry. The sinking feeling in the pit of his stomach made him realise that he too had hoped against the odds. But for what? 'It is so damned unfair,' he exclaimed.

Caro smiled tremulously. 'My feelings exactly. My father made it clear that unless I did as he bade me I had burnt my boats with him. I doubt he cares, but his unfeeling behaviour towards me, his singular determination not to see my side of things, has rather burnt *his* boats with me.'

'I wish I could say that is heartening, but I fear he has hurt you more than you care to admit,' Sebastian said. 'I know how much your family means to you. You may not like him, but you cannot help loving your father. And your brothers too, to deprive you of their company—I know, Caro, how deeply that must pain you.'

She shrugged, but Sebastian was not fooled. Secluded from society as they had been, caught up in their own private little idyll, it had been easy to pretend to be indifferent to the outside world, but today had demonstrated all too clearly the damage her presence here had already caused. To remain together at Crag Hall would undoubtedly court further outrage. He didn't give a damn for himself, he was accustomed to scandal, but Caro was another matter. She would bear the brunt of the notoriety and she would also bear the brunt of the consequences. 'I fear that our escapade has backfired somewhat,' he said morosely.

'Let us rather say that it has crystallised things,' Caro replied.

Watching her pull herself out of the tangle which her marriage had become, his admiration for her had grown. Seeing her today, witnessing the courage with which she faced the ill-disguised antagonism of the party guests, knowing how painful it was for her to come up against the appalling indifference of her parent, he felt a fierce pride combined with an equally fierce urge to protect her from all and sundry. The intensity of that desire took him aback. 'I would have been tempted to throttle your father had I been present at your interview,' he said grimly. 'Perhaps it's as well that I was not.'

'I was tempted to throttle him myself at one point,' Caro replied, this time with a more convincing smile. 'Having you with me got me across the threshold at Killellan. Knowing you were there, that you were on my side, gave me the strength to face my father, but that I needed to do on my own.' She reached for his hand and brushed it against her cheek. 'Thank you.'

Her words had an air of finality about them that instilled a strange sense of panic in him. 'You have no need to thank me. We social outcasts must look out for each other, since no one else will,' he said in a feeble attempt to make light of things.

'That is another thing my father made very clear. My being here is not just improper, it is exposing you to a—in short, he thinks that Sir Grahame could sue you for criminal conversation.'

'Nonsense. He would not dare.'

'Sebastian, listen to me. If my father is right, my husband would have your name bandied around the courts and the gutter press. Such cases are horribly sordid and very public, I could *not*…'

He yanked at the knot in his neckcloth and hurled the starched linen to the ground. 'How many times must I tell you, I don't give a damn about my reputation.'

'But you should.' Caro caught at his sleeve. '*I* care. I care that people are talking about you because of me, I feel terribly guilty about that, after all, you virtually saved my life. And I—I also care that the things they are saying of me are true. When it was unfounded rumours about boot boys and stable hands it didn't matter because I was blameless. But our actions have—don't you see, I'm not blameless any more?'

'Devil take it, your father has made an excellent job of heaping guilt upon your head.'

She winced. 'He said only what everyone else will say.'

Sebastian had no choice, thinking back to his conversation with Lady Armstrong, other than to accept this unpalatable truth. 'The fact is, Rider's is the only opinion which really matters.'

'I know. I have to see him.'

'I would do anything to spare you the need to confront the man. Perhaps I could arrange for a lawyer to speak on your behalf...'

'You cannot fight my battles for me, I must speak to him myself. It is not only that I have to understand what his position is regarding our marriage, I also need to put matters between us on some sort of more dignified footing.' She made a wry face. 'I find I am uncomfortable being the wrongdoer.'

He caught her to him. 'Damn your father, I am very proud of you, Caro. You've come a long way from the pitiful creature I found languishing in St John Marne's opium den.' He kissed her swiftly, tearing his lips from hers before passion could take hold of him. 'I will make the arrangements for your journey to town. The sooner the better, don't you think?'

'Yes, I agree. Thank you.'

'And while you are gone, I shall take the opportunity to write to my mother. You have not the monopoly on guilt. Whatever her reasons for leaving here, I owe her the opportunity to explain herself. I see that clearly now.'

He watched her go and the panicky feeling which had been gnawing at his belly intensified. What was wrong with him? Of course he was concerned for her, that was natural, but he had every confidence in her ability to handle the situation with her husband. She had to go, because without this meeting she would be in legal limbo. But he didn't want her to go. Not now. Not ever.

Why? Because he was in love with her. It was quite simple.

Sebastian discovered that it really was possible to feel as if the world had stopped turning on its axis. He was in love, for the first time in his life, and the woman he loved belonged to another.

Dammit to hell!

He began to prowl restlessly around the ruins of the orangery. He loved her, and she had more than enough problems to last her a lifetime without him declaring himself. Even if she did return his feelings…

Sebastian came to an abrupt halt in front of a long-dead vine. Last night, there had been an intensity in her love-making. A desperation in her kisses. A new depth to their passion. Last night they had truly made love. He swore under his breath. Of course she cared for him. And he realised too, with a sickening feeling, that last night had been her way of saying goodbye.

She was, as she had just admitted, at heart a moral woman. She would return to Crag Hall after seeing Rider, but unless by some miracle she could free herself without shame, she would not consider staying. Which meant, Sebastian told himself squarely, that they needed a miracle.

Love, he was discovering, was a most contrarily optimistic emotion, quite oblivious of logic and facts. It really was possible for a heart to overrule a head. He loved her. They were meant to be together. They would find a way because he simply could not contemplate a future without her.

Chapter Eleven

Caro reached London a few days later, weary but determined. It was tempting to pass the journey conjuring daydreams of what might have been had she not been married, but that way lay heartache. That Sebastian cared for her she did not doubt. That he could have grown to love her—had circumstances been different— she would not allow herself to contemplate. Circumstances were not different, and were highly unlikely to change. Indeed, it would be better if he felt nothing for her, for she would not—she *could not*—inflict the life to which she was likely to be condemned on him. The best she could hope for was freedom, from both her marriage and society's disapproval. And that was a great deal more than she had dared wish for when she had been so foolish as to seek oblivion with opium. To have finally known love, to have made love to the man she loved, that would have to be sufficient to sustain her on whatever path her future might take her.

Intent upon coming to a resolution with her husband as soon as possible, Caro was dismayed to discover that Sir Grahame had been summoned to his estates in Derbyshire, though was expected back any day. She had a note sent round to Aunt Sophia from the lodging-house she had booked into, thinking merely to confirm that this door too was closed to her, and was astonished when the lady turned up in person.

Her aunt, who had always had the demeanour of a grumpy camel, had aged considerably in the last year but though her back was no longer straight, her conversation was, as ever, to the point.

'You've certainly made a spectacular hash of things, young lady,' she said, dusting off a rickety chair with a lace handkerchief and lowering herself carefully down. 'Now, tell me exactly what's being going on.'

'I have to take my hat off to you, you may even have outdone your sisters in the behaviour-beyond-the-pale stakes, which takes a bit of doing,' she said, when Caro had concluded a brief and carefully edited summary of recent events. 'I was relieved to get your note, I must say. My brother won't even have your name mentioned. And yet you inform me that you had the gumption to walk in on Isabella's christening!' Lady Sophia cackled. 'Wish I'd witnessed that, but egad, Caroline, what on earth were you thinking? Henry can't abide being put in the wrong, you should know that.'

'So you agree then, that he *is* in the wrong?'

'It doesn't matter what I think.'

'I won't go back to my husband,' Caro said, crossing her arms over her chest. 'If that's what you've come to tell me...'

'I always did think there was a stubborn streak under that compliant façade.' Her ladyship's expression softened. 'Come here, child,' she said, holding out her hand. 'Is it true? Not that balderdash in the scandal sheets, no one believes that, but—did he mistreat you?'

Caro nodded.

'Why didn't you confide in me?'

'I was so ashamed. Besides, what could you have done? I was his wife. I still am.'

'I may be old, but I am not necessarily old-fashioned,' Lady Sophia said firmly. 'I don't subscribe to the popular belief that a wife is a man's property. I don't say that I'd have been able to make him stop, but I could have had words, warned him off. And I could have offered you some much needed respite.'

'Sanctuary. That is what I had at Crag Hall.'

'Aye. I remember you were always fond of young Conway. You look surprised. My body may be failing but I still have my faculties.' Lady Sophia's grim smile faded. 'Are you in love with him?' she asked sharply.

'It doesn't matter. I am married to Sir Grahame.'

'And Lord Ardhallow, what are his feelings towards you?'

'Sebastian has his estates to think of. He would deny it of course, but I really do think he has changed. Deep down, his heart belongs to his lands.'

Her aunt nodded. 'Which is precisely as it should be. It is an impossible situation, my dear. Painful as it is, I am pleased that you recognise that unfortunate reality for yourself.'

Which she did, though it was horribly difficult to have it articulated in such an unequivocal way. Caro managed a weak smile.

'I take it then, that this upcoming interview with your husband is to agree terms?' her aunt continued in a business-like manner. 'I am relieved that you will not be discussing divorce.'

'Would that be so terrible?'

Lady Sophia looked aghast. 'Caroline, you are not seriously considering—why, you would be forced to leave England. Your father would insist on that.'

'I am of age, Aunt. My father cannot insist on anything.'

'He can if he holds the purse strings,' Lady Sophia said tartly. 'How do you think you will live elsewise? As a divorcee you will forfeit your dowry, and it is not as if you are equipped to earn a living.'

'I hadn't thought about that.'

'Then you would do well to do so before you meet with your husband.' Lady Sophia threw her a sharp look. 'I have always thought you the most sensible of Henry's girls, Caroline. Difficult as this situation is, I am sure that given time, your father will come round.'

'Provided my behaviour is exemplary,' Caro said bitterly.

'Precisely,' her ladyship said, unaware that she was breaking one of her golden rules and agreeing with her brother. 'Now, one thing is certain, you cannot stay here while you await Sir Grahame's return to town, this place looks as if it might be overrun by vermin at any moment.' Lady Sophia sighed and heaved herself to her feet. 'Pack your bags. You'll have to use the side door to come and go, and you'll need to keep to your room when I have visitors, but you can stay with me until you resolve matters.'

'Aunt! Do you mean it? My father...'

Lady Sophia snorted. 'What Henry doesn't know cannot harm him. You're family, and no amount of proclaiming otherwise can change that. Now, are you coming or not?'

Some three days later, Caro paid off the driver and descended from the hackney carriage into Portman Square. The town house belonging to the Rider family was one of the smaller residences, a narrow three-storey building constructed in red sandstone, with a stuccoed frontage. She had never truly felt at home here, and had consequently never made any attempt to change the old-fashioned fixtures and fittings which dated from when Sir Grahame's grandfather had built the house eighty years ago.

A thick fog hung over the city like a damp blanket. In the manicured green space at the centre of the square, the leaves were already changing colour on the trees. Though it seemed to her that the weeks at Crag Hall had been golden, in fact the summer which had so rapidly ceded to autumn had been one of the wettest for years.

Her stomach was churning. Despite her father's threats and her aunt's dire warnings, Caro could not dispel the tiny seed of hope that today she would discover some resolution which would free her from both her husband and from scandal. It was unlikely in the extreme, she knew, but so much depended upon it. She could not bear the idea of remaining married to a man she had come to despise.

She had not spoken to her husband since the day she left him, almost six months ago. Though she had told herself she was no longer afraid of him, crossing the familiar dark reception hall in the wake of the ancient butler, fear turned her fog-damp skin clammy. He was just a man, she reminded herself even if, like it or not, she was still legally his property.

As the butler opened the panelled door, Caro summoned up Sebastian's image. She remembered him, tall, strong, unflinching, resolutely by her side that day at the christening. *Courage*, he'd said, and she'd found it because she didn't want to let him down. She found it now, not just because she wouldn't let him down, but because she wouldn't let herself down either. 'Courage, Caro,' she whispered to herself, and stepped into the morning room.

Her husband was standing by the window which looked out over the square, and had obviously observed her arrival. He was a tall man, well built, with a long narrow countenance and cheekbones so sharp that they made shadows on his face. Black hair receded from a sharp widow's peak to loose curls which she knew he despised and regularly weighted with hair pomade. He had a strong nose and a sensuous mouth. Caro had once thought him handsome. Hovering next to the door, uncertain how to greet him, she could not help but compare his pale complexion with Sebastian's tan, his grey eyes with Sebastian's brown ones, his thin smile with Sebastian's warm and endearing one. This was the man she had married more than five years ago, the man she had promised to love, honour and obey, the man to whom she had given her virginity and with whom she had hoped to have a family. The man who had destroyed her confidence and her reputation. The man who had hurt her, literally and metaphorically.

Looking at him now, she could not quite believe any of it. It was as if that life belonged to another Caro, not just younger but less formed and more uncertain. And Sir Grahame—she felt as if she did not know him, had never known him. It made her feel vaguely queasy to think of how intimate they had once been. She felt as if she was looking at a stranger. What she didn't feel, she realised as he crossed the room towards her, was fear.

'Hello, Caroline.'

She turned her face away so that his lips brushed her cheek, and slipped quickly from his embrace to take up position at the window, putting a table and a sofa between them. 'Sir Grahame,' she said, pulling off her gloves and setting them down on the half-table which spanned the gap between the windows. She kept her bonnet and her coat on.

'Won't you sit down? I've ordered tea.'

'I'm fine where I am, thank you.'

His mouth twisted into that smile which had always made her skin prickle. 'Sit down, Caro.'

In the old days, she'd have dropped her gaze and done as he bid her. Now, she looked him straight in the eye. 'As I said, I'm quite comfortable here.'

His smile became rigid, but eventually he shrugged and pulled a chair around to face her, carefully spreading out his coat skirts behind him, a habit which had always irrationally irked her. 'As you wish,' he said. 'I take it that you don't want tea?'

'I want to talk about an end to our marriage.'

'You did not use to be so blunt. Then again, you have been keeping uncivilised company at Crag Hall.'

'You know, then.'

'That you are an adulterous bitch?'

The filthy words, spoken in a silken tone brought back memories which made her shudder. A brief flash of real hatred coursed through her. It was true that she had technically been unfaithful, but she was not about to allow what had transpired between Sebastian and her to be cheapened by this vicious bully. It was also true that her husband, however he had come by his information, was reliant upon conjecture. 'I take it you are referring to the boot boy? Or perhaps the stable hand,' she said tightly, and had the pleasure of seeing him flinch.

'You know perfectly well that I never believed that rubbish.'

'Then why did you have it broadcast?'

'A tactical error, I admit. I confess to being somewhat taken aback when you left me. I had ample reason, as you well know, to think you lacked the nerve.'

'Because you beat it out of me,' Caro retorted. 'You mean it was simply spite?'

Sir Grahame shrugged. 'What emotive language you choose to deploy. It is true, my pride was bruised, but I was rather more concerned with the possibility of you blackening my name.'

'So you decided to get your retaliation in first and blacken mine instead. How little you know me.'

'Indeed, seeing you now, Caroline, I begin to think that there is some truth in that. You are looking very well, I must say, all things considered.'

'A tribute to my absence from you.'

To her surprise, he laughed. 'I had not taken you for a wit. There was a third reason for my spreading those scurrilous rumours, my dear. I wished to make you *persona non grata*. That way, you see, you would have no option but to return and I would be cast in a favourable light as the forgiving and magnanimous husband.'

She stared at him in dismay. 'You thought that saying those dreadful things would make me come back to you?'

'As I said, it was a tactical error. I underestimated you. Significantly, it seems. My compliments, Caroline, you have grown up. Seeing you now, I really do believe that we can start on a new footing. I said as much to your father some weeks ago, though I was not certain—but now I see that is a real possibility.'

She shook her head, wondering if she had mistaken his words. 'Grahame, I'm not coming back to you.'

Her husband abruptly got to his feet, making Caro shrink back instinctively. He held up his hands. 'For heaven's sake, woman, I have no intention of striking you.'

Annoyed at her temporary lapse, Caro drew herself up. 'And I have no intention of permitting you to. I won't be bullied.'

Once again, he astonished her by laughing. 'Damn me, I don't think you will. Won't you sit down, Caroline, and let us discuss this like civilised beings.'

She took a seat warily, on the opposite side of the table. 'As civilised beings, we must agree that we are not well suited.'

Her husband's smile thinned. 'Well suited or not, we are nevertheless married, Caroline, and I still require a son. As you know, my estates are entailed, an unbroken line from father to son stretching back more than two hundred years. I don't want the ignominy of being the first to break with tradition.'

She had not forgotten, for it was the reason he had married her, but she had managed to put to the back of her mind how very passionately he felt about having a successor to secure his lands.

Sir Grahame got to his feet and began to pace the room, keeping fastidiously, she noted, to the other side of the table. 'I have of course consulted my legal advisors. The fact of the matter is that there is no simple solution. I may divorce you for adultery, which would involve my suing Ardhallow for criminal conversation. Don't look so shocked. Unlike the mythical boot boy, I have every reason to believe your liaison with Ardhallow is all too real. I would be obliged to sue Ardhallow for damages if you continue your association with him, for I will not be branded a cuckold.'

Which was exactly, Caro realised sickeningly, what her father had said. 'I will not co-operate. Under no circumstances will I permit you to subject Lord Ardhallow to such a degrading experience,' she said.

'It is not a question of what you will permit, but rather a question of what I will allow,' Sir Grahame sneered. 'You are my wife, Caroline,

I will not stand by and allow another man to defile my property. We are married, and the fact is that the law and the church would prefer us to remain so, no matter how much you wish otherwise.'

'Then I humbly beg to differ with both the law and the church. I am not coming back to you. I won't! What if I went to—to Brighton. Hired a man to act as my paramour—a boot boy or a stable hand, if you feel that would add authenticity. There are professional witnesses who can be bought, are there not? I have read that is common practice in crim. con. cases.' Caro jumped to her feet, catching her husband's arm. 'Well?'

He gazed down at her, his face set. 'You would humiliate yourself in a public display of adultery in order to be rid of me? You certainly are full of surprises.' Distastefully, he removed her fingers from the sleeve of her coat. 'You are under a misapprehension, my lady. A crim. con. case does not in itself constitute a divorce. There must follow an application to the Ecclesiastical Courts for a legal separation, which can take years, and then I would require a private Act of Parliament to allow me to remarry, and that would put paid to my political ambitions which, as you know, burn almost as brightly as my desire for an heir.'

'Then if you will not divorce me, I will divorce you!'

Her husband laughed viciously. 'I am afraid that the law is even less amenable to such an action. You would have to prove both adultery and cruelty, and while you may think you have grounds for the latter, you would not dispute my fidelity, I trust.'

She shook her head slowly, appalled by the implications of what he had outlined. For the rest of her life, she would be forced to endure the humiliation of being married to a man who patently cared absolutely nought for her. She returned to the window seat, wishing to put as much distance between them as she could, anxious too that he would not have the satisfaction of seeing the devastation he had wreaked. 'Which leaves us then with a formal separation as the only viable option,' she said, trying to keep the despondency from her voice. 'I think it best that I consult my own lawyers. They will be better placed than I to discuss the precise terms.'

'Terms! You are in no position to demand terms.'

'My dowry…'

'I will not reward you for forcing my hand. My generous offer to take you back still stands. Your refusal to accept it not only deprives me of the heir I require but also makes you a deserter. I have no obligation to return your dowry nor to offer you any other form of support.'

Caro stared at him abjectly. It hadn't occurred to her that he would be so vengeful. She had assumed in fact, that remorse for his past cruelty would make him inclined to make his peace with her. Looking at her husband's pale face, she tried to conjure some vestige of sympathy for his plight, for he stood to lose any prospect of an heir, but felt only an acrid anger. 'So you will cast me out on the streets, having of course enlisted my father's support for your cause.'

'I have no more desire for scandal than your esteemed parent. I will provide you with adequate funds, but they will be on my terms.'

'And those are?' Caro asked, pleased to find that her voice did not betray her.

'Quite simple. You will leave England and you will behave with perfect propriety. You may trust that I will know if you do not. Your name is not unknown at the various embassies on the Continent. As I said earlier, I will not, repeat not, be made a cuckold. These are my terms, and they are non-negotiable, no matter how many lawyers you enlist. Naturally my offer to welcome you back into the marital fold remains open.'

'An offer which I can happily swear I will never accept.'

'In that case, may we agree on my terms?'

'No, we may not. You will hear from my lawyers in due course. Goodbye, Grahame.'

Caro picked up her gloves and made for the door, conspicuously avoiding his outstretched hand.

Outside, devastated but resolute, she took calming gulps of the metallic-tasting city air and decided to walk back to her aunt's house. Her bravado quickly deflated, a deep melancholy stole over her, for she knew her husband very well. He was an astute politician who would have made very sure of his facts. Her future lay abroad, alone, and probably impoverished. She could buy time by employing a lawyer, but unless Aunt Sophia provided her with the funds to do so, even that was not an option. She would still be married, far from her family, but at least she would also be far away from her husband.

And from Sebastian. He had saved her life.

She owed it to him to tell him what form that life would take. She should write to him, for in a letter she could depict an optimism which she had to hope would manifest itself eventually. It would be the sensible course of action, but she was going to have to be sensible for the rest of her life. She decided she would commit one last reckless act, and say goodbye in person.

Crag Hall—two days later

As the post chaise drew up in front of the stable block, Caro wondered if her shaking legs would actually support her descent from the carriage. She dreaded seeing Sebastian, and yet wanted to see him more than anything in the world. Pushing a stray lock of hair back under her bonnet, hoping that she did not look as travel weary and defeated as she felt, she declined Mrs Keith's offer of tea and entered the parlour.

'Caro!' Sebastian was sitting at the desk, but he was by her side almost before she had closed the door. He was dressed in his habitual garb of shirt, breeches and riding boots. Catching her to him, he surveyed her face anxiously. 'Are you well?'

She longed to throw her arms around him, to burrow her face in his chest and drink in his familiar scent, but she was holding on to her self-control by such a thin thread, it would be a mistake. She must not mar this last meeting with tears or confessions. Gently, she disengaged herself and untied her bonnet. 'A little tired from the journey.'

'I expected you back sooner,' he said, taking his customary seat opposite her.

He looked strained. The lines on his forehead seemed deeper. Had he missed her? It didn't matter. 'Sir Grahame was out of town. I had to await his return.'

'But you eventually saw him? How did the encounter go, Caro?'

She shook her head. 'I was apprehensive, but—you will think me foolish—I imagined you by my side, and I discovered that really, all it took was for me to stand up to him. I wonder I did not before. It was so strange, I felt as if I was quite a different person from the woman he married.'

He reached across and caught her hand. 'You are. I am proud of you.

She was in the process of lifting his hand to her lips when she remembered, and dropped it. 'I am afraid the interview did not go as well as I hoped.' Haltingly, she told him just as she had rehearsed it over and over on the journey here, her tone matter of fact, her explanation simple, leaving no room for doubt. She was conscious of his eyes fixed upon her, of his expression, set into stern lines, as if he was afraid to show his feelings. What feelings? She wouldn't think about that. 'So it appears that I have no option but to live abroad, at least for a while,' she concluded, managing a very weak smile. 'My aunt has been so kind as to permit me to remain with her for a few more weeks while arrangements are made, but her lawyers have confirmed the position is just as Sir Grahame told me.'

'But it's damnable!' Sebastian jumped to his feet and began to pace the room. 'Surely there is something else to be done. Your aunt...'

'Aunt Sophia has been extremely kind, but she still believes that the best solution would be for me to return to my husband, especially now that it seems—that I am not afraid of him. She has also offered to warn him off.' *He would not dare touch a hair on your head if he knows I am watching him,* had been her aunt's exact parting words.

'You will not succumb?'

She shook her head. 'No. No,' she said again, more confidently, 'I won't ever go back to him, but I had not realised—Aunt Sophia is my one supporter, and even she disapproves of my actions.'

'Not your only supporter, Caro. You will never find a stauncher supporter than me, or one less disapproving.'

The way he looked at her made her heart turn over. It was a look she had longed for and now dreaded seeing. Facing her father had been painful. Facing her husband had been extremely testing. Both paled in significance compared to this. 'Sebastian, it is very clear to me that only harm can come from our continued acquaintance. I am grateful beyond words for what you have done for me, but in return I have merely inflicted damage upon you. I already have to bear the weight of that guilt. I will not compound the felony by inflicting even more damage on you. Our acquaintance must come to an end, for your sake.'

'Our acquaintance,' he repeated flatly. 'You make it sound as if we have engaged in nothing more than the exchange of calling cards.'

'Sebastian, it is precisely because we have shared a great deal more than that—can't you see, I will not allow you to be tainted by association with me,' Caro exclaimed.

'Don't say that! Don't speak of yourself in that way.'

'When both my father and my husband called me an adulteress, I was horrified. It doesn't defile what you and I share, but it might, if it were said often enough.' She was on her feet now, pacing the room as he had done a few moments previously. 'Sebastian, I'm the wife of a fellow peer. My presence here as your mistress is a public stain on your honour—and don't say that you don't care about your honour, for I know perfectly well that you do.'

'Dammit, I don't want you to be my mistress.'

'Oh.' She stared at him, wondering frantically if she had misjudged the situation completely.

'I don't want a mistress, Caro. I want a wife. I want *you* to be my wife. I love you.'

She sat down abruptly, fearing she would faint clean away. Now her ears were deceiving her as well. She gazed at Sebastian in complete incomprehension.

He hadn't meant to say it, but seeing her, so bravely trying to hold back the tears, talking about the life her bastard of a husband was trying to condemn her to lead, had been too much to endure. Sebastian swore. 'The first time in my life I have said the words, and you're looking at me as if I have announced a bereavement.'

'Please don't.'

'Love you? I don't seem to have any choice in the matter,' he replied tersely.

'Please don't say it. I don't think I can bear it.'

'Why?'

'Because I love you too. So very, very much.'

'You do?' He swore again, and caught her in his arms, kissing her ruthlessly. For a brief moment he felt wild elation, his heart soared, his blood roared, he felt heady, joyous, and then he realised that she was not responding, lying limp in his arms, and he let her go.

'Sebastian,' she said gently, 'it doesn't change anything. It's still impossible.'

He had known that almost from the start, yet he had hoped. He had told himself that he would say nothing unless it were possible, but still he had spoken, and having spoken, he was not going to give up without a fight. 'There must be a way,' he said grimly.

She shook her head. 'I am married, Sebastian, and most likely I always will be, for Sir Grahame was quite intractable.'

'I don't care,' he declared, though he did. He would consider murder if it freed her of Rider.

And Caro knew that too. Her knowing him so well had been one of the things which made him love her. Now he cursed it as she took his hand and spoke to him gently, but firmly, as if she were speaking to a child. 'I am married. Even if my husband did eventually divorce me, I would not be permitted to marry again. And in the unlikely event that an Act of Parliament allowed me to do so...'

'Have such things been done before?'

'It is very rare.' Caro sighed heavily. 'What matters is not really my marital status, Sebastian, but my reputation—or lack of it. By keeping any sort of company with me, you would be shunned. A social leper. How long would it be before you began to resent me for keeping you from your life? And I would feel so guilty—heaven knows, I am riven with guilt at what people are saying of you already. Our love would be tainted.'

All of it made horrible sense, but he did not want to listen to sense. 'You think it would not survive?' Sebastian asked harshly.

'One cannot live on love alone,' Caro replied carefully. 'I think that it would destroy me, watching how I was slowly destroying you. I can't do that to you.'

One cannot live on love alone. A mere few

weeks ago, Sebastian would have agreed with her wholeheartedly. Now...

He dropped his head into his hands. Now, much as he longed to claim otherwise, he was beginning to see just how impossible it was. 'I could bear it,' he said, 'I lived the life of a nomad for four years on the Continent. It would be a sacrifice to give up Crag Hall to a tenant, but if it meant we could be together...'

'That is precisely the thing I could not ask you to do.'

'You are not asking, I am offering,' he said impatiently. 'But it would resolve nothing, dammit. I won't take you as my mistress. Just thinking about the whispers, the vicious gossip, the endless cold shoulders and direct cuts you would be subjected to makes my blood boil.' He gazed at her helplessly. She would put up a front, but he knew how much it would hurt her. Eventually it would wear her down.

'And then there is your family,' Sebastian said grimly. 'Your being with me would destroy all hope of a reconciliation. Even your Aunt Sophia would be forced to disown you.' He held up his hand when she would have interrupted him. 'Your father implied that he may see his way in the future to some reconciliation, as I recall.'

'My father holds out his promises like a carrot on a stick to a donkey. I am not interested in half-promises and I'm not going to be dictated to.'

The determination in her eyes filled him with admiration, but he knew how powerful an incentive it would prove. Lord Armstrong's reputation as a ruthless negotiator was not undeserved. 'I don't doubt that you can bear it, but in a year's time, or two or five—you love your family, Caro. I can't in all conscience deprive you of them for ever.'

He pulled her to her feet, clinging to her like a drowning man. 'It is hopeless. I love you too much to put you through that, and you are right,' he added with a grim little smile. 'My honour does matter to me in one important respect. I won't have it said that I ruined you.'

'Any more than I am prepared to ruin you.'

The break in her voice was almost his undoing. Sebastian gently disengaged himself. 'I have to let you go. Our being together will only make you unhappy. Best that you leave quickly, before I go down on my knees and beg you to stay.'

'Or I chain myself to the railings and refuse to go,' Caro said.

Her smile was a very poor attempt, but it

was her trying which almost broke him. He ran the flat of his hand over her hair, the nape of her neck, the curve of her spine. 'Goodbye, my darling.'

His voice was clipped, so tight was the rein he was keeping on himself. She raised her lips in mute invitation. Her kiss was sweet, tender and over far too soon. When she would have clung to him, he set her gently away from him. 'I'll have one of the grooms bring the post-chaise round.'

'Please, don't see me off. I don't think I could bear it. Goodbye, Sebastian. I wish— goodbye.'

She fled from the room without looking back. He watched her go, and wondered why doing what he knew to be the right and noble thing felt so dreadfully and utterly wrong.

Chapter Twelve

Crag Hall—six weeks later

Sebastian gazed listlessly out of the windows of the Gold Drawing Room. In the weeks since Caro's departure, he had thrown himself into the massive task of repairing and modernising the Hall in the hope that sheer volume of activity would help him to endure her absence. It did not.

At first he kept thinking to find her behind every door he opened. The rooms echoed with her voice. Every post brought bitter disappointment when she did not write. She had fled to her aunt's in London, he knew that from having dispatched her trunk there, but how long she would remain there he did not know. The not knowing was torture. What she was doing. Who she was with. Whether she dreamed as he did every night of their love-making. Whether she reached for him in her sleep, waking with a racing heart and a sinking feeling in the pit of her belly when she encountered only the empty space. She would not weep or wail, she would not sink into a decline, he knew that. But knowing she would be trying, valiantly trying, to get on with her life as he was, only made him miss her the more.

All the reasons for giving her up, which had seemed so clear at the time, were becoming hazier, less convincing, as the reality of their separation began to sink in. He had done the right thing. How many times would he have to repeat it before he believed it?

'Lady Emma, my lord,' Mrs Keith announced solemnly.

Sebastian whirled around. The woman who entered was small and slim, dressed modishly in a gown of russet velvet trimmed with jet beads which glittered in the weak autumn sunshine filtering through the windows. Sebastian, who had been unable to stop himself from pacing nervously while he awaited the appointed hour, found himself frozen to the spot. This complete stranger was his mother.

The door closed behind the housekeeper, and Lady Ardhallow stood hesitantly just inside the room. She wore a hat with a veil. 'Sebastian?'

Her voice had a distinctly nervous quiver which he found vastly reassuring. That she did not actually recognise him however rather confounded him. But then, he thought, finally uprooting himself and making his way towards her, he felt absolutely no pang of recognition himself. 'My lady,' he said stiffly, unable to bring himself to address her as mother.

She put back her veil and smiled up at him. 'Sebastian. I—you must excuse me, I am a little overcome. I think I need to sit down.'

He led her to one of the sofas from which the covers had only recently been removed. Under the pretext of pouring her a glass of Madeira, he studied her intently. He had naïvely expected to see the young woman in the portrait. It was a shock to find her aged. Not so aged though, in point of fact. She must be at least fifty and could easily pass for at least ten years younger.

'Thank you,' she said, taking the glass he proffered and sipping daintily at the amber wine.

Her hair was the same colour as his own, but

he had not her rich curls. She was not so slim as in her portrait, and there were lines around her eye, but as she smiled at him he felt a curious pang of recognition. It was like looking at his own face in feminine form.

'I am struck by your strong resemblance to me,' she said. 'It is quite remarkable. I'm not sure whether you consider that a good or a bad thing.'

'My father considered it a positive blight.'

Lady Ardhallow grimaced. 'I have not offered my commiserations.'

'It was two years ago. The time for commiserations is long past.'

'Better late than never.' Her smile crumpled. 'I'm sorry,' she said, searching frantically in her reticule for a handkerchief. 'I promised myself that I would not get upset, but just seeing you—I am so sorry, I know perfectly well that I have not the right to be sentimental.' She blew her nose with unexpected force for such a delicate woman. 'I can't quite believe that I am here,' she said. 'Your letter came so completely out of the blue. I never thought I'd be permitted to cross this threshold again.'

Her fingers plucked at the lace of her handkerchief, but her smile was pinned brightly in place. Her determined effort to keep control of her emotions aroused his reluctant admiration. He sat down on a chair at right angles to her. 'I wrote to you because I needed to know why you left. My father would never discuss the matter. He had your rooms locked up and your portrait removed from the gallery.'

'That does not surprise me in the least. He would not permit me to write to you, you know. That was one of the terms of our separation. Not that I am using it as an excuse. I cannot excuse what I did to you, abandoning you like that, and I don't expect you want me to.'

Her honesty surprised him. He began to see that he had endowed her with any number of character flaws over the years. 'When my father died, we were estranged. We were never close—no, truth be told, I thought he hated me. A few weeks ago I discovered your portrait, and I wondered if my resemblance to you may have been at the root of the matter.'

'But he is dead and you cannot ask him, so you wrote to me instead. So this meeting is about you and your father, not you and I. I see.'

His mother was folding her handkerchief into smaller and smaller squares. 'You must understand, you have given no indication over the years that you wished to have any contact with me, Lady Ardhallow,' Sebastian said, realising how defensive this sounded, realising too that he had not until this moment considered her own expectations of this reunion.

'No. I do see how it must have looked. It was foolish of me to expect—for why should you wish to be reconciled to your absent mother? I wish you would call me Emma. I know you cannot call me Mother, but I have not used that title since I left.'

'Emma, I'm sorry if it is painful for you to be here. If you prefer, we can rearrange this meeting for London.'

'No! I beg your pardon for sounding so vehement, but no. I have waited—I would prefer not to leave just yet.' She frowned down at her handkerchief, then put it away in her reticule before taking another sip of her Madeira. When she looked up, her expression was resolute. 'Very well, I will give you the unvarnished truth, you deserve that, though I am afraid it shows me in a very poor light. I was nineteen. Your father was a catch, much older, much more sophisticated than my other beaus, and he professed to be in love with me. I didn't love him, but I was flattered and ambitious, a fatal combination.'

'But it was an arranged marriage?'

'Oh yes, indeed, I would never have considered anything else. Your father was an extremely possessive husband, Sebastian, and a very jealous one. He showered me with gifts but he wouldn't let me out of his sight. I was suffocated. Then I had you and I hoped he would grant me a little more freedom but he did not and—it sounds inadequate but truly, I felt if I did not escape I would die. I tried to persuade him to give me a little more latitude but that made him worse. Finally, in desperation, I asked for a formal separation but he would not countenance it. So I'm afraid I employed the traditional means of escaping by taking a lover, and of course he found me out because I think that's what I wanted, to trigger some sort of dénouement.'

Her explanation had a horribly familiar ring to it. He did not like to think of the parallels between Lady Emma's story and Caro's situation, but he could not ignore them. 'And it did, I presume,' Sebastian said. 'My father threw you out?'

Lady Ardhallow looked surprised. 'Why no. He did find me out, but he begged me to stay. I simply couldn't. I know you will not understand, but this place had become a prison.'

The parallels were so strong as to be almost unbelievable. 'A prison,' Sebastian repeated dumbly, his mind only half on what his mother was telling him.

Lady Emma nodded. 'I was actually afraid he would literally lock me up, so I fled without even packing so much as a change of clothes. I left you, even though it broke my heart, because I knew, in all conscience, you would be better off with your father. I had no money, I knew my family would only send me back to him, and you were only four years old.'

'But what about your lover?'

'He was married. I did not elope. Is that what he told you?'

Sebastian shook his head in utter confusion. 'He didn't tell me anything.'

'Goodness. Well then, it was *my* father who brokered our arrangement in the end, though it took over a year before *your* father finally accepted that I was not prepared to go back to him. I was to be allocated a generous fixed allowance provided that I never set foot in England, that I took no other lover, and that I—that I sever all contact with you.'

He stared at her, wondering if this was some sort of sick joke. Lady Emma finished her Madeira, oblivious to the turmoil she was raising in his mind. 'I had no option but to obey,' she continued, every word like a terrible echo of

Caro's 'My family were insistent that I accept the terms and I had no other means. I am very, very sorry.'

Though he rarely imbibed, and almost never during the day, Sebastian poured himself a large brandy and drank it in a single draught before pouring another and topping up his mother's glass. 'He banished you, like some mediaeval lord. And your family agreed to this. Do you mean you have not been in England since?'

His mother shook her head. 'To be honest, that was the least of my worries.'

'And he forced you to live—all these years, you have been alone? Surely there must have been another way. What about divorce?'

His mother shuddered. 'The scandal. Your father would have died rather than face it, and my family too—you can have no idea, Sebastian, it would have been a black mark on all of us for generations to come.'

Just as Caro had insisted. But he did not want Caro to endure his mother's fate.

'As to my being alone,' Lady Emma continued, blushing faintly—I simply learned how to be extremely discreet. I will not lie to you, Sebastian. My life has turned out very differently from that I imagined. I have missed you dreadfully, and missed my sisters almost as much, but I have not spent the last twenty-seven years weeping and wailing. That would only serve to add yet another wasted life to the list of those damaged by the whole sorry mess.'

Caro would neither weep nor wail, but she would be alone, without the comfort of her sisters or her brothers. Alone. Without him. As he was without her. He got to his feet and resumed the path his pacing had taken before his mother's arrival. 'I can only apologise on behalf of my father. I had not realised—but Caro was right, I should have written to you sooner.'

'Caro?'

'Lady Caroline. It was she who first pointed out my resemblance to you. She is—she is…' He stopped, because there was only one way to express what Caro was to him. 'I'm in love with her,' he said abruptly.

Lady Emma crossed the room and put her hand tentatively on his arm. 'I take it she does not return your affection?'

'It is rather a case of will not. Unfortunately Caro is married.'

'Oh, my dear. I am so sorry.'

'She has left her husband, just as you did. And just as you did, she is to be forced to come to terms which require her to live abroad.'

Lady Emma nodded. 'Some things do not change. What an appalling situation for you both to have to endure.'

She did not condemn him. It was her pity which struck him. She knew what Caro would suffer. He had tried so hard not to think about it, tried so hard to look to the future, but the future he saw now was unbearably bleak.

They had agreed to part because it was what the world expected of them. The world would condemn them for being together. But being apart was making him miserable and he was pretty damn sure Caro was the same. By being true to convention, they were surely being untrue to themselves.

His mind seething, he spent the afternoon showing his mother around the Hall. Her fondness for the place, now it was no longer her prison, surprised him. In the course of the afternoon, she made light of her life in exile, though he was certain this was done in deference to Caro. She also steadfastly refused to condemn either his father or her family for their treatment of her, saying only that there had been no alternative. She made no attempt to ingratiate herself with him, was careful to avoid any but the most trivial of contact, and her very restraint endeared her to him.

He could not stop comparing Caro and Lady Emma's fate. He didn't want Caro to live the life of an exile. The truth was, he didn't want Caro to live her life anywhere else but with him. All very well to be principled and noble, but dammit, he was bloody miserable without her and he was sick of pretending otherwise.

Standing on the steps awaiting her carriage at the end of the day, Lady Emma held out her hand to him. 'I have very much enjoyed today. It means a great deal to me. I would ask to see you again, but I fear I forfeited that right when I left you.'

'What is it you said earlier—there is no point in regrets?' Sebastian brushed a kiss on to her glove. 'If it pleases you, I shall have another agreement drawn up, one without conditions. Then, if you wish to, you may visit England any time you wish.'

'Why, thank you, Sebastian, I should like that very much.'

'I confess, I would like it very much too. I did not think I wished for a grand reconciliation, but now that we have met, I would like to become better acquainted.'

His mother smiled. 'Then I shall confess in

return that I was quite terrified about meeting you for fear you would be like your father, but you are a very, very pleasant surprise.'

It was while he was watching his mother's carriage recede down the drive that it came to him. In their determination each to have a care for the feelings of the other, neither he nor Caro had actually said what they wanted. What a pair of self-sacrificing nincompoops they had been, trying to make the best of being apart when what mattered, all that mattered, was being together.

London

'A visitor has arrived for you,' Lady Sophia said.

Caro looked up frowning from the letter she was transcribing for her aunt. 'For me?' Her heart sank. 'It can only be my father,' she said, looking at her aunt in dismay. 'I thought...'

'I have not informed Henry of your presence here, so you can remove that disapproving look from your countenance,' her aunt said acerbically. 'Your visitor is in the library. Please assure me, Caroline, that you will not succumb to the urge to do something foolish.'

'Foolish? What do you mean—Aunt! It is not...'

'It is indeed Lord Ardhallow. Looking as if he has just rolled in from the high pampas of South America, judging by the cut of him. Riding boots and leather breeches are not at all proper attire for a morning call. In my day...'

But Caro had already left the room, smoothing down her frumpy woollen gown. Sebastian was here. He had no reason to be here. She had every reason to wish he was not here but oh, she could not wish him anywhere else. She had missed him so much. Her fingers were inky, she noticed with dismay, and she suspected that her hair was a mess for she had a terrible habit of sticking her pen into it when she was thinking. Should she go and tidy herself?

But she had already kept him waiting at least five minutes. Caro threw open the library door. He looked exhausted. His coat and breeches were spattered with mud. Had he ridden all the way from the country? 'Sebastian.'

'Caro!' He strode towards her, then pulled himself up short with a conscious effort.

'Is something wrong?'

'Everything, but I hope—I have something to say to you.'

'What is it?' His eyes had a glitter that was almost feverish. He looked—nervous? 'Sebastian, if it is something dreadful, I beg you not to spare me.'

'It is nothing dreadful. At least I hope you do not view it as such—Caro, sit down.'

She took a seat on the sofa which was set into the window embrasure. Sebastian dug his hands deep into the pockets of his breeches and began to pace. He was definitely edgy.

'I can think of nothing more painful than the words we exchanged the last time we met,' Sebastian said, coming to a halt in front of the hearth and leaning his shoulders against it.

'We said goodbye. We agreed it was the right thing to do, for both our sakes.'

'I know, but that was arrant nonsense. No, listen to me. I know it was all right and proper and I know we spoke as we ought, but it was wrong all the same, Caro. When I saw my mother...'

'Your mother!'

'I wrote to her, as I promised I would, and she came to visit me at Crag Hall. I'm so glad I did—not for that reason—well, that one too but mainly because... Look, I'm not here to talk about my mother, except that she made me realise...' He broke off, giving her a rueful look and came to sit beside her. 'I'm making a terrible hash of this. Let me put it simply.

I miss you like the devil. I think I can put up with anything other than being without you. I thought I had no right to ask you to sacrifice all the things we talked about when we said good-bye, but I realise now that they are nothing compared to what we are really sacrificing.'

'What is that?'

'Our life together.'

'I have not dared imagine that,' Caro whispered.

'Nor had I, until the other day when I met Lady Emma—my mother. You would not believe how much you have in common—or would have in common if—Caro, I don't want you to live her life. In truth, it would not just be you who would be alone. What use will society be to me, when the only society I crave is you?'

'Oh Sebastian, that is one of the most romantic things I've ever heard.'

He smiled his upside-down smile and her heart turned over. 'I had something rather more romantic planned.' He dropped on to his knees before her and took her hands in his. '*"Come live with me and be my love."* They are not my words…'

Caro slid on to the floor beside him. 'Not your words, but perfect.'

'I can't offer you marriage, my love, but you can have my heart, I offer it willingly.'

She scanned his face anxiously. 'Are you certain?'

'Are you? It will be a rocky road to travel, if we choose to embark on it. The obstacles we discussed are very real. They may never be overcome. But at least we will travel the road together.'

She was under no illusions. There would be times when it would seem impossible, times when guilt would overwhelm her. There would no doubt be times when she would be overcome with homesickness for they would almost certainly have to flee England. But there would not be a time when she would be as miserable as she had been these last weeks, without him. Caro smiled softly. 'I could survive without you, but I could never be happy. Let me live with you and be your love, Sebastian. I will take a chance on happiness if you will.'

'I love you so much, Caro.'

His kiss was sweet, but she was not in the mood for sweetness. '"*And we will all the pleasures prove,*"' she murmured.

'What?'

'That is the next line of the poem. Do you think we shall?' she asked wickedly.

'Of that, my love, I have no doubt at all.'

He caught her up in his arms, pulling her on top of him, kissing her wildly. His body was hard beneath hers, just as she remembered. He kissed her passionately, his hands stroking down her back, cupping her bottom, holding her fast against him, kissing her.

She shuddered. Her nipples hardened. 'I was only teasing,' she said in an anguished tone. 'We cannot possibly—my aunt...'

'Ah yes, your aunt.' Sebastian rolled over, jumping to his feet. 'You are quite right to re-mind me, I have no desire whatsoever to be interrupted,' he said, turning the key firmly in the library door before rejoining her on the hearth rug. 'Where were we?'

He kissed her. A deep, passionate kiss that sent her senses spinning. Still kissing, he quickly rid himself of his jacket and waistcoat, boots and breeches. Still kissing, he pushed up her skirts and removed her undergarments. 'Much as I would love to see you naked, I think it would be prudent not to undress completely, just in case your aunt sends one of her ancient retainers in search of us,' he murmured. 'We would not like to be the cause of her butler's apoplexy and subsequent untimely demise.'

Caro giggled. 'Nor my aunt's! Sebastian, don't you think we should…'

'Stop? Certainly not. You know what they say, Caro. *Once a rake!*' Still kissing, they touched, stroked, becoming feverish, heated, in moments. Still kissing, wildly kissing, he rolled her underneath him. His erection jutted up towards her belly. She touched him in wonder, wrapped her legs around his waist, and cried out as he entered her. Fast and furious, they clutched and kissed and thrust and pulsed, to a climax that caught them suddenly, leaving them shuddering, panting. And sated.

The future would have to wait, but at least the prospect existed when none had before. And that would do very well for now.

Epilogue

Crag Hall—December 1831

My Dearest Son,

I trust this finds you and darling Caro well—which is a silly thing to say, for I doubt I have ever met a happier and more contented couple. I am writing this in the library, where myself and Mrs Keith have just finished hanging the new curtains. Please tell Caro that the colour she settled upon is absolutely perfect, it has quite transformed the room. Outside it has just begun to snow. My first winter in England in more years than I care to count, thanks to your exceedingly kind offer, and it is even more beautiful than I remember. Though I hope the snow does not fall too thickly, for my sister Agatha— one of your newly discovered aunts!—is expected at any moment. I trust you are comfortable in my little Italian home and enjoying more clement weather.

I am actually the bearer of glad tidings. You will recall from my last letter that I suggested there might be a possible mechanism to free Caro from her marriage and, more importantly, open up the possibility of your marrying—something I know would mean everything to you both. As I explained, I was made aware of its existence during the negotiations surrounding my own separation from your father. It was never a viable option for me since your existence somewhat disproved the grounds, but it occurred to me that Rider might be more amenable to an annulment since he also has something to gain. Therefore, as you suggested, I consulted with Lord Armstrong upon the subject.

He was, as Caro herself predicted, somewhat reluctant to enthuse over a proposal which did not originate from himself, but by the end of our meeting, he had quite persuaded himself it was his own idea, and has promised to pull every one of the many diplomatic strings to which he has access in order to expedite the matter. There remains, naturally, the issue of persuading Sir Grahame to swear the marriage was not consummated before it can be placed before the Consistory Court, but Lord Armstrong is of the opinion that Sir Grahame's desire to remarry in order to produce an heir will overcome any scruples he may have about this. It is not, his lordship assures me, a matter of lying, but merely of adjusting the truth! All being well, my dear son, Caro may be free to marry you in the summer.

It would seem that Lord Armstrong is already pulling strings in our favour, for I have, you will be surprised to learn, had several morning callers. Sir Timothy Innellan arrived sporting a most magnificent beard—is this a new fashion? He had his mother in tow, a snob of the first rank with a vastly inflated notion of her own consequence. I remember her from my salad days, but I smiled most politely and gave her tea and pretended, as she did, that it was the first time we had met. Lady Armstrong, Caro's stepmother, also called, with the sweetest little girl. She was most insistent that I pass on her warmest regards—and from what Caro has told me of her stepmother, I know that will make you both smile.

I will close now, my dear boy, for my sister is due to arrive at any moment. I enclose a note from Lady Sophia to Caro. Her aunt is resting upstairs. She is over the worst of her head cold, but is still rather weak. I imagine you and Caro reading this letter together, sitting in my lovely south-facing salon looking out over the lemon trees. I very much look forward to being reunited with you both when I return to my little house in Florence in the spring.

In the meantime, I kiss you both.

* * * * *

Historical Note

In England, up until the end of the 19th Century, as Lawrence Stone informs us in his excellent book *Uncertain Union and Broken Lives,* marriage was second only to inheritance as a method for the transfer of property. As a consequence, litigation about marriage was in reality litigation about property.

Until the *Married Woman's Property Act* was passed, a wife could not own any property in her own right. In effect, marriage made her the property of her husband, to do with as he saw fit. He was responsible for her upkeep (so she could, as Caro does, run up reasonable debts if he refused to keep her), but he could also force her to return to live under the marital roof if she deserted him and he could, as Caro's husband does, beat her (to a degree!) with impunity. There are some particularly heart-rending cases cited by Lawrence. The law, as Caro points out in my story, was very much weighted in favour of the man, and also, as her husband states, very much weighted in favour of keeping marriages intact, no matter how unhappy the relationship.

The options open to couples in the Regency period to dissolve a marriage, particularly where property was involved, were limited. They could agree on a formal separation, which gave the wife entitlement to alimony (aliment in Scotland) provided she signed away her right to incur debts in her husband's name. Children (as property of the marriage) almost invariably remained with the husband, no matter whether or not his behaviour contributed to the marital breakdown.

Suing for 'criminal conversation', a common law procedure in England, also stemmed from the notion that a wife is her husband's property, making her lover guilty of trespass. While some husbands sued purely to avenge themselves on their adulterous wives, and some were more interested in the damages awarded as a result of a successful suit, many crim. con. cases were the necessary prelude to a parliamentary divorce. They were quite often what Lawrence calls 'collusive', the husband and wife in cahoots in order to obtain a legal separation. The wife, with a paid paramour and two paid 'reliable' witnesses, are conveniently discovered in some sort of pre-arranged *flagrante* which can then be cited as evidence in the separation case.

Once criminal conversation has been proven, the next stage in dissolving a marriage was for the husband to apply for legal separation in an ecclesiastical court. Assuming this was successful, he could then take the final step of applying for a private Act of Parliament, which would finalise the divorce and in some, but not all cases (it very much depended upon the value of property at stake) win the right to remarry. This was an expensive and very long, drawn-out procedure, with as few as four or five cases a year succeeding. And, it is worth noting, it was a procedure which very much favoured the husband. Rare indeed was it for a wife to be permitted to remarry. It was far more likely, even in collusive cases, for the wife to be given a pittance to live on and packed off abroad.

Adultery was not the only grounds for separation and divorce, but it was the most straightforward, and hence it was the most utilised. Sadly, because of the legal quirk which required wives to prove two grounds (such as adultery and cruelty) it meant that in the vast majority of cases, the 'blame' (and the law required there to be a guilty party) was placed upon the wife—even where the husband was equally guilty, and even in cases when the wife was actually innocent! Women who had left their husbands, separated from them, or, worst of all, who had been divorced from their husbands, were stigmatised, ostracised, usually permitted no contact with their children and families, and were, I would guess, pretty miserable. The pressure on couples to remain together cannot be over-emphasised, which makes those like Caro who refused to succumb extremely brave women indeed, in my view.

A final word on annulment. It was late on in my research, when I was desperately trying to find some hope of a happy ending for Caro and Sebastian, that I remembered the case of John Ruskin and Effie Gray. Without going into the scurrilous details, the marriage was declared null on the grounds of non-consummation. Digging a little deeper into this process, which was the province of the ecclesiastical courts, I discovered several dubious cases where non-consummation was conveniently proved. Since it resulted in the marriage being declared null and void, and granted both parties the freedom to remarry, as you can imagine, it was an attractive option for desperate couples with money and access to influential contacts who were willing to twist the truth under oath.

HISTORICAL

IGNITE YOUR IMAGINATION, STEP INTO THE PAST...

My wish list for next month's titles...

In stores from 6th December 2013:

- Not Just a Wallflower — Carole Mortimer
- Courted by the Captain — Anne Herries
- Running from Scandal — Amanda McCabe
- The Knight's Fugitive Lady — Meriel Fuller
- Falling for the Highland Rogue — Ann Lethbridge
- The Texas Ranger's Heiress Wife — Kate Welsh

ailable at WHSmith, Tesco, Asda, Eason, Amazon and Apple

Just can't wait?

t us
ine

1113/04

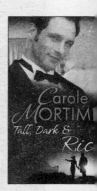

£8 12/13

MILLS & BOON®
Book Club

Join the Mills & Boon Book Clu

Subscribe to **Historical** today for 3, 6 or 12 months and you could **save over £50!**

We'll also treat you to these fabulous extras

- **FREE L'Occitane gift set worth £10**
- **FREE home delivery**
- Rewards scheme, exclusive offers…and much more!

Subscribe now and save over £50
www.millsandboon.co.uk/subscribem